"You're pretty

twelve-year-old Dee Dee said with what Mandy knew was high praise. "I wouldn't mind if *you* were my dad's girlfriend."

"It sounds as if he has enough of them without me," Mandy commented dryly.

The young girl looked at her thoughtfully. "Women usually fall for him like a ton of bricks. He's quite a stud."

"That's no way to talk about your father!" Mandy had to express disapproval—although she privately agreed with Dee Dee.

"Why do grown-ups always get so uptight about sex? Haven't you ever wondered what it would be like to kiss him?"

"No!" Mandy *refused* to think about Connor Winfield's firm, sensual mouth moving over hers.

"Okay, but watch out if he decides to make a move on you." Dee Dee grinned impishly. "I've seen my dad in action. And he's awesome...."

Dear Reader,

It's that joyful time of year again! And Santa has some wonderfully festive books coming your way this December.

Bestselling author Marie Ferrarella brings you our THAT'S MY BABY! for December. This holiday bundle of joy is still a secret to his or her dad...and Mom is sure to be a *Christmas Bride*.

And the patter of little feet doesn't stop there. Don't miss *A Baby for Rebecca* by Trisha Alexander, the latest in her THREE BRIDES AND A BABY miniseries. *Holly and Mistletoe* is Susan Mallery's newest title in the HOMETOWN HEARTBREAKERS miniseries, a tale filled with Christmas warmth and love. And for those of you who've been enjoying Tracy Sinclair's CUPID'S LITTLE HELPERS miniseries, this month we've got *Mandy Meets a Millionaire*—with the help of some little matchmakers.

December also brings Diana Whitney's *Barefoot Bride*—the heroine is an amnesiac woman in a wedding dress who finds love with a single dad and his kids at Christmastime. This is the second book in Diana's wonderful PARENTHOOD miniseries. *The Sheriff's Proposal* by Karen Rose Smith is a warm, tender tale that takes place during the season of giving.

I hope you enjoy all our books this month. All of us here at Silhouette wish you a happy, healthy holiday season!

Sincerely,

Tara Gavin
Senior Editor

Please address questions and book requests to:
Silhouette Reader Service
U.S.: 3010 Walden Ave., P.O. Box 1325, Buffalo, NY 14269
Canadian: P.O. Box 609, Fort Erie, Ont. L2A 5X3

TRACY SINCLAIR

MANDY MEETS A MILLIONAIRE

Published by Silhouette Books
America's Publisher of Contemporary Romance

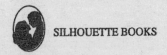

SILHOUETTE BOOKS

ISBN 0-373-24072-4

MANDY MEETS A MILLIONAIRE

Copyright © 1996 by Tracy Sinclair

This edition published by arrangement with Harlequin Books S.A.

® and TM are trademarks of Harlequin Books S.A., used under license. Trademarks indicated with ® are registered in the United States Patent and Trademark Office, the Canadian Trade Marks Office and in other countries.

Printed in U.S.A.

Books by Tracy Sinclair

TRACY SINCLAIR,

author of more than forty Silhouette novels, also contributes to various magazines and newspapers. An extensive traveler and a dedicated volunteer worker, this California resident has accumulated countless fascinating experiences, settings and acquaintances to draw on in plotting her romances.

DEE DEE WINFIELD'S "ESCAPE" ITINERARY

1) Sneak out of this hoity-toity Swiss girls' school and stowaway (first-class, of course) on the first jet outta here.

2) Arrive unexpectedly on Dad's temporary doorstep in Tangier and discover an ally. (Thank goodness for Mandy!)

3) After much pleading, spend an exotic, fun-filled week in Tangier, sightseeing with Mandy—and Dad, of course.

4) Return to San Francisco, hang out with Mandy. (She's really cool.)

5) Catch Mandy and Dad making funny eyes at each other—pretend I'm too young to understand what's happening between them.

6) Visit Mandy and overhear something fabulously horrible! Run and tell Dad. *"I'm gonna be a sister. Now I want a mom!"*— and it better be Mandy!

7) Marry Dad off to a super stepmom like Mandy and become permanently assigned to stand-by baby-sitting duties—NO MORE HOITY-TOITY SWISS GIRLS' SCHOOLS!

Chapter One

It started out as an ordinary Monday morning at the Jet Away Travel Agency. Mandy Richardson and her partner, Alexandra Reynolds, chatted idly about the weekend while one opened the mail and the other made coffee. Then the telephone rang, and suddenly the day ceased to be ordinary.

Mandy answered the phone. "Jet Away Travel, Mandy Richardson speaking. How may I help you?"

"Connor Winfield wishes to speak to one of your travel agents," a woman's crisp voice informed her. "Will you hold please?" It wasn't really a question.

The name sounded familiar, but where had she heard it? Mandy searched her memory, then remembered it was a name mentioned frequently in the society columns. Connor Winfield also turned up regularly in the accompanying pictures, usually with a beautiful woman by his side. He was a strikingly attractive man, even in the grainy newsprint photos. The columnists gushingly referred to him as "the dashing, much-sought-after venture capitalist", or "that handsome man-about-town and bon vivant, the CEO of Winfield Enterprises."

Mandy had no idea what a venture capitalist did, but it must be lucrative. He was always jetting off to Europe or some other faraway place—when he wasn't yachting or attending formal balls.

She had a lot of time to think about him, because the wait was endless. Connor Winfield's time was evidently more valuable than other people's, Mandy thought resentfully.

"Who are you talking to?" Alexandra glanced over curiously. "You haven't said a word in five minutes."

"I'm on hold for the head honcho at Winfield Enterprises."

"Don't you just hate that? Some people have no consideration."

"Unfortunately, you have to—" Mandy broke off abruptly.

Connor Winfield didn't apologize for keeping her waiting when he finally came on the line. His voice was deep and authoritative, and he got straight to the point. "I'm unhappy with my present travel agency and I want to make a change. What I'm looking for is someone capable of booking airline tickets, hotel reservations and meeting rooms—often on short notice—for cities all over the world. Can your agency handle that sort of thing?"

Dollar signs danced in front of Mandy's eyes. This could be the account of a lifetime! "Oh, yes, I'm sure we can meet your requirements," she said breathlessly. "We try very hard to satisfy our clients."

"No doubt," he said dryly. "But I require more than good intentions." He paused imperceptibly. "What is your position with the agency?"

Mandy could have kicked herself for sounding so young and eager. He seemed to be having second thoughts. "I'm one of the partners of Jet Away," she said with belated dignity.

"I see. Well, you were recommended highly," he remarked grudgingly. "Why don't we have a meeting? I can give you half an hour at four o'clock. Could you come to my office?"

"Let me check my appointment book." She didn't intend to make the mistake of sounding as if she'd drop everything for the chance. "Yes, I can manage to work you in."

But after he'd given her his address and concluded the call, Mandy's cool self-possession changed to elation. Connor Winfield's account could be a bonanza!

"He sounds like a difficult man," Alexandra commented. "You're going to earn every dollar."

"He's a man like any other, only richer. I'll have him eating out of my hand," Mandy boasted.

Alexandra took stock of her friend's assets: long, glossy black hair, cornflower-blue eyes fringed with thick, dark lashes, perfect skin and an enchanting smile. All of that, plus a slender yet curved figure, had attracted more than her share of men. Maybe Mandy was right, and this one would be as charmed once he met her in person. Except that Connor Winfield was used to beautiful women.

"He's had more experience than you have," Alexandra warned. "Just be careful not to promise more than you're prepared to deliver."

"Are you worried about the agency, or me, personally?" Mandy grinned.

"Both. Someday you're going to meet a man you can't wrap around your little finger, and it's going to come as a big shock."

"Maybe that's the kind I'm looking for. The guys I know are such wimps," Mandy said disdainfully.

"Look for your dream man somewhere else. Just remember that Connor Winfield is strictly business."

"That describes him perfectly." Mandy laughed. "He sounded so cold on the phone that I'm tempted to wear gloves and earmuffs to our meeting."

The offices of Winfield Enterprises, in downtown San Francisco, were what Mandy expected—elegant, dignified and redolent of serious money. She was passed through a series of receptionists and secretaries to Connor Winfield's inner sanctum, a large corner office with a glorious view overlooking the city.

Connor saw her promptly at four o'clock. He was sitting behind a large desk covered with papers and manila folders. It faced the room, rather than the distracting view outside the wide windows.

He glanced up when she was shown in. "You're on time. I like that. Please have a seat, Ms. Richardson." He indicated the chair across from his.

Connor Winfield was even more handsome in person. The black-and-white newsprint couldn't capture his vibrancy or the penetrating quality of his smoky gray eyes as he sized her up.

The admiration Mandy usually generated in the opposite sex was completely absent—or awfully well masked. That was good, she told herself. All she wanted from this man was his account.

He lounged back in his chair, continuing to appraise her. "Forgive me for saying so, Ms. Richardson, but you seem rather young to handle a corporate account. How much experience have you had?"

"I was one of the founding partners of Jet Away. I've planned trips for clients to places all over the globe."

He studied her for a few moments longer. "I'd like you to be honest with me. It will save a lot of problems down the line. Do you feel your agency is capable of handling extensive travel arrangements, including extra services?"

"I'm not quite sure what you mean by extra services," she said cautiously.

A look of amusement flitted across his strong face and was gone in an instant. "I require a complete package when I send my people on assignments—a car and driver at their disposal, meeting rooms in hotels, that sort of thing."

"Jet Away can handle that," Mandy said with relief. Connor didn't look like the kind of man who had to pressure women for "extra services," but it was always wise to spell everything out in the beginning.

"I'll be quite frank with you," he said. "The two travel agencies who handled my arrangements before were totally incompetent. That's why I've taken over the selection myself. One thing I can't tolerate is sloppy performance. I require expertise, not excuses."

"That's understandable," Mandy murmured.

He looked at her skeptically. "How large is your organization? I'll need the full-time services of at least one person to handle various details for a meeting I have scheduled. That's in addition to airline tickets and so forth, the normal function of a travel agency. Are you equipped to deal with that?"

"I'll take care of your account personally." Her voice was calmly matter-of-fact, but she couldn't hide the sparkle of excitement in her blue eyes.

"This meeting I spoke of is in Morocco. People are flying in from all over the world, and I just discovered the arrangements my former agency made are hopelessly inadequate. I want to make sure there are no more slipups. You'd have to leave for Tangier immediately to get things set up while your office here at home takes care of the routine details. Do you have the personnel to handle the job?"

"No problem," Mandy answered airily.

"How many people are there in your office?" he persisted.

"I wouldn't assign your account to an agent," she said evasively. "My partner and I take personal care of corporate clients—with the help of our staff, of course. We can also call on an associate in Rome who assists us with foreign travel."

Mandy felt justified in stretching the truth a bit. Their former partner, Penny Drake, did give them tips on restaurants and special events in Europe. She had married a dreamy Italian and now lived in Rome.

"Frankly, I'm in a bit of a bind here. Time is growing short and I have to make a decision." Connor gazed at her silently for a few moments. "You did come recommended. Although, so did the last agency."

"Who told you about us?" Mandy asked quickly, before the memory could tip the balance against them.

"One of my vice presidents, John Kleinhold."

"I remember him. We planned a cruise of the Greek Islands for Mr. Kleinhold and his wife. They were very pleased with the trip," Mandy said persuasively.

"So he told me." He paused as the intercom buzzed.

"Your four-thirty appointment is here, Mr. Winfield."

"Tell him I'll be right with him." Connor stood and held out his hand. "It looks as though we have a deal, Ms. Richardson."

His unexpected smile transformed him from an autocratic tycoon into a charming, sexy man. Mandy felt his impact as her hand was swallowed up in a clasp that was firm, but not crushing. Connor didn't have to prove his forcefulness—he had nothing to feel insecure about.

She gazed up at him, feeling her pulse accelerate. "Thank you, Mr. Winfield. We won't disappoint you."

Something flickered in his eyes for just a moment before he released her hand. "Talk to my secretary on your way out. She'll give you all the information you'll need to get started."

* * *

"You're going to Morocco!" Alexandra exclaimed when Mandy returned to the office with the news. "Why? Our business is sending *other* people on trips."

"We never planned one like this. Wait till you hear about it! I'm flying to Tangier to make arrangements for a big meeting Winfield Enterprises is having—and everything had better run smoothly. His Highness doesn't tolerate anything less than perfection."

"From your description of him, it's no wonder his last two agencies couldn't please him. Do you think we can?"

"It will be a challenge," Mandy admitted. "But on the other hand, the job pays well."

"I'll bet that's what his wife told herself when he proposed," Alexandra remarked derisively.

"He can't be married. Every time I see his picture, he's with a different woman."

"That should tell you something about him. I pity the woman who does marry him."

"There would be compensations," Mandy answered dryly, remembering Connor's lean physique and ruggedly handsome face. He could make a woman forgive any shortcomings—at least while she was in his arms.

"Well, yes, I guess he's wildly rich," Alexandra conceded.

"That, too." Mandy grinned.

Alexandra looked at her sharply. "I hope you're not attracted to the guy. He sounds like twenty pages of bad news."

"Maybe for his girlfriends, but not for us," Mandy said confidently. "Connor Winfield is going to make us rich—or at least mildly affluent." She laughed. "Just wait and see what a change he makes in our lives."

Mandy pressed her forehead against the window, staring at the exotic landscape as the plane circled for a landing at

Tangier. The domed mosques and slender spires pointing like fingers at the sky were something out of the *Arabian Nights*.

The impression was reinforced during the taxi ride to the hotel along streets crowded with colorfully dressed people. Many of the older women wore long robes and scarves over their heads. A few even had their faces covered, leaving only their eyes to peer out at the strange mixture of ancient and modern. Cars clogged the streets, along with wooden carts and an occasional camel.

Mandy's head swiveled back and forth as she tried to get a better look down the twisted lanes that led off the main street. They were filled with little shops that displayed robes and dresses and slippers outside. It was like looking at the inside of an untidy closet.

She longed to go exploring, but that would have to wait. Her first priority was to check out the Ayoubi Palace, supposedly the best hotel in Tangier. The guidebook had given it five stars.

Mandy was a little dubious after her first glimpse of Tangier's scenic yet crumbling walls and buildings. Everything looked so weather-beaten. But the Ayoubi Palace lived up to its rating. The spacious lobby had a mosaic-tiled floor centered by a splashing fountain, and the rich tapestries on the walls were reassuring. It was reminiscent of a Moroccan castle, and the plentiful personnel seemed dedicated to the guests' well-being.

The manager, a man named Abdallah, was especially helpful. The rooms he had chosen for Connor's guests were just what she had in mind. After she explained her other requirements, Abdallah offered to assemble a household staff for her as soon as she found a suitable house for Connor to rent.

Mandy expected to look at several properties before she found the right one. Connor had instructed her to rent a house so he'd have somewhere to entertain. It would also give him a measure of privacy that he wouldn't get if he stayed at the hotel with his associates. Mandy worried that things in Tangier wouldn't meet Connor's rigid standards, but the first house the real estate agent took her to was absolutely perfect. The word *house* was hardly an adequate description. It was a mansion, surrounded by lush green lawn, set far back from the street behind a high wrought-iron fence.

The rooms downstairs were furnished in period French and had tall windows that gave a stunning view of the formal gardens in front. The windows in the back of the house overlooked more lawn and flowers, plus a swimming pool that glowed like an oval turquoise.

Upstairs were about a dozen bedrooms. Mandy didn't bother to count. They were all furnished exquisitely, but she was only interested in the master suite. That was what Connor would occupy. The rest of the bedrooms wouldn't be used, since his associates would stay at the hotel and be driven back and forth. That reminded her to arrange for a fleet of limos.

The large dining room would double nicely as a conference room. After the sessions were finished, cocktails could be served in the living room while the table was set for dining on the nights Connor preferred to entertain at home. The estate was absolutely perfect for his purposes. Even *he* couldn't find anything wrong, she thought with satisfaction.

When Mandy returned to the hotel, the manager had the promised household staff waiting to be interviewed. There was a cook, a butler and a couple of maids—all very experienced, Abdallah assured her. Never having hired servants before, Mandy had to take his word for it, but they seemed competent. She asked a few questions, crossed her fingers and hired them on the spot.

Mandy was pleased that everything had gone so well, but that meant there was nothing left to keep her there. She'd hoped the arrangements would take a few days, leaving time to sneak in a little sight-seeing. Tangier was such a fascinating city, and she might never get here again. Well, at least Connor should be pleased with her efficiency.

She telephoned him with a detailed report. "The cook and butler can handle an informal cocktail party between them, but for something fancy, or if you intend to have more than eight for dinner, they'll need to bring in extra help. Don't worry, though, they'll take care of it. Just give them a little advance notice. The cook's name is Salima. She can prepare either Moroccan or French cuisine, whichever you prefer. I think that about covers it. Any questions?"

"You accomplished all of that in one day?" Connor asked. "I'm impressed."

"I was hoping you would be. Jet Away would like to have all your business."

"If this meeting goes smoothly, we'll certainly talk about it. Is the cook capable of planning menus?"

"Uh . . . I didn't ask her." Wouldn't you know he'd zero in on the one thing she'd forgotten?

"Find out," Connor said crisply. "Somebody has to do it. If she can't, you'll have to find someone else."

The cook and butler were a husband-and-wife team. Mandy was afraid he might get insulted and quit if she fired his wife without even giving the woman a chance. They were perfect for the job. What if she couldn't get anyone as competent?

"Perhaps I could arrange for the chef at the hotel to plan the menus before I leave," Mandy suggested. She was sure Abdallah would help her out again. She had filled all of his best suites. "Just tell me how many dinners you'd like to have, and the number of guests."

"How can I know ahead of time? The scheduling isn't that rigid. I'll have a cocktail party the first night to welcome everyone, but from then on I plan to play it by ear. It will depend on what the group wants to do. The staff has to be flexible.''

"I see," Mandy said slowly. This was a potential disaster. Salima was an experienced cook, but Connor required more than cooking skills. "Maybe I could hire a housekeeper to oversee everything."

"Whatever. I definitely need someone who can take charge."

"All right, I'll get on it first thing in the morning and report back to you."

After a moment of silence he said, "Would you consider taking over yourself? It would only be for a week, and I'd pay extra for your services, naturally."

"You want *me*? I don't have any experience planning fancy dinners."

"How difficult can it be?" he asked impatiently. "I'm sure you've been to plenty of parties. It's not like I'm asking you to do the cooking."

What he said was true. It wouldn't be much different than selecting from a menu in a restaurant. Although Mandy couldn't boil water without scorching the pot, she'd gathered a lot of knowledge about fine cuisine from dining out regularly.

An added plus would be the all-expenses-paid vacation in Tangier. It was enough to make up her mind. "Okay, you've got yourself a deal. I'll check out of the hotel tomorrow and move over to the house."

"Splendid. I'll be there the following day."

Connor frowned slightly as he hung up the phone. This meeting was important to him. Millions of dollars were at stake, yet he'd just entrusted the details to someone who admitted she didn't have experience for the job. That wasn't like him at all.

He was under no illusions about Mandy. He knew her agency was small and she was eager for his business, but there was nothing wrong with being hungry. He admired ambition and he didn't mind a little bluffing—as long as it was backed by the ability to deliver. And he was fairly certain Mandy could. She would do anything it took to get ahead—well, almost anything.

A grin softened Connor's hard features as he remembered her startled expression when he'd asked if she was prepared to provide extra services. Too bad he didn't operate that way. She was a beautiful woman. Would her eyes sparkle with the same blue fire, and would she call out his name in that breathless little voice, while he explored her lovely body with his hands and mouth?

His smile faded as the intercom buzzed. "Your daughter is calling from Switzerland on line 1, Mr. Winfield," his secretary said.

Connor seized the phone. "Dee Dee? What's wrong? Are you in trouble again?"

"What did you hear?" a young girl's voice asked cautiously.

"Nothing, yet. Prepare me," he said with a clenched jaw.

"It wasn't my fault! You can't do anything at this crummy school without breaking some kind of rule. We even have to wear uniforms. I might as well be in the army," she complained.

"You could benefit from a little military discipline. Unfortunately, our army doesn't take children."

"I'm not a child! I'm practically a teenager."

"Don't rush things. You just had your twelfth birthday."

"So, I'm in my thirteenth year."

"Barely, and don't try to change the subject. What's the reason for this phone call?"

"I want to come home. I hate it here!"

Connor sighed. "We've been through all this, Dee Dee. It's natural at your age to be homesick in the beginning, but you've been there less than a month. It's supposed to be a very fine school. You haven't really given it a chance. If at the end of the term you're still not happy there, we'll discuss making a change."

"But that's months away! What am I supposed to do until then?"

"You might try studying," he answered dryly.

"You don't care that I'm miserable. You just want me out of your hair."

"I'm sorry you feel that way, because it isn't true. I'd bring you home in a minute if I thought it was in your best interests. Whether you believe it or not, I miss you."

"Yeah, sure!"

He hesitated. "Maybe I could stop by and visit you for a day. Would that make you happy?"

"You're gonna fly over here for one day?" she asked skeptically.

"I have to go to Tangier day after tomorrow for a meeting. It will last for most of the week. After that I could fly to Switzerland before coming home."

There was a short silence at the other end of the line. "Tangier's in Africa, isn't it?"

"That's right, in Morocco. You *have* been paying attention in class." Connor chuckled.

Dee Dee didn't react indignantly. Her voice was filled with interest instead. "That's one of the places where the women wear veils and long robes, and they have casbahs and camels, don't they?"

"Right again. Would you like me to send you a caftan?"

"Maybe. What hotel are you staying at?"

"I've rented a house." He looked down at the slip of paper with the information Mandy had just given him. "It might be a good idea to give you the phone number there. Although you're not to call me unless it's a dire emergency. Just being homesick doesn't fit that description," he warned.

"Okay. What's the number?"

As he finished giving it to her, his secretary appeared in the doorway. "I don't want to interrupt, Mr. Winfield, but Mr. Yamaguchi is calling from Tokyo on line 2."

"Tell him I'll be right with him." Connor returned to his daughter. "I'll phone you from Tangier. Be a good girl."

"Yeah, right—like I have a choice!"

He shook his head, smiling and frowning at the same time, as he pushed a button on the desk console.

Early the next morning, Mandy moved over to the rented estate. While the servants were getting settled in their quarters, she selected a room for herself—well down the hall from the master suite.

Not that she anticipated any unwelcome attention from Connor. All of his energies would be focused on this meeting. He probably didn't even think of her as a woman. And yet . . . there had been just an instant's awareness in his eyes when they shook hands.

Remembering his charismatic smile and the male energy that flowed out of him, Mandy wondered what it would be like to have a man like that in love with her. To see his gray eyes darken with passion, and listen to his husky voice in the velvet night.

She shook her head disgustedly, deciding she sounded sixteen instead of twenty-six.

The house came completely equipped, but it took all morning to locate and inspect the china and glassware, the linens and all the other necessities of a household. The things men took for granted. Connor would only notice them if they weren't there.

After she had discussed menus with the cook, Mandy went to check out Connor's suite. It was fit for a pasha. A king-size bed was set on a raised platform. It had a canopy overhead and a bedspread made of maroon silk with an oriental design embroidered in gold thread.

Outside the bedroom was a wide balcony overlooking the swimming pool and the landscaped grounds. The air was fragrant with the perfume from long borders of colorful flowers.

Mandy inhaled appreciatively before going to check on the bathroom. A sunken black marble bathtub with gold faucets was the focal point of the large room. It was reflected in the floor-to-ceiling mirrors that covered two walls. Another wall had a view of the garden through a wide picture window.

Mandy made sure the bathroom was stocked with the necessities—a stack of towels and washcloths on the ledge of the tub and additional ones on the towel bars, facial tissues and bars of soap in the appropriate places. Then she checked the bedroom closets to see that there were enough hangers, and that the drawers of the chests were all lined.

After a last look around, she said, "Mission accomplished. The only thing missing is a nubile maiden to share his bed, and he'll have to supply *her* himself."

By early afternoon, Mandy was satisfied that the house was ready and waiting for Connor's arrival. The help were busy with domestic chores and there was nothing left for her to do, so she felt justified in taking a couple of hours off.

Her destination was the medina in the old Arab section of town, where narrow, winding streets formed a fascinating maze. Mandy wandered happily through them, stopping to look at all the merchandise, both genuine and junk.

In addition to what was displayed in the tiny shops, street peddlers stopped her to offer everything from jewelry to T-shirts. She'd been to countries where the street merchants were annoyingly insistent, but these weren't. They coaxed rather than bullied. She was so charmed that she bought a number of useless trinkets.

It was late when she reluctantly hailed a cab to go back to the house. There was so much more to see, but she'd been told that it wasn't wise for a woman to go wandering about alone after dark. No matter what her own feelings were, she'd learned to follow the customs of her host city.

Rock music was blaring loudly when Mandy opened the front door. She frowned. The servants evidently didn't expect her back so soon, but this mustn't happen while Connor was here. Fortunately, she had time to speak to them about it before he arrived.

As Mandy was starting for the kitchen to have a talk with the staff, a young girl came down the staircase carrying a portable radio. That was the source of the music. She looked to be about sixteen—a very streetwise sixteen. She was wearing a miniskirt, a tight sweater and spike heels.

Mandy stared at her in amazement. "Who are you?"

"I was wondering the same thing about *you*." The girl peered at her from under long false eyelashes. "Are you one of my dad's bimbos?"

Mandy couldn't help laughing. "I don't mean to be insulting, but you fit that description better than I do."

The girl seemed pleased rather than insulted. "Do you really think so? These shoes are killing me, but if they do the trick they're worth it."

"You *want* to look like a bimbo?"

"I want people to treat me like an adult, not some little kid who has to be told what to do every minute of the day." Suddenly she looked much younger than sixteen.

Mandy tried to hide her amusement under a casual tone. "I know that must be a pain, but adults can't always do whatever they want, either."

"My dad can. He's a big wheel."

Mandy began to get an inkling—but the idea was crazy! "Who is your father?"

"You must know him if you're here in his house. His name is Connor Winfield. He's the head honcho of some kind of business that buys and sells companies. I don't exactly understand it, but he makes lots of money."

Mandy was scarcely listening. "I could have sworn Connor wasn't married!"

"He isn't anymore. He and my mom got a divorce a couple of years ago. She lives in New York now."

"And where do you—? No, wait. I have a lot of questions, so let's go into the den where we can be comfortable."

"Okay." The girl teetered after her on the ridiculously high heels. She paused at the entrance to the den, looking around appraisingly. "Not bad, but I hope there's a TV set behind one of those doors."

The luxurious room had two walls paneled in teak wood. It was furnished with deep couches and chairs, and the floor was covered with an Oriental rug that was a mixture of deep reds and blues.

"Let's start by introducing ourselves," Mandy said. "I'm Mandy Richardson. What's your name?"

"I'm thinking of calling myself Desiree," the young girl said thoughtfully. "Kind of sexy, don't you think?"

"Not bad. But what name were you born with?" Mandy asked casually.

"I wasn't born with it, it was wished on me! Can you imagine parents giving their kid a dorky name like Doris?"

"I've heard worse. In the sixties people named their children things like Sunrise and Moonbeam."

"Hey, cool! Maybe I'll call myself Hurricane, and my middle name can be Cyclone." The girl grinned mischievously. "My dad ought to approve of that."

"Doris, I—"

"Now you sound like the teachers at that dumb school he stuck me in. I asked them to call me Dee Dee like everybody at home does, but a lot of good it did," she finished resentfully.

"Your father sent you to a school here in Africa?" Mandy asked incredulously.

"No, it's in Switzerland. One of those places that's supposed to make a lady out of you. Lots of luck," she said grimly.

Mandy gave her a bewildered look. "Then what are you doing here?"

"I've never been to Tangier. When Dad said he was having a meeting here, I figured this was my chance."

"He didn't tell me to expect you."

"That's because he doesn't know I'm here," Dee Dee answered calmly.

"You just left school without telling him?" Mandy gasped. "Your father will be furious!"

"He's always ticked off about something. You ought to know that. Or are you two still in that dorky romantic stage? Don't worry, I won't cramp your style. I'll keep myself busy checking out Tangier."

Mandy had trouble deciding which misapprehension to address first. "I don't know your father very well, but I seriously doubt that he's going to let you cruise around Tangier alone. And you're wrong about our relationship, too—it's strictly business."

"What kind of business?"

"I'm in charge of seeing that his meeting runs smoothly, and you're not making my job any easier."

"I won't be any trouble. This place looks like a hotel, but if all the bedrooms are taken, I can sleep in here on the couch."

"That's not the problem. The guests have accommodations at a hotel. Only your dad and I are staying here. Don't let that give you any ideas, though," Mandy warned. "I'm sure he has a lot of women in his life, but I'm not one of them."

"You're his type. Dad goes for beautiful women, although the last one was a blonde—*Bar-ba-ra.*" Dee Dee pronounced all three syllables in an affected voice. "She gave me a royal pain! Always pretending we were best buddies. I wish Dad's girlfriends wouldn't use me to try and score points with him.''

"That can't be much fun," Mandy agreed. "How long have he and your mother been divorced?"

"She split about two years ago."

"Your mother left you?" The exclamation just slipped out. Mandy could understand a woman wanting out of a bad marriage, but how could she leave her child behind?

Dee Dee shrugged. "She and Dad weren't happy together, so what was the point in hanging around?"

It was a matter-of-fact statement, but Mandy suspected the girl felt rejected. How could she not? Abandoned by her mother and sent away to school by her father. And not just any school, one thousands of miles away! Mandy's sympathy was aroused.

"Do you ever see your mother?" she asked gently.

"Not very often, but she phones sometimes."

That was big of her! Mandy tried to hide her indignation. "Sometimes marriages don't work out, but I'm sure both of your parents love you very much."

"I know." Dee Dee changed the subject. "I guess Dad's gonna be pretty steamed. Will you help convince him to let me stay?"

"You're overestimating my influence. I'm just an employee, and a brand-new one, at that."

"Well, at least stick around when he gets here. He won't go too ballistic in front of you."

Mandy gave her a shocked look. "He wouldn't get physical, would he?"

"You mean, whack me one? He never has, but I never gave him this much reason to." Dee Dee grinned. "I wouldn't want to be around when he gets his credit-card bill."

"You charged your plane ticket to him?"

"To Winfield Enterprises. Dad has an account with all the airlines."

"He told you he'd be in Tangier, but how did you know where? Did he give you the address here?"

"No, but he gave me the telephone number. That was just as good. I called from the airport and asked for directions to give the cab driver."

Mandy stared at her in amazement. "You're a very enterprising young lady. How old are you?"

"How old do I look?"

"Oh . . . sixteen or seventeen," Mandy lied.

"Cool!" It was Dee Dee's favorite word, along with *dorky*. "Everybody but Dad can see that I'm grown up."

"How old *are* you?"

"Practically in my middle teens." When Mandy raised an eyebrow, she said, "Okay, I'm twelve, but that's just my chronological age. Emotionally I'm much older, and that's what counts."

"You might be right, but unfortunately the law says you have to abide by your father's rules until you're eighteen."

"I'm not going back to that school." Dee Dee set her chin stubbornly.

"What don't you like about it?"

"The food is rotten, and my bed is hard, and they have rules about everything." Dee Dee recited a litany of complaints until she got to the real one. "And they're all a bunch of snobs," she muttered.

"It's hard being the new kid in town," Mandy remarked sympathetically. "But you'll make friends if you hang in there. Just give yourself time."

"You don't understand any more than my dad does. I don't *want* to be friends with them. They don't know anything about rap music or television shows. All they're interested in is how important their families are. One girl's father is a duke, and another's uncle is a lord. To hear her talk about him, you'd think he was the real thing," Dee Dee said disgustedly.

"We don't have royalty in our country, but I'm sure your father is just as important in the business world."

"I couldn't care less. Titles and money shouldn't matter. It's whether you're a good person or not," Dee Dee said earnestly.

Mandy was impressed. Somebody had taught this girl good values. "Have you told your father that?"

"I tried, but he just says the same things you did—stick it out, you'll get to like it there, it'll be good for you."

"I'm sure he feels it will be." Mandy wasn't at all sure. Connor probably wanted to get rid of his daughter so he could live it up with all his blond Barbie dolls.

"Well, he's wrong. I can get into just as much trouble in Switzerland as I can in San Francisco."

"Were you in trouble at home?"

Dee Dee's gaze wavered. "So, I cut classes a few times. Big deal."

"It is if it gave your father the impression that you're irresponsible."

"I got myself on a plane from Switzerland to Tangier. Doesn't that prove I'm responsible?"

Mandy couldn't help smiling at the youngster's convoluted thinking. "No, it proves you're resourceful."

"It's the same thing."

"A debatable point. Right now we have to call your father and tell him where you are, in case the school alerted him that you took French leave."

"Do you have to?" Dee Dee looked like an apprehensive twelve-year-old, in spite of the makeup and outlandish clothes.

"I really do. What if he calls the police? You don't want them looking for you, do you?"

Mandy dialed Connor's office number, calculating the time. It was the dinner hour in Tangier, which made it only around eleven in the morning in San Francisco. Too early for him to be out to lunch, she thought as the telephone rang. Although that would only postpone the inevitable blowup.

"Mr. Winfield left for the airport," his secretary informed her, after Mandy had identified herself.

"Oh...I didn't expect him until tomorrow."

"That's correct, he won't be there until then. He plans to stay overnight in London and fly to Tangier tomorrow evening. Are there any problems? I can get in touch with him if there are."

"No, everything here is fine." It would be pointless to tell Connor's secretary what was going on.

Dee Dee looked relieved when Mandy relayed the news to her. "Great! Let's go out and live it up."

"Are you trying to get me fired? Your dad will be in a foul enough mood when he finds you here. He'll send us both packing if he thinks I encouraged you in any way."

"I'm already here. He can't blame you for that. And as long as I *am* here, I might as well see Tangier."

"Tomorrow," Mandy said firmly. "Women don't go out alone at night in Morocco—especially in outfits like that. I hope you brought some other clothes with you."

"All I had were school uniforms, and they're dorky. I bought these clothes on the way to the airport."

"Well, you can't let your father see you looking like that. You're in enough trouble already. Tomorrow we'll just have to give his credit card another workout."

"Okay, and then can we go to the casbah?"

"Sure, that's what I planned to do. There's also a spice market I read about that sounds fascinating. We'll make a whole day of it."

"You're pretty cool," Dee Dee said, with what Mandy knew was high praise. "I wouldn't mind if *you* were my Dad's girlfriend."

"No thanks. It sounds as if he has enough of them without me," Mandy commented dryly.

The young girl looked at her curiously. "Women usually fall for him like a ton of bricks. Don't you think he's handsome?"

"I suppose so."

"He must be quite a stud, too," Dee Dee said thoughtfully.

"That's no way to talk about your father." Mandy felt she had to express disapproval, although privately she agreed with Dee Dee. "It isn't respectful."

"Why do grown-ups always get so uptight about sex? You can be honest with me. Haven't you ever wondered what it would be like to kiss him?"

"No, I have not." Mandy refused to think about how Connor's firm yet sensual mouth would feel moving over hers. "Come on, let's get cleaned up for dinner."

"Okay, but watch out." Dee Dee grinned impishly. "My dad grows on you."

Chapter Two

Dee Dee was precocious and outspoken, but nobody could ever accuse her of being dull. Mandy thoroughly enjoyed their evening together. They discussed clothes and dating, among other things. Boys were a big part of the conversation, especially how to know when you're really in love with one.

"If you asked a dozen people, you'd get twelve different answers," Mandy commented. "Poets say you can tell because your heart beats faster and you feel light-headed. To me, that sounds like a case of the flu."

"Don't you know what it feels like?" Dee Dee demanded.

Mandy wasn't sure she did. She'd been attracted to a few men, but the initial excitement hadn't developed into anything deeper and lasting. It bothered her sometimes. Was she looking for something that didn't exist?

When she hesitated, Dee Dee said, "You must have been in love lots of times. You're almost as old as my dad."

"That's pretty doddering, but we're both still fairly well preserved." Mandy grinned.

"You know what I mean. You're the same generation."

"I'll agree to that. Why don't you ask for your father's advice? He's had more experience than I have."

"Yeah, but it's hard to tell how he really feels about anything. His girlfriends never last more than a couple of months, sometimes less. Maybe he's one of those guys who doesn't want to make a commitment. I guess he was in love with my mother when he married her, but it didn't seem to bother him a lot when she left."

Connor must have felt rejection, if nothing else. He probably hadn't experienced it very often. "Some people are better than others at hiding their feelings," Mandy remarked.

"Yeah, that's my dad. Mom is just the opposite. We talk about everything under the sun. She tells me about her dates, and all the exciting places they take her, and which guys she really goes for. Mom falls in love all the time."

Mandy had heard about mothers who prided themselves on being pals with their daughters, but this seemed rather excessive. "Have you ever asked *her* how to tell when it's the real thing?"

"Oh, sure, but she wasn't very helpful. Mom says not to bother with a lot of introspection. It spoils all the fun."

"I guess I can see why your parents got a divorce," Mandy said slowly. "Your mother sounds rather impulsive, and your father strikes me as a person who thinks everything through."

"It's not a great combination," Dee Dee agreed. "But Dad's really a good guy when he isn't putting on the stern-father act. We have a lot of fun together."

Mandy was thoroughly confused. If they had the good relationship Dee Dee seemed to indicate, why had Connor sent her so far away?

"You'll like him when you get to know him," Dee Dee continued. "All women do."

"We're on a first-name basis, but I doubt if we'll ever get any closer than that."

"You will if he decides to make a move on you. I've seen him in action, and he's awesome!"

Mandy was torn between amusement and annoyance. "You need to spend more time at that school in Switzerland. Normal twelve-year-olds don't comment on their parents' sexual prowess."

"That's the trouble with your generation. You've got all these hang-ups."

Mandy laughed helplessly. "You sure know how to hurt a gal! I never thought twenty-six was old enough to create a generation gap."

"My mom says age is just a state of mind."

"She sounds like a very...unusual woman."

"She is. So's my dad." Dee Dee grinned. "I've got crazy, mixed-up genes."

"Do you look like your mother?" Mandy examined her curiously. The young girl showed signs of growing up to be a beauty. She had blond hair and the fair coloring that went with it—evidence of Connor's preference for blondes—but she was more than candy-box pretty. Her blue eyes held intelligence, and her firm chin indicated character.

"Everybody says so, but people always say that. Why does a girl have to look like her mother and a boy like his father? I'm *me!*"

"I don't think anyone will ever dispute that." Mandy smiled. "You're quite remarkable."

"I can talk to you. Is that 'cause you know a lot of kids my age?"

"Not really, although I enjoy teenagers. I always wanted a younger sister, but it never happened. I'm an only child."

"Me, too." Dee Dee looked at her appraisingly. "If you hang out with my dad, I'll be your little sister. You're cool."

Mandy was touched. "That's the best offer I've had in a long time, but it doesn't have to be a package deal. Maybe we can get together on a Saturday and go shopping, or to a movie—if or when your father lets you come home."

"There's no *if* about it." The young girl said firmly. "You can count on it."

"Yes, well, we have a lot to do here first." Mandy changed the subject, since she wasn't optimistic about Dee Dee's chances. Connor was formidable even when he wasn't challenged. "After we get you outfitted tomorrow, we'll hit the casbah and then the spice market. How does that sound?"

They started early the next morning and put in a full day. Their first stop was a boutique in the hotel where Mandy had stayed. She hadn't been interested in shopping at the time, but she'd noticed they had nice things.

The store didn't carry children's clothes, which delighted Dee Dee and challenged Mandy's ingenuity. It wasn't easy to talk the youngster out of the glittery sweaters and tight satin pants she was attracted to.

"I don't want to influence you, but the fashion magazines say that stuff is out," Mandy remarked casually. "Women are into simple clothes they can wear all day and dress up at night with a scarf or jewelry. It's certainly made *my* life a lot easier."

Dee Dee looked doubtfully at the pleated skirt and matching blouse the saleswoman was holding up. "They don't have any pizzazz."

"Not on the hanger, but I'll bet they'd be smashing with ballet flats and the right belt. That's the way I'd wear them."

"Okay, I'll try them on." As Dee Dee followed the saleswoman to a dressing room, she said over her shoulder, "But I'm not wearing them if they make me look like a dweeb."

"The choice is strictly up to you," Mandy answered, managing not to smile.

Eventually Dee Dee was coaxed or maneuvered into a suitable wardrobe. As they left the shop after arranging for the rest of her purchases to be sent to the house, she finally looked like what she was, a bright and beautiful twelve-year old.

The rest of the day was pure pleasure. Mandy was as fascinated as Dee Dee at the sight of two camels lounging in a trash-strewn vacant lot. The animals were viewing the passing traffic with disdain, while their handlers, dressed in long flowing robes and small flat caps, held an animated conversation.

"Isn't this neat?" Dee Dee's eyes were shining. "I want to ride on a camel while I'm here."

"So do I," Mandy agreed. "There must be someplace we can rent them." Her head swiveled around. "Quick, look at the sheep, right here in the middle of the city!"

A man was dodging and weaving his way through the vehicles on the crowded street, pulling a couple of sheep tied to a short rope.

Mandy and Dee Dee stared avidly at the exotic blend of ancient and modern buildings, the mix of people dressed in everything from business suits to caftans and head scarves. It was an incredible scene. Horns blared as taxicabs and automobiles challenged each other for space, ignored by little old ladies dressed all in black, trudging along the cobbled streets carrying string bags filled with vegetables and even live poultry.

The medina, or marketplace, was equally captivating. Mandy had gotten too brief a glimpse the day before. She and Dee Dee wandered happily through the warren of meandering little lanes, stopping to examine the jewelry and leather purses, the souvenir key rings and native clothing.

Dee Dee was so engrossed that she refused to stop for lunch. "We can get something from one of those stands. I don't want to waste time in a restaurant."

Since Mandy felt the same way, they bought huge rolls filled with meat, salad and pickles at a take-away snack bar. Mandy could only eat half of hers, but Dee Dee ate the whole thing and still had room to sample a kebab—barbe-cued meat wrapped in bread on a skewer.

"This is great," she mumbled with a full mouth. "You ought to try one."

"I would have if I'd seen them sooner. I'm too full now."

"You only ate half your sandwich. Are you one of those women who brags about eating like a bird? Barbara was one of those. She used to tell Dad food wasn't important to her, she could live on love." Dee Dee made a gagging sound.

"No man is that good," Mandy said disdainfully.

"That's what *I* think, but hey, I'm only twelve years old." Dee Dee grinned. "Maybe he really is that terrific."

"You'll have to get your information elsewhere, because I don't intend to find out."

"Dad's a gorgeous hunk. Women won't leave him alone. Aren't you even a little bit curious about his technique? That's not normal—unless you're frigid. Is that your prob-lem?"

Mandy was once again caught between amusement and annoyance. "I'm beginning to sympathize with your fa-ther—and not because he's besieged by women. Do you mind if we change the subject?"

"Okay, but I don't know why sex is such a big deal with grown-ups—everybody except my mom, that is."

"It must be hard to be so far away from her. Did she agree with your father about sending you to school in Switzer-land?"

"I don't know. He never asks her about stuff like that." Dee Dee caught sight of a pair of dangling gold earrings in a shop window. "Wow, look at those! Aren't they awe-some? Let's go inside."

Mandy was filled with indignation as she followed the young girl into the store. How could Connor try to cut Dee

Dee's mother out of her life? Obviously he had the money
to hire better attorneys than the poor woman. The courts
seldom favored the father—unless he was super rich. It was
unconscionable! Dee Dee was at an age when she needed her
mother. To make matters worse, it appeared that Connor
had only sued for custody out of spite. If he really cared that
much about his daughter, he wouldn't have sent her half a
world away.

Dee Dee wasn't nearly as troubled by the situation as
Mandy was. She haggled over the price of the jewelry like a
seasoned shopper, and left the store wearing both the earrings and a broad smile.

Her enjoyment was infectious. Mandy forgot about
Connor as they continued to explore the quaint little alley-
ways. It was late afternoon before either of them realized it.

"We'd better start looking for a taxi," Mandy said. "I
should be there when your father arrives."

Dee Dee looked apprehensive. "When's he coming?"

"His secretary said he'd be here this evening. I don'
know when, but I told Salima to expect him for dinner, jus
in case."

"It should be a jolly little meal. We'd better have antacid
tablets for an appetizer," Dee Dee said wryly.

"For you and me, anyway." Mandy laughed. "From
what I've seen of your father, he doesn't get ulcers, he gives
them."

Connor spent the entire morning in meetings, with more
scheduled for the rest of the day. It was standard procedure
on a business trip. What was unusual was the way his attention wavered in the afternoon.

The upcoming meeting in Tangier was important, but
everything had been arranged. He was used to delegating
responsibility and then putting the details out of his mind.
So why was he doodling a face on the notepad in front of
him while the treasurer of a company he was interested in

buying was giving some very important figures regarding the company's fiduciary position?

Connor never doodled aimlessly. Usually he made notes to himself or wrote down columns of figures and did rapid calculations. This face had nothing to do with high finance. The long-lashed blue eyes were seductive, and the soft lips were parted. How did he know the eyes were blue? Because the face was Mandy's.

Connor shook his head in irritation, as though to root her out of his mind. Mandy was an employee, one whose capabilities had yet to be determined. That was probably why he was thinking about her, not because of her flowerlike face and alluring figure. He knew plenty of beautiful women, and they didn't interfere with his work.

Mandy had talked her way into this job because he prized initiative. She lacked experience but, properly trained, she could be a valuable asset to his company. It made good sense for him to keep an eye on her.

After coming to a decision, Connor looked at his watch. "I think we've covered everything. You can fax me anything further that you think is pertinent. Thank you for your input, gentlemen. I have a plane to catch." He picked up his attaché case and strode out the door, ignoring their sputtered protests.

The estate Mandy had rented brought an approving nod from Connor as his limo traveled through the gates to the circular drive in front of the house. So far, so good.

Jemal, the uniformed manservant who answered the door, passed muster, too. Connor was feeling benevolent as he introduced himself. He was also looking forward to congratulating Mandy and perhaps having a drink with her to celebrate.

Jemal put a damper on those plans. "The lady is not here, sir."

"Where is she?"

"I do not know. She and the young one went out before lunch. They have not returned yet."

Connor gave him a puzzled look. "What young one? Do you have a child?"

"I have three beautiful children." The man beamed at him. "Two boys and one girl."

"Staying here this week?" Connor asked incredulously.

"Oh, no, no, no!" Jemal laughed merrily. "They are at home with their grandmother."

"But you just said— Never mind." Connor took a deep breath. "Who is the young one who went out with Miss Richardson?"

"The little blond girl? She said her name is Desiree."

"What the devil is she doing here?"

"I do not know, sir. It was not my place to ask."

"All right, you can take my bags upstairs."

Connor wandered through the downstairs, getting acquainted with the house. Although the rooms were beautifully furnished and spotlessly clean, his good mood had evaporated.

After the inspection tour, he went into the den and fixed himself a drink he didn't particularly want. Then he opened his briefcase and got out some paperwork. Connor had always been able to immerse himself in work no matter where he was, but today that ability deserted him. Where was Mandy? Didn't she know it wasn't safe for a woman to go wandering around Tangier alone? The mysterious little girl was forgotten in his concern for Mandy.

When he heard the taxi stop outside, Connor got to the front entry ahead of Jemal. Throwing the door open wide, he said, "It's about time you got back. I was starting to—" The words died briefly when he saw his daughter. "Dee Dee! What are you doing here?"

"Hi, Dad. Isn't this a nice surprise?" she asked brightly, ignoring his question.

Connor's face was ominous. "Did you get kicked out of school?"

"No!"

"Then why are you here?"

"That's a fine way to greet your only daughter!" She put on a pretense of indignation. "You haven't seen me in a month."

"Our reunion is going to be very brief," he answered grimly.

Dee Dee's chin jutted out to match his, and her eyes sparkled with anger. "Thanks for all the concern. For all you know, I could have been sent home from school because I'm suffering from a terminal disease, but do you even bother to ask? That'll be the day! All you want to do is get rid of me again."

"I must say, you're looking remarkably well for someone with a fragile grasp on life." His derisive expression darkened once more. "Let me rephrase my earlier question. Did you run away from school?"

"Why don't we all go inside?" Mandy asked hastily.

Connor's eyes were cold as he turned his attention to her. "What part did you play in my daughter's little caper?"

"Get real, Dad! I just met Mandy when I got here yesterday."

"You don't have to defend me." Mandy's quick temper was starting to simmer, but she realized Connor had a right to overreact. Her tone softened as she said to him, "I don't blame you for being upset, it was a crazy thing for her to do. But she's here now, and thank goodness nothing happened to her along the way."

"Until now," he snapped. "Come inside, Doris. I want to talk to you." He turned and strode through the open door.

"Bummer," Dee Dee muttered. "Dad only calls me Doris when he's *really* mad."

"You've just learned a valuable lesson," Mandy told her. "There's no free lunch."

"I thought you were on my side."

"It isn't a question of choosing sides. I might sympathize with you, but I can also see your father's point of view. Something serious could have happened to you."

"But it didn't. I'm not a total dweeb. I can take care of myself."

"I'm waiting," Connor reminded his daughter in an implacable voice. He stood in the doorway of the den, watching enigmatically as they walked slowly toward him.

"Stay with me," Dee Dee whispered, clutching Mandy's hand.

"I will if I can, but he might not let me," Mandy whispered back.

Connor's expression didn't change, but diverse emotions filled him—laughter and tenderness, among others. Their apprehension made them look like two naughty children. At that moment, Mandy didn't seem much older than Dee Dee.

They were both unaware of any chink in his armor as they filed into the den and sat next to each other on the edge of the sofa.

Connor closed the door and faced them, crossing his arms over his impressive chest and gazing at his daughter. "Before I accuse your headmistress of criminal negligence, I'd like to hear what story you told her. I know you have an inventive mind, but what could possibly persuade a presumably responsible woman to allow a child to travel to Africa all alone?"

"I didn't tell anybody," Dee Dee answered in a small voice. "I just left."

"You walked out with a suitcase and nobody thought to ask where you were going? I presume you did bring some clothes with you?"

Dee Dee and Mandy exchanged a glance. "I just had a tote bag," the young girl mumbled.

"Good, then you won't have much to pack for your return trip."

Dee Dee sprang to her feet. "I'm not going back there!"

"Oh, yes, you are. On the first available plane."

"You can send me back, but I'll just run away again. And this time I'll disappear for good. You don't care what happens to me, anyway."

"Stop talking like a child," Connor said impatiently.

"It's true! I told you I hate it there, but you wouldn't listen."

"That's not true. We've had long discussions on the subject. I said I'd consider making a change if you'd stick it out until the end of the term."

"No way!"

"You don't understand. I'm not giving you a choice."

Father and daughter faced each other with equal determination, neither prepared to give an inch. Somebody had to intervene before they both made a grave mistake.

"I'm sure it's a good school, but perhaps it isn't right for Dee Dee," Mandy said hesitantly. "Maybe you should listen to her reasons for wanting to make a change."

"I can already guess," Connor said. "They refuse to let her slide by with half an effort. My daughter is a bright girl, but you wouldn't know it by her grades."

"Okay, so maybe I goofed off a little," Dee Dee admitted. "You didn't have to stick me in a Swiss jail! All I'm gonna learn there is how to be Susie Supersnob."

Connor gave her a perplexed look. "I realize it's a big change for you. I'm just asking you to give the school a chance."

"I did!"

"Why don't you let Dee Dee stay here this week?" Mandy said placatingly, when it appeared another impasse was imminent. "You can discuss the matter calmly and perhaps come to some compromise."

"It isn't negotiable," Connor stated flatly.

"I'm sure that isn't the way you conduct your business," Mandy coaxed. "Your way, or none at all."

"This happens to be a lot more important than my business," he snapped. "Whether either of you believe it or not, Dee Dee's welfare is of primary importance to me."

"Then listen to what she has to say. *I* have, and a lot of it makes sense."

He looked at her with annoyance. "It's easy to give advice when you don't bear any of the responsibility. I know my daughter better than you do, Ms. Richardson. She can be very convincing. She's obviously made a convert out of you."

"You don't have to tell me this is none of my business. I know that. But sometimes an outsider can see things with a little more perspective. I think you and Dee Dee need to talk frankly to each other, and this week would be a good time."

The young girl held her breath as Connor considered the idea. Finally he said, "As long as she's already here, I suppose a few more days won't make that much difference. I'll admit I'm less than pleased with the supervision at that school. The headmistress and I are going to have a long talk."

Dee Dee threw her arms around Mandy's neck and whispered, "Thank you! You're the greatest!"

Connor gave her a level look. "You're not out of the woods yet, young lady. When I hear all the details of this little escapade, you might be grounded until you're twenty-one."

"Just pour yourself a stiff drink and keep telling yourself she got here safely," Mandy advised.

"That might necessitate two drinks." He walked over to the built-in bar. "Can I fix you one?"

"While you mellow out, I'm gonna see if they delivered my new clothes," Dee Dee said.

Connor paused with a decanter in his hand. "New clothes?"

"You don't want to know." Mandy laughed.

"Probably not," he said as his daughter hastily left the room.

Mandy changed the subject. "Are you happy with the house?"

"Yes, it's exactly what I had in mind. You did a good job."

"Thanks," she said matter-of-factly, to cover her pleasure. A lot of people were vocal when you goofed, but not all of them expressed appreciation. "Everything is set for the welcoming cocktail party here tomorrow night. I also booked a restaurant near the hotel for dinner afterward, since it's the first night and they might be jet-lagged."

He nodded. "Good thinking."

"You said you wanted to remain flexible, so the only other reservation I made is at a restaurant that serves an authentic Moroccan dinner with entertainment afterward—a snake charmer and belly dancers, that sort of thing. This is subject to your approval, of course."

Connor looked amused. "I suppose the men would enjoy that."

"Anybody would. It's something you don't get a chance to see very often."

Her slightly wistful tone registered. "You can come along if you like."

"I wasn't hinting for an invitation."

"I know that. But there's no reason you can't attend all the social events. In fact, it's a good idea. I'd like you to act as my hostess."

"Is that really wise? One woman in a whole group of men might inhibit them."

"You won't be the only woman. Several of the heads of these corporations are female." Connor smiled at the look of surprise on Mandy's face. "I'm not the male chauvinist you think I am."

"I never said you were," she protested.

"But it's what you were thinking."

Was that her opinion? Mandy examined her feelings. "I don't really know you," she said slowly. "My first impression was that you're a very forceful man, demanding yet fair."

"So far I can't quarrel with your assessment." He smiled. "However, I sense a *but* in there somewhere."

"Not really." Belated caution caught up with her. It didn't do to be *too* honest.

"Don't start pulling your punches now. I have a hide like a rhinoceros."

"I'm not just being polite. That's really all I know from my own experience, and I don't believe in being influenced by things I hear."

Amusement glinted in his gray eyes. "What have you heard?"

"Most of my information comes from the society columns," Mandy said reluctantly, since she knew he'd insist on an answer. "You're the preferred escort of all the beautiful women in San Francisco."

"Not all of them." He looked at her appraisingly. "You said most of your information. Where does the rest come from?"

"It isn't important."

"Now I'm really curious. Who's been feeding you spicy gossip?"

"I don't listen to gossip," she said, avoiding his eyes.

"Everybody does, it's human nature. If you don't want to tell me who told you, at least tell me what was said. I have a right to defend myself."

"It wasn't anything derogatory. If you must know, I heard you have a preference for blondes, and your attention span isn't very long. There, are you happy now?"

"Not especially, since your information is faulty." He gazed at her classic features, like a connoisseur examining a work of art. "I can appreciate beauty in any form. Women with pale skin and a cloud of dark hair are just as appealing as blondes, maybe more so, because the contrast is so striking.''

Mandy knew better than to attach any importance to the compliment. ''You don't have to be gallant with me,'' she said tartly. ''I work for you.''

''That means we can be honest with each other, which I was being. You're a very beautiful woman, Mandy. I'm not the first man to tell you that.''

She was uncharacteristically rattled. It was true that many men had been in love with her, but the feeling had never been mutual. She certainly wasn't in love with Connor, but he held a powerful attraction for her. There was no use denying it. She was acutely aware of everything about him—his lithe body, so deceptively relaxed, his intelligent face, not merely classically handsome but filled with character. It was no wonder women fought over him—but she had no intention of joining their ranks.

''I realize you're trying to be nice, but I'd prefer to keep our relationship strictly business,'' she said crisply.

''Nobody has ever accused me of trying to be 'nice.''' He chuckled. ''Especially not when a lovely woman is involved. Men are predatory animals, and I can't claim to be unique. But I don't let my personal feelings interfere with business. Let me assure you that you're perfectly safe with me.''

As Mandy wondered how safe any woman could be with a man like that, Dee Dee came bouncing back into the den.

''Do I have time for a swim before dinner?'' she asked. ''That swimming pool is awesome!''

''We can have dinner anytime your father likes.'' Mandy looked inquiringly at Connor. ''Why don't you and Dee Dee go for a swim?''

''Is that your way of making peace between us?'' he asked. ''Father and daughter find understanding in togetherness?''

"Unless you'd prefer to pursue your private war."

"Point well-taken." He looked at her speculatively. "I never realized what a designing woman you are."

"I wouldn't say that." Mandy smiled enchantingly. "People sometimes back themselves into a corner. I just show them the way out."

"Or cut off their escape route. I pity the man you set your sights on," Connor remarked ironically. "He won't stand a chance."

Mandy felt vindicated a little later, when she glanced out the window and saw Dee Dee and her father in serious conversation on the edge of the pool. The young girl was making her point passionately while Connor listened intently. The important thing was that neither was letting anger interfere.

Mandy was careful not to ask questions when they all gathered for dinner later. She didn't have to. Dee Dee was only too happy to supply the details.

"Dad agreed with me that those snooty girls are dorks," she crowed.

"That doesn't mean I condone your actions," he warned.

"Yeah, I know, but I'll bet you would have flown the coop, too. You always told me bigotry is wrong. I learned from the best."

"Don't try to butter me up, young lady. I agree with you on that particular school. It was an unfortunate choice, but I'm not convinced that boarding school is a bad idea."

"But, Dad! You can't—"

"You'll have all week to discuss it." Mandy stepped in deftly.

"Unfortunately, this isn't the best time for a father-daughter conference," Connor said. "The entire week is closely scheduled."

"I won't get in the way," Dee Dee promised. "You won't even know I'm here."

"You've never been the self-effacing type," he remarked dryly. "All I ask is that you refrain from doing anything outrageous. Millions of dollars are riding on this meeting."

"Wow! Can I have a raise in my allowance?"

"Nice try. Just consider yourself lucky that I don't make you pay for your ticket here. By the way, where did you get the money?"

"This was sure a good dinner," Dee Dee said hurriedly. "I think I'll go in the kitchen and tell Salima. May I be excused?"

"I suppose so," Connor said indulgently. "I've had enough surprises for one day. I don't really want to hear any more." He watched his daughter leave the room. "If this doesn't discourage you from having kids, nothing will," he told Mandy.

"You're a real softy." She smiled. "I never would have suspected it."

"I'm a pushover for manipulative females. It's a challenge to try and outwit them, although I never do."

"I don't believe that for a minute. You're a very successful man. I'm sure you don't lose very often."

"That depends on whether you're talking about business or pleasure." A little smile played around his mobile mouth as he gazed at her. "Business relationships are a lot more straightforward than personal ones. A man has never tried to cloud my judgment by batting his eyelashes at me or dishing out compliments."

"No woman with any self-respect would, either."

"Some women are distracting without even trying to be," he murmured.

Mandy felt her pulse quicken at his deep velvet tone. She was glad when Jemal provided a diversion.

After they had both declined more coffee, Connor said, "It's a beautiful night. Would you care to take a stroll through the grounds? You can show me around."

"I'd like to, they're simply beautiful," she said.

* * *

A full moon bathed everything in a silvery light. They strolled along neat paths bordered by flower beds whose colors were muted in the semidarkness.

"This is such a perfect setting for entertaining," Mandy remarked. "What would you think about having lunch served by the pool? I could have a bar set up out here, and maybe pipe in some music. There are speakers on the terrace."

"This is a business meeting," Connor reminded her. "We don't linger over lunch."

"You just eat and go right back to work? Those must be very high-powered meetings. I don't really understand exactly what you do."

"We implement acquisitions and mergers." He laughed at the puzzled look on her face. "That doesn't make things any clearer, does it?"

"Not much. There doesn't seem to be any product involved. All you make is money."

"That's the general idea, although there are risks involved." They had circled back to the pool area, and Connor pulled out a chair for her. "Let's sit here, and I'll try to explain it to you." He sat facing her. "There are a lot of small companies that are mismanaged. Some of them make a good product, but they're losing money. We buy up those companies. That's one phase of our business."

"Why would you want something that's losing money?"

"Often it's simply a case of their equipment being outdated, or perhaps the payroll is too fat. If the company is basically sound, we make it productive. Retool if it's a factory, and cut out the deadwood."

"You mean, fire people?"

He shrugged. "If they're not pulling their weight."

"But that's so heartless!"

"There's no room for sentiment in business." His features looked hawklike in the moonlight. "Actually, that's not as cold as it sounds. We don't fire people summarily. We offer them early retirement, or a realistic wage based on the work they do. After we turn the company around and make it profitable, we sell it and move on.''

"You said that was only one phase of your business.''

"Another aspect is buying small companies and merging them with larger ones. Sometimes that entails moving the operation to a different state.''

"What happens to the employees of the smaller companies? Do they all lose their jobs?''

"I'm not Attila the Hun, Mandy,'' Connor said patiently. "I don't roam the country looting businesses and destroying the workers. Nobody is fired. Everyone is given the opportunity to relocate in a comparable position.''

"But it's like playing chess with real chessmen. You're the one who makes the decisions about their lives.''

"There's another way of looking at it. The companies we take over are shaky to begin with. If they didn't sell to us, the majority of them would go under and then nobody would have a job. Would that be any better?''

"No,'' she admitted.

What Connor said made sense, but the amount of power he wielded made Mandy uneasy. Did he really care about anyone, or were people just pawns to be used for his convenience? Even his personal relationships weren't permanent. As she gazed uncertainly at his autocratic face, he smiled, and the illusion of ruthlessness disappeared.

"Now you know more than you ever wanted to know about acquisitions and mergers,'' he said. "Tell me about your industry. I'm sure it's much more interesting.''

"If you like living vicariously. We spend all day planning glamorous vacations for other people.''

"Don't you get perks like free cruises and discounts at hotels?''

"Sometimes, but it's hard to get away now that there are only two of us in the office.''

"How about your large staff?" Connor's eyes danced with amusement. "Can't they handle things?"

Mandy bit her lip, chagrined at her slip of the tongue. She had allowed herself to become too relaxed. Never a good idea with a man like Connor.

"It's all right." He chuckled. "I know you run a small operation. I had you checked out after our meeting."

"And you still took a chance on us? That was very generous of you."

"I admire guts. You have to go after what you want, even if it means bluffing to get it. I've stonewalled myself, on occasion."

"I might have given you the idea that our agency was a little larger than it is, but I didn't really lie to you," she said carefully. "I said we could do the job. You're satisfied, aren't you?"

"I have no complaints so far."

"The rest of the week will go just as smoothly. That's what I'm here for."

"Is this fouling up your private life?"

"I'm a professional. My clients get top priority."

"Very commendable, but it must be hard on your personal relationships," he persisted. "Is there someone special who's annoyed with me for monopolizing you this week?"

"It wouldn't change anything, but no, there's nobody special."

"You'd rather drive a lot of men crazy instead of just one?" He grinned.

"I don't play those kind of games."

"Every woman does," he answered cynically.

"You'd find out differently if you dated career women instead of dilettantes. Women who are capable of pulling their own weight don't need to manipulate men."

"You didn't want anything from me when I interviewed you?" he teased.

"That was different," Mandy protested. "Yes, I wanted your business, but in exchange for expert services."

"There's usually a quid pro quo involved," Connor said dryly.

A warning bell rang as she realized the kind of services he was referring to. "When you told me we had a deal, I spelled out exactly what I was prepared to do. I thought we were in agreement."

"Don't worry, I haven't changed the rules," he said with amusement. "You're very lovely, and I'd like to make love to you. I know it would be a memorable experience for me, and I'd try to ensure that it was equally enjoyable for you. Unfortunately, it would complicate matters, which is why you have nothing to worry about."

Mandy forced herself to match his clinical detachment—not an easy feat, when her body was as taut as a violin string. "I'm not worried. I know you're just amusing yourself by trying to get a rise out of me."

"Do you always underestimate men so badly?" Getting to his feet, he held out a hand to her. "Well, tomorrow is going to be a big day. Are you ready? I think it's time we turned in." When she looked up at him warily, Connor laughed. "I meant to our respective bedrooms."

"I knew that," she said hastily, taking his extended hand, because she didn't have much choice.

He talked about some last-minute details as they strolled into the house. They parted at the top of the stairs. Connor went in one direction and Mandy in the other. She was grateful for her foresight in selecting a room far from his.

Not that it would have made any difference if they were next door to each other. She was sure her assessment of him was correct. Connor had only been teasing her because he sensed that she was uncertain around him.

Mandy couldn't understand why, and nobody who knew her would ever have believed it. The shoe had always been on the other foot. Men jumped through hoops to try to

please her. So why did Connor rattle her so inexplicably? He
was just a man like all the others. Well, maybe a little richer
and more experienced, but that was no reason to act like a
star struck schoolgirl around him.

As she climbed into bed, Mandy vowed not to react from
now on, no matter what Connor did or said. Not even if he
wasn't joking when he said he wanted to make love to her.
She reached up quickly and turned out the light.

Chapter Three

Mandy was up and dressed early the next morning. As Connor had said, it was going to be a busy day. His associates were coming not only from all over the world, but also at different times during the morning and afternoon.

Mandy had arranged for a fleet of cars and drivers to meet their planes and drive them to the hotel. But to make sure everyone received the VIP treatment, she needed to be at the airport to see for herself.

It was late afternoon before she returned to the house to check on the arrangements for the welcoming cocktail party. This was equally important. Nothing must go wrong.

Luckily, it looked as though nothing would. The house was spotless and filled with flowers, and a catering crew was busily at work in the kitchen. The only potential problem was Dee Dee. She wanted to come to the party.

"You'll have to take that up with your father," Mandy said.

"Couldn't you ask him for me?"

"No, I can't. I've already meddled enough, and besides, I have a lot to do."

"Like what? There's a whole army of people swarming around. What's left to do?"

"Somebody has to make sure they don't forget anything. I went to a party once where the hostess forgot to serve an entire tray of hors d'oeuvres."

Connor appeared at the door of the den. "Oh, good, you're back. Can you come in here for a moment, Mandy?"

She joined him, with Dee Dee trailing along behind.

After asking whether everyone had arrived without incident, he said, "The hotel was supposed to send over a secretary, but she didn't show up. I phoned them, but nobody seemed to know anything about it. Are you sure you arranged for one?"

"That was one of the first things I did. Don't worry, I'll take care of it." Mandy looked at her watch. "It's getting rather late. If they say they can't send anyone until tomorrow morning, will that be acceptable?"

Connor frowned. "I have some invitations to be addressed. I wanted to hand them out this evening."

"I can do that," Dee Dee volunteered.

He looked at her doubtfully. "How is your handwriting?"

"I don't use a crayon anymore," she answered sarcastically. "And I can print in big block letters now."

"Okay, I get your message." He laughed. "The list of names is on the desk, next to that stack of envelopes. I appreciate your help."

"No problem. I'll hand them out for you at the cocktail party," Dee Dee said casually.

His response was prompt and firm. "You're not coming. It's a party for adults."

"That's not fair! I'm practically an adult."

"You aren't even a teenager yet—although, God knows, you act like one."

"I'll leave you two to slug it out," Mandy said.

"Stay here," he said. "I want to go over a couple of things with you." When she hesitated, he asked, "Do you have something else to do?"

"Nothing important. I was just going to run over to the hotel and try to find something suitable to wear tonight. I didn't expect to need anything dressy. It's all right, though, I'll manage somehow."

"No problem. Call the shop and have them send over a selection for you to choose from. You'll need several outfits. Have them charged to me."

"Tell them to send something in my size, too," Dee Dee said.

"You are not coming to the party, young lady."

The girl's lower lip jutted out, but she appealed mutely to Mandy instead of her father.

"It might be educational for her to meet such a cosmopolitan group," Mandy suggested tentatively.

"A cocktail party is no place for a child," Connor stated.

"A minute ago I was a young lady. Now I'm a child?" Dee Dee asked indignantly. "By the end of the week I'll be back in a crib!"

"Cocktail parties are really overrated," Mandy consoled her. "You won't be missing anything."

"Yeah, sure! You'll all be down here having fun, and I'll be upstairs in the nursery!"

Connor gave her a level look. "Perhaps you'd be happier in school. I'd be glad to put you on a plane."

"Okay, okay, but when I have children I'm not going to treat them like second-class citizens!" Dee Dee stormed out of the room.

He sighed. "She was such a sweet little girl, just last year."

Mandy smiled. "She's still a sweet little girl. She just can't wait to grow up. You're right about the party tonight, but maybe she can come with us when we go to the show with the snake charmer.''

''I suppose that would be all right.''

''Then why don't you go upstairs and tell her so? It will give her something to look forward to.''

Connor smiled wryly. ''You're manipulating me again. But I must admit you've made my life a lot easier. By the time this week is over, you'll be indispensable. Would you consider moving in with us?''

Mandy laughed. ''I might, if I can have my own room and kitchen privileges.''

His expression changed as he gazed at her soft mouth. ''I can make you a better offer than that.''

The phone rang. When Connor answered it, his manner changed. He was once more the remote tycoon as he listened to a report from halfway around the world.

This was the real Connor Winfield, Mandy reminded herself. Any woman who took him seriously was in for heartbreak.

A selection of dresses was delivered to the house a little later. When Mandy was sure everything was running smoothly, she went upstairs to see if they'd sent anything suitable. That was no problem. All of the outfits were stunning.

Dee Dee appeared in the doorway. ''Can I help you decide?''

''Yes, I can use another opinion.''

In her right hand, Mandy held up a pink satin cocktail suit with a short jacket fastened with rhinestone buttons. The hanger in her left hand held a slinky paisley chemise, beaded and sequined in all the colors of the Taj Mahal. It had a short skirt and a deeply scooped neckline.

''No contest. The beaded one, for sure,'' Dee Dee proclaimed. ''It's *mucho* sexy.''

''I don't want to look sexy. I want to look competent.''

"There's no law that says you can't look glamorous, too. Go for it. Dad will be blown away."

Mandy doubted it, but the dress was very tempting. "It's awfully expensive," she said dubiously.

"He won't mind. He told you to pick out a bunch of stuff, didn't he? Dad's very generous."

"Why don't you ever tell *him* nice things like that?"

Dee Dee grinned. "If I didn't give him a hard time, he'd think there was something wrong with me."

"Well, you might lighten up a little this week. Your father has a lot on his mind."

"Okay," Dee Dee answered meekly. "If you say so."

Mandy was already downstairs when Connor came down. She was outside on the terrace, looking approvingly at the gardenias drifting slowly over the glassy surface of the swimming pool, almost in rhythm with the soft music that played in the background.

Connor stood inside the French doors, gazing at her for the few moments before she became aware of him. His eyes held a predatory gleam as they traveled over her slender figure and long, slim legs.

When she turned her head and noticed him, he joined her on the terrace. "I see you found something to wear." The feral desire on his face had changed to mild approval.

"I hope this isn't too extreme. Dee Dee talked me into it."

"My daughter has good taste, although you'd never know it from the torn jeans and T-shirts she wears at home."

"Enjoy it before she moves into haute couture. This dress was terribly expensive."

"It's a business expense," he said dismissively.

"You don't think it's too sexy?" Mandy persisted, trying to goad him into a compliment.

Connor was far from being blown away as Dee Dee had predicted. Not that she wanted him to be, but it wouldn't hurt him to express approval, if nothing else. She had to settle for faint praise.

"I think it's in very good taste," he said.

The guests started arriving a few minutes later, and Mandy was too busy to be annoyed with Connor. There were seven men and three women in the group, from such diverse locations as Europe, Australia and the Far East. Two of the women were CEOs of large companies. The third was the petite wife of a Japanese businessman.

Connor made the introductions, and at first everyone was formally polite, as strangers often are at a party before they get to know each other. Mandy did her best to break the ice.

While chatting with a man from Germany, she discovered that he traveled regularly to Tokyo. Maneuvering him over to the Japanese couple, she suggested that perhaps they had mutual acquaintances. They were soon in animated conversation, and she moved on to someone else.

Mandy wasn't aware of it, but Connor was watching her. She finally got the approval she wanted—although it wasn't exactly personal.

He came over to her when she was alone for a moment. "I'm impressed," he said. "You're handling this beautifully."

"Thanks. I had my fingers crossed, but the caterers are really great. Everyone seems to like the hors d'oeuvres."

"That's nice, but it wasn't what I was referring to. You're very good with people. I admire the way you're able to get them to loosen up."

"I've always been good at parties." She smiled. "It's one of my more trivial talents."

"On the contrary, I consider it an asset. These business affairs can be quite awkward until everyone gets to know one another. Thanks to you, we're off to a good start."

"I'm glad you're pleased with my efforts. Jet Away would certainly like to have all your business." She wouldn't get a better chance to pitch her cause.

He stared at her consideringly. "I was thinking of making you a different kind of offer."

She gave him a startled look. That would sound like a proposition from any other man, but the look on Connor's face was business. Still, you never knew about men.

"What kind of offer did you have in mind?" she asked cautiously.

"This isn't the time or place to discuss it. Perhaps we can talk later tonight, when we're alone."

Mandy stared at him searchingly, but she couldn't detect anything personal in his expression. Before she could comment, they were joined by one of the women guests.

Isabella Romano was the head of an Italian company—that was all Mandy knew about her. She was a stunningly attractive woman with an excellent figure, glossy dark hair and an air of confidence. The hand she put on Connor's arm was tipped with long red nails.

"I am looking forward to our meeting tomorrow." Her voice was low and throaty.

"I expect it to be quite productive," he said. "We all share mutual interests."

"I felt that immediately." She gazed at him with a little smile. "I am sure we will reach a satisfactory arrangement."

Mandy wondered cynically if Isabella was talking about business or pleasure. It was obvious that she found Connor sexy. Was he receptive? She couldn't tell by his face. He wore a charming smile that concealed any real feelings.

"Isabella is the CEO of Fabbrica Italia," he told Mandy. "Their mills make fabrics for some of the leading couture houses."

"How interesting," Mandy said to her. "You must get inside information about the new styles before they're shown."

"I am afraid not. The collections are guarded fiercely, but I do have some indication of what colors will be predominant."

"The gown you're wearing is lovely." Mandy admired the other woman's chic black dress. "Is that your fabric?"

"Yes, this is peau de soie. I have a marvelous dressmaker who designs most of my things."

"I'll leave you ladies to discuss fashion. My presence here is clearly superfluous," Connor said.

"You are too modest. Any woman would welcome your company," Isabella said in a velvet voice.

"You don't have to be polite." He laughed. "Enjoy your conversation."

The Italian woman watched him walk away. "He is a very charismatic man," she commented. "Have you been with him long?"

Mandy wasn't sure what Isabella was implying, but she hastened to set the record straight. "Connor hired me to make arrangements for this meeting. I only met him a short time ago."

"Then you are not . . . involved?"

"Only in seeing that everything runs smoothly. Our relationship is strictly business."

Isabella continued to watch Connor as he moved around the room with the coordinated grace of an athlete. "That is appropriate during working hours, but the nights are another matter."

"Not to me," Mandy answered evenly. "I don't believe it's wise to get involved with one's boss."

"With a gorgeous man like that one, who wants to be sensible?" Isabella murmured. "Excuse me, I think I will sample the canapés." She drifted off in Connor's direction instead.

A man came over to take her place. "At last, I have you alone," he said. "My patience is rewarded."

Jacques Gallet was in his early fifties, but he kept himself in top physical shape. He could have passed for a much younger man, in spite of the touch of gray at his temples. It gave him a distinguished look, and he had the legendary charm of a Frenchman.

Mandy pretended to misunderstand his meaning. "Is there something I can get for you—another drink, perhaps?"

"The pleasure of your company is enough. You are an enchanting woman."

"And you are very direct," she answered with amusement.

"Alas, I do not have time to spare. At any moment our host might return to claim you. He would be a fool if he did not."

"There seems to be a misconception going around. Connor is my employer. I'm here solely to see that his guests are happy."

"You have succeeded admirably with me."

"You're easily pleased, Mr. Gallet," she said lightly.

"Jacques, please, and may I call you Mandy?"

"Certainly."

"Have you ever been to Paris, Mandy?"

"Yes, but not for quite a while. I'd love to go back. Paris is such a fascinating city."

"I would like to show you the parts a tourist does not see."

"That would certainly be a bonus," she said brightly. "Although there's a lot to do even if you don't know anyone there."

"But how much nicer if you do." He took her arm. "It is quite warm in here. Let us stroll outside by the swimming pool."

She didn't have much choice, but there was no reason to refuse. Jacques wasn't the first man who had come on strong with her. Mandy was adept at discouraging amorous men without damaging their fragile egos.

She was smiling at a comment of his as he led her through the French doors, unaware of Connor watching from across the room. The look of displeasure on his strong face deepened as they disappeared from sight.

Mandy was startled when Jacques took her in his arms. As she stiffened instinctively, he waltzed her around the terrace in time with the soft music. She relaxed, glad that she hadn't overreacted.

"Dancing is a very civilized pursuit, is it not?" he murmured in her ear.

"I never heard it described that way," she answered, trying to put distance between them.

"Think about it, *chérie*. Suppose a man meets a woman and his desire for her is instantaneous. If he gives in to his first impulse, he is at risk of having his face slapped. But on the dance floor, all is possible."

"Not *all*, Jacques." Mandy drew away. "You're moving too speedily for me."

"I meant no disrespect." He took both of her hands. "It is my nature to worship perfection when I find it."

As she glanced away, trying to figure out how to discourage him without creating a sticky situation, Mandy noticed a shadowy figure on the balcony overlooking the terrace. Dee Dee was leaning over the railing watching them. When she saw she'd been discovered, the young girl gave a thumbs-up salute. Mandy couldn't help laughing.

Jacques's dignity was ruffled. "You find that amusing?" he asked stiffly.

"Not at all. It's a lovely sentiment, one that I'm sure our little eavesdropper will repeat to all her girlfriends." She gestured toward the upper story.

Dee Dee wasn't a bit embarrassed. "Hi, I'm Desiree."

Jacques smiled up at her, his good humor restored. "I thought perhaps your name was Juliet."

"You can be my Romeo any day. This guy's a keeper," she told Mandy.

"Meet Connor's daughter," Mandy said. "Sometimes known as Dee Dee."

"I did not know he had a grown-up daughter," Jacques said with a twinkle in his eyes.

Dee Dee didn't notice it. "You see? Everybody but my dad can tell how mature I am."

"You have a lot of growing up to do if you believe everything a man tells you," Mandy said dryly.

"Surely you are not referring to me?" Jacques asked in mock dismay. "I cherish women too much to try to deceive them."

"I'll buy that." Dee Dee was hanging over the railing, clearly having the time of her life. "You can go ahead and kiss her if you want. It's okay."

"With whom?" Mandy asked crisply. "Don't you have something better to do than hang out on the balcony?"

"What else is there to do around here? I can't come to the party, and I don't have a television set in my room."

"Poor underprivileged kid," Mandy said with exaggerated sympathy. "Why don't you read a book? You might even learn something."

"Watching you two is just as educational. When I start to date—like when I'm around twenty-five if Dad has anything to say about it—I'll know what moves to expect."

Jacques exchanged an amused look with Mandy. "As much as I would like to contribute to your education, I find myself distracted in the company of two such fascinating ladies. I can give neither the attention she deserves." He blew a kiss toward the balcony. "Farewell, Juliet. Call me when you are twenty-five and your father lets you go out with men."

"Count on it!" Dee Dee answered.

Jacques had his arm lightly around Mandy's shoulders, and she was laughing up at him as they strolled back into the house. A flash of annoyance crossed Connor's face and was gone in an instant. When Isabella linked her arm through his and murmured a few words, anyone would have thought she had his full attention.

That was the impression Mandy got—and she reacted with the same disapproval he'd shown. She couldn't care less about his love life, Mandy told herself, but he wasn't being very professional. These were his guests and potential business associates. Did he expect her to carry the entire social responsibility while he pursued his own interests?

Mandy's criticism wasn't strictly fair. Connor wasn't devoting himself entirely to Isabella. The Italian woman's eyes never left his face, but he was including Nigel, the banker from London, in their conversation.

Mandy turned away and beckoned to one of the waiters. "Would you care for some hors d'oeuvres?" she asked Jacques.

"I would prefer to find a quiet spot where we can continue our talk," he answered.

"This is a party," she chided him. "You're supposed to get acquainted with the other guests."

"I will be spending the rest of the week with them. You are the one I want to know better."

"You'll be seeing me all week, too."

"Someplace more private than this, I would hope. Can we not slip away and have a quiet dinner together?"

"I'm afraid not. I've made reservations for the entire group at a restaurant that was highly recommended. I'm sure you'll like it."

"Only if you will be my dinner partner."

"I'll have to confer with Connor on the seating arrangements," she said evasively.

Jacques glanced over to where Isabella was still glued to Connor's side. "I think our host has already decided on his own partner for the evening."

"Yes, well, will you excuse me for a moment? I must speak to the caterer."

It was the only excuse she could think of to get away. Jacques's attention had been flattering at first, but he was a little too persistent. She continued on to the kitchen, in case he was watching.

After chatting with the caterers for a few minutes and expressing her satisfaction with their work, Mandy returned to the living room. Jacques was talking to the Japanese couple, so she went over to join a group that included Margaret Bradbury, an American woman who was president of her own company. She was chatting with Robert and Wesley Conover, two brothers from Australia who owned sheep ranches.

"Does anybody need another drink?" Mandy asked.

"No, your help is very efficient," Margaret answered. "I wish I could find people like them at home."

"Where are you from?"

"Metropolitan New York."

"My very favorite city," Mandy said.

"Have you ever been to Sydney?" Robert asked.

"No, but I've always wanted to visit Australia. I've sent a lot of people there, and they all came home raving about your country. I operate a travel agency in San Francisco," Mandy explained.

"I thought you worked for Connor," Wesley said.

"He's one of our clients. I made all the arrangements for this trip. If you have any problems, just let me know and I'll take care of them. Are your rooms at the hotel satisfactory?"

"Very comfortable." Margaret nodded. "I must admit I was surprised to find such first-rate accommodations in Tangier."

"There are good hotels outside of New York City," Robert teased. "We even have some in Australia. You should come and visit us, so you'll know what to recommend to your clients," he told Mandy. "I'll show you Sydney in depth."

"You will have to wait your turn." Jacques had come up behind Mandy. He put an arm around her shoulders. "The lady has promised to visit me in Paris."

Mandy turned aside casually, so that his arm was dislodged. "I'd like to visit all the great cities of the world, but unfortunately I'm a working woman. I have to get back to my business."

"You can take a flight from Paris," Jacques coaxed. "At least we could have a weekend together."

Mandy was very conscious of Margaret's raised eyebrows and the knowing looks the two other men exchanged. It was difficult to conceal her irritation with Jacques, but she couldn't afford the luxury of telling him to buzz off.

"Weekends are the busiest days of the week for working women," she said with a tight smile. "That's when we take our clothes to the cleaner, try to revive all the plants we neglected from Monday to Friday and plead with a repairman to give us an appointment in this century."

"You're so right," Margaret agreed. "It's a lot easier to deal with the president of a bank than it is with a plumber."

"And will someone tell me why plumbing always gets stopped up on a weekend?" Mandy laughed.

"It's Murphy's Law of economics," Margaret said. "Plumbers get double time on Sundays."

Jacques had a one-track mind, and he didn't intend to be derailed. "Surely you are joking about the way you spend your weekends," he said to Mandy.

"Those are the peaceful ones. Sometimes they get really frantic."

"All the more reason to seize a few days of rest and relaxation while you can."

"I don't even allow myself to think about it," Mandy replied lightly. She glanced across the room. "Excuse me, I think Mr. Nakamura wants to speak to me."

She walked across the room and joined the group around the Japanese couple, but it was no use. After a few moments, Jacques followed her.

Mandy was beginning to lose patience with him, but it was a catch-22 situation. She had assured Connor that this week would run smoothly. He wouldn't be impressed if she had a problem with one of his associates on the first night—regardless of the fact that she'd done nothing to encourage Jacques.

While she was struggling with the dilemma, Connor joined their group. He was very affable, the perfect host, but Mandy could tell something was wrong. His smile didn't reach his eyes, especially when he looked at her. It wasn't long before she found out why.

After making small talk for a few minutes, Connor said, "Would you excuse us for a moment? I have a little matter to straighten out with Mandy."

As he took her arm in a firm grip and led her away, she tried to figure out what had upset him. The guests were clearly enjoying themselves. What possible complaint could he have?

Connor wasted no time in telling her. "In case you've confused this cocktail party with a social event, let me remind you that it's a business gathering. In your role as hostess, you are supposed to circulate among the guests."

"That's what I've been doing. You even complimented me on the way I was handling the job."

"That was when the party first started—before you began to devote all of your attention to one guest."

Mandy's first impulse was to tell him it wasn't by choice, that Jacques didn't understand the word *no* in any language. But she didn't want Connor to get the idea that she couldn't handle such a minor problem.

"What you do on your own time is your affair," he continued. "It's scarcely businesslike, however, to ignore everyone else in your... pursuit of happiness, shall we say?"

Mandy gasped at the injustice of his accusation. "You're a fine one to talk! How about *your* grab for the gold ring with that Italian sexpot?"

Connor frowned. "I have no idea what you're talking about."

"Oh, really? You and Isabella have been closer than Siamese twins all evening."

"That's ridiculous! We've been standing in the middle of the room, talking to other people. I didn't take her outside for a romantic stroll in the moonlight."

"Jacques said it was warm in here and he wanted to go outside for a breath of air. What was I supposed to do?"

"He's a grown man. I'm sure he could have found his way out and back without your help. What were you doing out there all that time? You were gone for over fifteen minutes."

"Were you timing me?" Mandy asked incredulously.

"Of course not! I just happened to notice that you weren't around when...uh...when Isabella brought up your name."

"It's hard to believe she even remembered it. Her only interest in me was making sure I wasn't going to give her any competition. When I assured her that you and I have no interest in each other, she purred like a cat."

Connor's face became even more austere. "I don't require your affection, but I think I have a right to expect professionalism. From now on I'd like you to distribute your attention more evenly. Is that clear?"

"Perfectly," she answered, gritting her teeth in an effort to contain her anger.

As they faced each other tautly, Dee Dee appeared unexpectedly. She had exchanged her jeans for a pretty blouse and skirt, and her sneakers for shoes with little heels.

"Oh, is the party still going on?" she asked in mock surprise.

"It's almost over." Connor looked at his watch. "Shouldn't we be leaving soon?" he asked Mandy. "It's almost eight forty-five."

"Yes, we'd better go," she answered. "I made a reservation for nine o'clock. If you want to start rounding everyone up, the cars are waiting outside."

"Aren't you going to introduce me?" Dee Dee asked quickly. "I got dressed up especially so you'd be proud of me."

"I thought you came downstairs because you assumed the party was over," Connor said dryly.

"Oh...well, I did, but I changed clothes just in case I was wrong."

His hard face relaxed in a smile. "How exceedingly thoughtful of you." Putting his arm around his daughter, he led her around the room, introducing her with obvious pride.

When they came to Jacques, Dee Dee said, "I've already met Mr. Gallet. Hi again."

He took her hand and kissed it. "You look ravishing, my dear Juliet."

Dee Dee grinned. "I cleaned up pretty good, didn't I?"

Connor's eyes narrowed. "You get around, Jacques. Where did you meet my daughter?"

"It was outside, earlier tonight." Dee Dee answered first. "I was watching him and Mandy dancing on the terrace. He said I looked like Juliet up on the balcony. It was cool."

"You're no doubt well versed in the role of Romeo." Connor gave the other man a thin smile.

"That is my favorite of Shakespeare's plays," Jacques replied. "It surprises me that an Englishman could be so romantic. I have always thought he must have had a French ancestor somewhere in his past."

"You could learn a lot from Mr. Gallet, Dad," Dee Dee said. "He has an awesome line with women. You should have heard the stuff he was handing Mandy."

Jacques gave her an amused look. "I am wounded that you think I was being insincere."

"I'm sure Mandy bought every word of it," Connor remarked coolly.

"One can but hope," Jacques observed with twinkling eyes.

Mandy appeared next to Connor. "I really think we'd better go," she said.

"Can I come with you?" Dee Dee asked.

"No, you may not," her father said. "I told you that earlier."

"You said I couldn't come to the cocktail party, but that's over. Why can't I go to dinner with you?"

"Because you can't."

Mandy had a suspicion that Connor's irritation was really directed at her. He shouldn't be taking it out on Dee Dee. His curt refusal was bound to provoke a reaction from the girl. Mandy attempted to defuse the situation.

"Didn't you have dinner already?"

"I only had a snack," Dee Dee answered with a stormy look at her father.

"Then tell Salima to make you something more," he said.

"It's no fun to eat alone," she said sulkily.

"If you'd stayed in school where you belong, you wouldn't have that problem."

"Every time I want to do something you don't want me to do, you threaten to send me back to school. That's really rotten!"

"Don't make a scene," Connor said sternly.

The two were on a collision course when Mandy stepped in to smooth things over. The others were politely pretending not to listen, but it was an awkward situation.

Raising her voice slightly she said, "I'm sure everyone is ready for dinner. If you'll go outside now, cars are waiting to take you to the restaurant. Connor will be with you in a moment."

After they filed out, Mandy said to him, "I'll stay home with Dee Dee. You go ahead with your guests."

"That's ridiculous!" he said. "There's no reason for you to stay home and baby-sit her—even if she is acting like a two-year-old."

"What do you expect, when you treat me like one?" Dee Dee demanded.

"I really don't mind," Mandy said hastily.

"That's not the point," he said. "I won't have you miss dinner because my daughter decides to throw a tantrum."

"You're the one who threw your weight around," Dee Dee said resentfully. "Sheez! I make one little request and you go ballistic on me!"

Mandy gave her a quelling look. The youngster wasn't helping matters any. "You'd better go," she told Connor. "The others are waiting."

"Then come with me."

"Go ahead." Dee Dee sighed, accepting defeat. "You don't have to stay home on account of me."

"I really don't want to go," Mandy insisted, which was the truth. She'd had enough of Jacques for one evening— and Connor, too, for that matter. Things would only get worse as the evening progressed.

Connor gave her a moody look. "Leave us alone, Dee Dee. I want to talk to Mandy."

"Can't it wait?" Mandy asked. "There are three cars full of hungry people outside."

He paused until his daughter had left the room. "I'm sorry if I was harsh with you earlier. Jacques is a charming man. He's also married. I don't know if he thought to mention the fact."

Her eyes widened with surprise. "No, he didn't."

"I didn't think so."

"It doesn't really matter." When Connor frowned, she added hurriedly, "I mean, I was only trying to be a good hostess—in spite of what you think."

"Perhaps I overreacted," he conceded. "I don't approve of sexual predators. I'm even more judgmental when they're married and the game means more to them than the prize."

"That doesn't say a lot for my charms," Mandy said wryly.

Connor's eyes wandered over her lovely features. "You don't need me to tell you how desirable you are."

She slanted a glance at him. "Speaking of sexual predators, is Isabella married?"

"The subject didn't come up. You can find out at dinner tonight."

"I'd really prefer to stay home, Connor. It has nothing to do with Dee Dee, or our slight misunderstanding. I'm just a little tired. It's been a long day, and you don't really need me anymore. I checked earlier, and everything is all set up at the restaurant."

"How about your dinner?" he protested. "You have to eat."

"I'll have a little something with Dee Dee, and then we'll both turn in early. You'd better go, before all the goodwill we generated is overcome by hunger pangs."

"Well, if you're really sure," he said reluctantly.

"I am. Have a good evening."

Dee Dee returned when she heard the cars drive away. She gave Mandy a wary look. "Dad's really teed off at me, isn't he?"

"He's not one of your cheerleaders at the moment, but he'll get over it."

"Do you think he'll send me back to school tomorrow?"

"I doubt it. His meetings start early in the morning, and he'll be too busy to make the arrangements. To be on the

safe side, though, I'd suggest you don't go out of your way
to aggravate him.''

"I didn't *this* time. I got all dressed up, and I was real
polite to everybody. I was nicer than he was to Mr. Gallet.
Dad was smiling and everything, but his eyes were kind of
cold, like they get when he's mad about something but he
doesn't want to let on." She looked reflectively at Mandy.
"They got that way when I told him about you and Mr.
Gallet dancing on the terrace. I wonder if Dad was jealous.''

"I can assure you he wasn't.''

"How can you be so sure?''

"Because he didn't come near me all evening except once,
to complain about something. An Italian woman was as-
suring him of his virility.'' Mandy's voice held annoyance as
she remembered the fatuous way he kept smiling at Isabella. Men were such pushovers for the hero-worship act!

"Did she really have the hots for him? I'll bet it was the
woman in the slinky black number. She's a real fox. You
think they're an item, huh?''

"I'm not an authority on your father's reactions, but he
seemed attracted to her,'' Mandy said coolly.

"Now *you* sound jealous.'' Dee Dee grinned.

Mandy gave her a level look. "Don't start getting any
ideas just because you're bored and you want to stir things
up. I'm beginning to understand why your father sent you
away to school.''

"I'm sorry,'' Dee Dee said, but she didn't look it. "I just
think it would be neat if you two fell in love and got married. Dad's getting older. He needs to stop running around
so much and settle down.''

"He has a few good years left,'' Mandy observed dryly.

"I guess so, but I don't want him to marry somebody like
that dorky Barbara.''

"How do you know I'd be any better? You don't know
me that well.''

"I can tell you're cool."

"I have to be, in this job." Mandy sighed.

"I'm sorry you had to miss dinner because of me," Dee Dee said with belated remorse. "I would have been okay."

"I know that, but I had enough socializing for one night. Let's go in the kitchen and eat up all the leftover hors d'oeuvres. There's a lot of good stuff, like smoked Scottish salmon and beluga caviar."

"Okay." Dee Dee said without enthusiasm. The delicacies were wasted on her. "As long as we can have ice cream for dessert."

"If there isn't any in the freezer, we'll lay in a supply tomorrow," Mandy promised.

As they walked together toward the kitchen, Dee Dee said, "It's nice to have somebody to talk to about stuff. I wish you could be around all the time. Are you sure you don't want to marry my dad?"

"Very sure, but you and I can still be good friends."

"Unless he marries some nerd like Barbara." The young girl gave Mandy an appraising look. "She wouldn't want somebody as sexy as you hanging around."

"Then we'll just have to weed out all the nerds. Between the two of us, I'm sure we can change your father's taste in women," Mandy joked.

"Cool!" Dee Dee exclaimed, giving her a high five.

Chapter Four

Mandy and Dee Dee both slept late the next morning. Connor's meeting had already started by the time they came downstairs. There was a steady hum of voices coming from behind the closed doors of the dining room that was being used as a conference room.

"I'll have to buy an alarm clock," Mandy commented as she and Dee Dee ate breakfast at one of the umbrella tables out by the pool. "I should have been up ages ago."

"Why?" Dee Dee asked. "What do you have to do today?"

"Actually, nothing until tonight. Your father and the rest will be in meetings all day, and they won't want to be disturbed. I planned the menu and told Salima to have Jemal serve lunch whenever Connor requests it."

"Then there was no reason for you to get up."

"I suppose not, but I feel I should be doing something for the money he's paying me. I mean, I should at least be available."

"Don't worry, if he wants you, you'll know it. What do you have to do for them tonight?"

"I made reservations at another restaurant, and this time I guess I'll have to go." Mandy shot a look at the young girl. "You'd really be terribly bored. I'd get out of it myself if I could. They'll probably talk business all night."

"Not Jacques." Dee Dee grinned. "I bet he'll be all over you like fleas on a dog."

"You make it sound so appealing," Mandy said with distaste.

"Don't you like him? I thought he was kind of cute. For an old guy, that is."

"An old *married* guy."

"No kidding! What a bummer. Why don't you just tell him to get lost?"

"Adults don't have the luxury of being that direct," Mandy said wryly.

"I'm always gonna say what I think," Dee Dee declared.

"I don't doubt it for a minute. You might spend your life as an unemployed, friendless spinster, but you won't be an inhibited one."

As they were laughing together, Jacques strolled onto the terrace. "I thought I heard voices out here. What a pleasant surprise."

"Surely the meeting isn't over already!" Mandy exclaimed. "Is anything wrong?"

"No, we are just taking a break. I missed you last night," he said in a deepened voice.

"Was the dinner all right?" she asked.

"Without you it was merely adequate."

Mandy smiled brightly. "I hope you didn't tell Connor that. You could cost me my job."

Dee Dee had been listening silently, which was unusual for her. But she had an ulterior motive. She was waiting for the right moment to send Jacques a message, and it finally arrived. "Don't worry, Dad wouldn't fire Mandy. They're an item."

"An item?" Jacques asked cautiously.

"Yeah, they're crazy about each other."

"Dee Dee!" Mandy gasped. "How can you say a thing like that?"

"I'm sorry. They don't want anybody to know," the young girl explained. "It sounds dumb to me, but they think it would look unprofessional if people knew about them."

"I see." Jacques looked thoughtfully at Mandy. "So that was why you were not interested in my company last night."

It was a wonderful out. His feelings would be spared, and he'd be out of her hair. But what would Connor say if he found out?

"You're a very charming man, Jacques. . . ." Mandy began hesitantly.

"But Connor is younger and richer." He chuckled. "It is all right. I understand."

"I'm glad you realize it was nothing personal," Mandy murmured, allowing the misconception to stand. What else could she do without creating an even bigger mess?

"It is too bad. You are utterly enchanting. I hope Connor knows what a lucky man he is."

"You won't tell him I told you?" Dee Dee said quickly. "He'd be seriously ticked off at me."

"I will keep your secret, little one. And yours, too," he said to Mandy.

"Somehow I thought I'd find you here, Jacques," Connor drawled as he strolled onto the terrace.

"Surely you do not begrudge me a glimpse of your two lovely ladies," Jacques answered.

Mandy and Dee Dee exchanged an apprehensive look. "How is your meeting going?" Mandy asked Connor hastily.

"Everything is still in the early stages." He looked from her to Jacques.

"Do not fear, my friend. I have no intention of challenging you," the Frenchman said.

Connor gave him a slightly puzzled look, but before he could comment, the secretary he'd hired appeared at the French doors.

"The others are waiting to resume the meeting whenever you are, Mr. Winfield," she said.

As the two men disappeared inside, Mandy said, "If that was your idea of a joke, it wasn't funny, Dee Dee. How could you tell Jacques that your father and I are involved?"

"I was only trying to be helpful. You said he was a drag, and I figured he'd leave you alone if he thought you were Dad's main squeeze."

"Don't they teach you English in school? Where on earth do you learn that kind of language?"

"At the movies, mostly. All the kids my age talk like me. Except for those wimps at that school in Switzerland. What's wrong with the way I talk?"

"Never mind, I have more important things on my mind right now. You've gotten me into an awful mess."

"I don't know why. Mr. Gallet won't hit on you anymore, and he said he wouldn't tell anybody. You ought to thank me."

"You'll excuse me if I'm not grateful," Mandy said acidly. "And what makes you think Jacques will keep his promise?"

"You think he'll tell Dad?" Dee Dee looked apprehensive. "I might as well start packing."

"Connor probably won't make that big a deal out of it," Mandy said with confidence she was far from feeling. "But it might be a good idea if we made ourselves scarce today. How do you feel about doing some sight-seeing?"

"Yeah, that would be great! Where can we go?"

"I'd like to see Malcolm Forbes's house. He was the American tycoon who owned *Forbes* magazine, among other things. Before his death he gave wonderful parties for all kinds of celebrities. The family still owns the house, but the first floor has been turned into a toy-soldier museum to exhibit his collection.''

''That sounds like a blast.'' Dee Dee jumped up. ''I'm ready if you are.''

The Malcolm Forbes house was large, but not ostentatious. Across the back was a lovely black-and-white tiled patio, and beyond that a swimming pool and landscaped lawns with a view to the sea.

The first floor of the house was a child's delight. It was filled with one hundred and twenty thousand toy soldiers set up in battle position, facing each other with cannons and rifles. Dee Dee was enchanted. She ran from one exhibit to another, calling Mandy to come look at each new discovery. They lingered there for a long time.

''Where to now?'' Dee Dee asked when they were finally back in the car.

Mandy looked in her guidebook. ''We can either go to the medieval town of Asilah, or the Caves of Hercules.''

''Let's go to the Caves,'' Dee Dee said.

''Why did I have a feeling that's what you'd choose?'' Mandy smiled as she started the car.

''We can go to the other place if you'd rather.''

''No, I want to see the Caves, too.''

It was a good choice. They climbed down a steep, slippery path to a series of cavernous underground caves where, in ancient mythology, Hercules had killed a fearsome dragon. Candles set in niches cast shifting shadows, making it easy to imagine monsters still lurking in the murky depths.

The day flew by happily as they explored the exotic surroundings, which were so different from any place either had ever been. They were completely compatible. Dee Dee might have given her father a hard time, but not Mandy. No generation gap existed. They laughed and talked together as if they were best friends.

All the problems with Connor and Jacques were forgotten. It wasn't until she and Dee Dee were driving home in the late afternoon that Mandy remembered them. It had been such a carefree day that she decided she was worried over nothing. Jacques would have no reason to break his word.

Mandy revised her opinion when they reached the house. The meeting had broken up, and everyone had gone back to the hotel to change for dinner.

As she and Dee Dee crossed the hall to the staircase, Connor came out of the den. "I'd like to speak to you for a moment, Mandy."

She tried not to let her trepidation show. Although he didn't look seriously upset, she knew him well enough by now to recognize the danger signs.

"Certainly," she answered casually. "You can go on upstairs, Dee Dee. I'll be up in a few minutes."

"No, I'll stay with you." The young girl faced her father. "It wasn't her fault. I was the one who did it."

"Did what?" He gave her a puzzled look.

Mandy put a warning hand on the girl's arm. "What did you want to talk to me about?" she asked cautiously. It might not have anything to do with Jacques.

"Maybe you can explain to me why Jacques is acting so strangely," Connor said, dashing her hopes.

"That's what I want to tell you," Dee Dee said.

"I can handle this," Mandy told her in a low voice. "There's no need for you to get involved."

"But it isn't fair for you to take the rap for me," Dee Dee protested.

Connor gave her a sharp look. "What mischief have you been up to now, young lady?"

"Go!" Mandy gave her a little push before she could answer. "I mean it," she added sternly. When Dee Dee had reluctantly complied, Mandy stalked into the den and confronted Connor angrily. "She's a wonderful child. You should be proud of her instead of always suspecting her of being up to something."

"I *am* proud of her, but I know my daughter better than you do. She usually *is* involved in something guaranteed to turn me prematurely gray."

"All kids get into little scrapes."

"What has she done this time?"

"Nothing major." Mandy changed the subject hastily. "We had a wonderful time today. There are so many interesting things to see here. If your people have some free time, I can arrange a tour for them."

"I can see I'm not going to get any answers, so let's talk about Jacques."

"What about him?" Mandy asked warily.

"After we came back from our coffee break this morning, he told me I was a lucky dog."

"That's not so strange. You do have everything a man could possibly want."

He looked at her without expression. "That's open to debate. But you didn't let me finish. Jacques also mentioned that you were a very desirable woman and he envied me. Could you tell me why?"

She avoided his eyes. "I have no idea. Unless he means you're lucky to have someone competent to handle details for you."

"Somehow, I don't think that's the right answer."

Mandy decided to go on the offensive. "He's your associate. You know him better than I do. What do *you* think he means?"

"I think he believes we're more than business associates."

"That's ridiculous! Where would he get such an impression?"

"That's what I'm trying to find out. Someone gave him the idea that we're involved, and I'd like to find out who."

"You surely don't think I'd do a thing like that!"

"I can't imagine why you would," he answered slowly. "But Jacques made those comments right after our coffee break this morning—after he'd spoken to you and Dee Dee on the terrace." Connor's gaze sharpened. "Did she have anything to do with this?"

Mandy hesitated, unwilling to tell an outright lie. She tried to figure out a way to play down Dee Dee's involvement. "I might have made the mistake of talking too freely to her," she said cautiously. "You know how kids are. They have a tendency to overreact."

"To what? What did you tell her?"

"Well, I might have mentioned that Jacques was coming on a little too strong."

Connor stared at her as comprehension dawned. "So Dee Dee decided Jacques would back off if he thought I had a prior claim."

"Something like that," Mandy said uncomfortably. "She didn't realize what complications it would cause."

"On the contrary." He smiled broadly. "I think my daughter handled a sticky situation brilliantly."

"She got *me* off the hook, but she put you in an awkward position."

"Why would I mind having people think a beautiful woman was in love with me?"

"For one thing, Isabella won't be pleased if she thinks the feeling is reciprocated."

"I guess I'll just have to make the sacrifice."

He seemed more amused than annoyed. Of course, one woman more or less was no big deal in his life. Still, it made things easier that he was taking it so well.

"I'm really sorry," she said.

"Don't be. These little flirtations sometimes occur, especially when the group includes free spirits like Jacques and Isabella. But they're distracting. I'd prefer that people keep their minds on the reason we're here."

"Was your meeting productive?"

"I think it will be ultimately. Everyone is wary of making any commitments in the beginning."

"Well, this is just the first day." Mandy looked at her watch. "I guess I'd better get ready. I arranged to have cocktails at the restaurant before dinner, and I want to go over early to be sure they're all set up for us."

"There's plenty of time." Connor continued to gaze at her speculatively. "You and my daughter seem to have developed quite a rapport."

"She's a delightful youngster." Mandy had hoped he'd forgotten Dee Dee's indiscretion. "You won't be too hard on her, will you? She was only trying to be helpful."

"Don't worry, I'm not going to punish her. This was minor compared to some of the stunts she's pulled."

"I'm sure they were never malicious," Mandy said earnestly. "Dee Dee is an only child, which can be lonely. I know, because I'm one, too. She needs somebody to talk girl talk with—things like clothes and boyfriends. That's probably why she's become attached to me in such a short time."

"I'm not complaining." Connor smiled. "I'll take all the help I can get. Maybe you can give me a short course in child psychology."

"I don't imagine there's such a thing as a shortcut. Besides, it's easy to give advice when you don't have any children of your own," Mandy said self-deprecatingly.

"You're good with them. You'd make an excellent mother."

"First I have to find a husband," she answered lightly.

"That should be the easy part."

"Not so far. I seem to attract the ineligibles like Jacques."

"You should have told me he was bothering you. I'm sorry I didn't understand what was going on last night."

"No problem," she said dismissively. "I run into difficult people in my own business. You learn to consider it part of the job."

"That reminds me of something I wanted to talk to you about. Would you consider coming to work for me full-time? I didn't realize how handy it is to have an advance person right on the scene. Things run a lot more smoothly. You could handle all the details from beginning to end. Are you interested?"

So that was the offer Connor had alluded to last night. She should have known it wasn't anything personal. "That isn't really my field," she said.

"It could be. You have excellent people skills."

"Thanks, but I prefer to use them in my own business."

"You haven't heard what I'm prepared to offer."

"It wouldn't matter. I couldn't leave my partner in the lurch. Three of us started the agency together, but we're down to just two since Penny left."

"She evidently didn't share your loyalty."

"Penny didn't leave because of a better offer. She married a fantastic man and moved to Rome."

"Is she the European connection you claimed to have?" Connor teased.

"Maybe Penny isn't exactly part of the agency anymore, but she does give us a lot of valuable information. I might have misled you slightly, but I knew we could handle the job."

"So the end justifies the means?" He smiled.

"You're not unhappy with me, are you?" she countered.

He leaned back and gazed at her alluring body and lovely face. His eyes lingered on her sweetly curved mouth. "I think you could make any man happy," he answered finally.

"I can see why you're such a success with women," she remarked in a light tone.

"I'm not sure that's a compliment."

"That's the way I meant it. You can be very charming."

"Am I a success with you, Mandy?" He watched her like a lazy tiger, pondering whether it was worth the effort to spring.

"You're smart and capable. I admire those qualities," she replied evasively as she rose to her feet, and moved toward the door. "I really must get ready."

Mandy was still fuming ten minutes later as she took one of her new outfits out of the closet. Whenever Connor was bored or at loose ends, he amused himself by coming on to her. It was annoying, because she knew he had no more real interest in her than he had in Isabella. Connor was like a beaver that had to keep sharpening its teeth—he had to keep practicing his technique. At least she hadn't let him rattle her this time. Mandy was proud of the way she'd managed to appear completely indifferent.

She was almost ready to leave when Dee Dee came into her bedroom.

"You look really cool!" the girl exclaimed.

Mandy finished fastening the pearl-and-rhinestone buttons of her pink satin cocktail suit. "At least this isn't as sexy as the beaded dress last night. That was a definite mistake."

"Hey, if you've got it, flaunt it."

"Oh, sure! Look where it got me," Mandy said wryly.

Dee Dee gave her an apprehensive look. "Did Mr. Gallet blab to Dad about what I told him?"

"Not in so many words, but I'm afraid your father got the idea."

"Did you tell him I was responsible?"

"I tried to get around it, but he asked me a direct question. I couldn't lie."

Dee Dee sighed. "How mad was he?"

"Luckily, he seemed to think it was funny. But I'd keep a low profile for a while if I were you."

"I will, I promise! You're the greatest, Mandy. I'll do something for you someday."

"You don't owe me. It was no big deal." She picked up her purse. "I have to run. Try not to get into any mischief."

"Now you sound like Dad." Dee Dee grinned.

Connor and Mandy arrived at the restaurant ahead of the group, which wasn't really necessary. Everything was ready for them. Cocktails were served at one end of a large room reserved for their party. At the other end was a long table set for twelve.

Mandy intended to make sure she wasn't seated next to Jacques, in spite of Dee Dee's propaganda. A man who would cheat on his wife wasn't likely to consider another man's girlfriend off-limits.

Connor must have had the same thought. During the cocktail hour he stayed close to her. Mandy didn't mind, but she considered his other little attentions unnecessary—like holding her hand, and gently brushing a lock of hair off her forehead. It made her uncomfortable.

Jacques came over to her during one of the brief interludes when Connor left her side. "You look very lovely tonight."

"Thank you." She changed the subject. "Did you have a productive meeting today?"

"Did Connor not tell you?"

"We don't talk about business."

"He shows more sense than most American men. They have this driving passion for success, whereas the French are more romantic. They have a passion for beautiful women."

"Even married men?"

He slanted a glance at her. "You heard that I am married?"

"Not from you," she said dryly.

"That troubles you? It should not. My wife and I have an arrangement."

"She's more understanding than I would be. I don't share."

"You would never have to." Connor had come up beside her in time to overhear their conversation. "What more could a man want if he had you?"

Connor didn't touch her, but she was tinglingly aware of his hard body only inches from hers. The gaze he gave her was intimate, and a little smile curved his firm mouth, as though in remembrance of shared passion. Mandy had to remind herself that it was only an act for Jacques's benefit. If Connor had really meant it... But he didn't.

She took a deep breath. "I believe dinner is served. Would you get everyone to the table, Connor?"

He also took charge of the seating arrangements, putting Jacques and Isabella at the far end of the table, and Mandy in the place next to his own. To her relief, he lightened up during dinner, playing the perfect host, charming everyone.

It was a very pleasant evening. Mandy was sorry when the party broke up soon after dinner. But the others had been together all day, and several of them wanted to go over their presentations for the next morning.

Mandy was completely relaxed with Connor on the ride home. They talked about the evening and the plans for dinner the next night. That was the special one, with entertainment.

When they arrived home, he said, "It's still early. Would you care to go for a swim?"

"Sounds like a winner, if you don't have to prepare for tomorrow's meeting. That's why some of the others made it an early evening."

Connor grinned. "They're still working on their game plan. I already know mine."

He seemed confident that everything would go his way. Maybe because everything always had. "Have you ever gone after something and not gotten it?" she asked curiously.

"Nothing I really wanted."

No wonder Connor kept gobbling up companies and collecting beautiful women, Mandy thought as she changed into her bathing suit. He was looking for a challenge, something or someone he couldn't have—or at least had to work hard to get. It might make him more human if he encountered such a challenge.

When she started down the hall, Mandy thought of asking Dee Dee to join them. But the girl's bedroom door was closed, and she decided that Dee Dee had turned in early after their strenuous day. The thick carpet muffled her footsteps as she went past Dee Dee's room and continued down the stairs.

Connor was already in the pool. Mandy paused to watch as his powerful arms and shoulders propelled his lithe body through the water like a guided missile.

He swam over to the edge of the pool when he caught sight of her standing there. The moonlight sparkled in his eyes as he looked her over with a grin. "I like that outfit best of all."

Mandy's bikini wasn't overly skimpy, but his male scrutiny made it feel that way. She was very aware of his gaze on her partially exposed breasts. "This didn't cost you anything," she managed to say carelessly. "I brought it from home. How's the water?"

"Great! Come on in."

Mandy sat on the edge of the pool and pinned her long hair on top of her head while Connor watched. "Go ahead and swim. You don't have to wait for me," she said.

"I can think of worse things to do than look at you."

"You can knock off the act," she said lightly. "Jacques isn't here."

"I have to keep in practice, don't I?" he teased.

She was startled when he put his hands around her waist. Mandy braced her own hands against his shoulders, but Connor only intended to lift her into the water.

"Come on, I'll race you to the deep end," he said.

"That wouldn't be much of a contest. I watched you just now. You're a champion-class swimmer."

"I'll give you a head start."

"Something tells me I'd need more than that to beat you."

"You'll never know unless you give it a try. Or are you afraid of looking bad?" he taunted her.

"No way! Just tell me when you're ready."

Mandy was a good swimmer, but she was no match for Connor, even with a head start. He closed the distance between them easily. She doubled her efforts as they approached the finish line, even though she knew it was no use. Connor was even with her. He could have passed her, but he didn't. Mandy touched the tile coping seconds before him.

"Congratulations." He gave her a big smile. "See what self-confidence can do for you?"

"I didn't really win. You could have beaten me easily." She was breathing hard, while he was barely winded. "Why did you hold back?"

"Does that sound like something I'd do?" he joked.

"No, but we both know you did, and it's insulting. I'm not a child, Connor!" Mandy was clinging to the edge of the pool under the diving board while she caught her breath.

"I'm well aware of that," he answered softly, putting an arm on each side of her so that she was penned in.

It was dark under the diving board. The automatic timer had turned off the pool lights earlier, and the moonlight didn't penetrate their little niche. Mandy couldn't see Connor's face clearly, but she could feel his warm breath on her cheek. That was how close they were.

As she tried to ignore the excitement building inside her, the buoyant water brought their bodies together. His legs tangled with hers, and their hips were joined for a brief, tantalizing moment.

Mandy tried to defuse the tension. "Why did you let me win? Don't you think I can handle defeat?"

"I'm sure you can. I just hope you never have to," he said in a husky voice.

"Then answer my question."

"It wasn't a fair contest, as you guessed. But everybody likes to win. Maybe I just wanted to make you happy."

"That's very nice," she said hesitantly.

"I'm not really such a bad fellow."

His head moved slowly toward hers, blotting out the small amount of light. A warning alarm rang in her brain, but Mandy ignored it. Her star-pointed lashes brushed her cheek as she closed her eyes and parted her lips.

"Hey, you guys, where are you?" Dee Dee's voice shredded the still night. She was standing on her balcony, peering down at the pool. "I heard you in there a minute ago, and I went to put on my bathing suit. Are you still there?"

Connor swam out to the middle of the pool. "What are you doing up at this hour?"

"It isn't that late. Where's Mandy?"

"I'm here." Mandy swam out from under the diving board.

"Why didn't you tell me you were going swimming?" Dee Dee complained. "I would have come, too."

"Your door was closed and I didn't hear any sound from your room, so I thought you'd gone to bed," Mandy said.

"I fell asleep reading a book. There wasn't anything else to do," Dee Dee said pointedly. "But I'm awake now and I have on my suit. I'll be right down."

"You can swim with your father. I'm going to bed." Without looking directly at Connor, Mandy remarked, "That race really winded me. I guess I'm out of shape."

"It isn't apparent," he murmured.

She swam over to the edge of the pool without answering. After hoisting herself out, she said good-night and went into the house, conscious of his eyes following her.

While she was showering, Mandy tried to figure out the best way to handle Connor. She knew he was only teasing her by continuing his act even when Jacques wasn't around. But she also knew he wouldn't back off from a casual affair if she proved willing. Connor was a very virile man, without a lot of scruples.

Not that there would be any problem if she said no. At least he wasn't the kind of man who used sex as a bargaining chip. Any business she got from him would be on merit, which was the only way she'd accept it. What she had to work on was her own attitude. Connor wasn't going to stop testing her, so she had to stop letting him get to her.

Jet Away Travel had a good shot at getting all of Winfield Enterprises' business, and Mandy had no intention of blowing that chance. From now on, she would treat his little tricks and innuendos with amusement, as though she were used to all this sexual sparring. He wasn't the only one who could play that game.

Mandy didn't have to worry about dealing with Connor until the next night. She and Dee Dee left the house while he was in his meeting, and when they returned after a full day of sight-seeing and shopping, it was time to get ready for dinner.

Dee Dee had been eagerly looking forward to the evening. Her excited chatter in the car didn't leave Connor any time to devote to Mandy.

The dinner was held in a tent. Two camels were tethered outside for the guests to mount for a short ride around a ring. Handlers in long Moroccan robes led the animals and made sure the notoriously ill-tempered beasts didn't take a nip out of anyone. It was very picturesque, a change from the elegant dinners and cocktail parties Mandy had arranged up until now.

After a dinner featuring native dishes, the show began. The first act was a belly dancer dressed in a skimpy bra and long, filmy pantaloons that rode low on her generous hips. She undulated sensuously around the room before extending a hand to Connor, coaxing him to join her. When he declined with a smile, she chose Jacques.

"Why didn't you go for it, Dad?" Dee Dee asked. "You could put on a sexier show than Mr. Gallet."

"I perform better without an audience." He slanted a mischievous glance at Mandy.

She was saved from having to comment when Dee Dee said to her, "You have a better figure than she does."

"So I've noticed," Connor remarked.

"You might try to behave in front of your daughter," Mandy whispered in his ear.

"I always try to be on my best behavior," he answered blandly. "Even when I've suffered a disappointment."

Mandy acted amused, belatedly remembering her vow. "Nobody can have everything he wants."

"I've never accepted that," he murmured as the music ended and the master of ceremonies took the stage.

The next act was a snake charmer. Everyone was fascinated as a man in a turban sat cross-legged on the floor, playing an eerie tune on a flute while a hooded cobra undulated in front of him.

After putting the cobra in a basket, he brought out a long green snake and asked for volunteers from the audience. Dee Dee jumped up immediately.

When Connor started to call her back, the master of ceremonies whispered in his ear that the snake was harmless. Connor conveyed the information to Mandy, who was urging him not to let Dee Dee anywhere near the reptile.

"Harmless is a matter of opinion." She shuddered as the snake charmer draped the snake around Dee Dee's neck. "I wouldn't let him do that for anything in this world!"

Connor's arm was lying across the back of Mandy's chair. He leaned toward her. "You should try everything at least once. You never know what might happen."

His soft voice drew her attention away from the show. She turned her head to look at him squarely. "I have a fairly good idea."

"Do you?" he murmured. "I wonder."

Dee Dee returned, eyes sparkling with excitement. "That was really cool! Snakes aren't yucky and slimy, like you'd expect."

"I'll take your word for it," Mandy said.

"Would I lie to you?" Dee Dee grinned.

"You've learned a lot from your father," Mandy commented dryly.

The evening was a big success. Mandy had been slightly worried that the event might be too touristy for such a sophisticated group, but they loved the novelty of it. When the party broke up, they were all vocal with their praise.

The days went by too quickly for Mandy. She enjoyed the exotic flavor of Tangier, and living in the lap of luxury wasn't too bad, either. She was going to miss it. She would miss Connor, too, Mandy admitted to herself.

As the week drew to a close and the pressure of putting together a high-powered merger of multinational companies increased, Connor didn't have time for games. Their conversations were relaxed, and Mandy got to know and like him better.

Connor's relationship with his daughter had also improved. The deep affection between them was apparent, in spite of their head-on confrontations. But there were no more of those—until the day before it was time to leave.

Dee Dee took it for granted that she'd be returning to San Francisco with her father. "You agreed with me about that school in Switzerland being the pits! How can you even think of sending me back there?"

"Only for a short time," Connor explained. "Until I can look into other schools. And this time I'll be more thorough, I promise you."

"Thanks a lot! What's the next one gonna be like? Someplace with bars on the windows?"

"Don't be childish, Dee Dee."

"That's the problem, you still treat me like a child. When are you gonna realize I'm growing up and I have a right to some say about my own life? Why can't *I* pick where I want to go to school?"

"If you'd gone to school we wouldn't be having this discussion."

"Okay, I cut a few classes. Does that make me a world-class criminal? I didn't hurt anybody."

"Except yourself. How can I convince you of how important it is to get an education?"

"I know that. I'm not a complete dweeb. If you'll let me come home, I promise I won't cut class anymore."

Connor hesitated. "There's nothing I'd like better. It's lonesome without you. But I do realize that you're getting older. I think you need the female guidance you'll get in a girls' school."

"There are lots of women teachers in public school," Dee Dee pointed out. "And your girlfriends are always making up to me. Sheez! How many women do I have to be around?"

His jaw tightened. "You're exaggerating as usual, and my personal life is not the issue here. Your well-being is. I have an obligation as a parent to do what's best for you, and that's what I intend to do."

"Can't you make him listen to reason, Mandy?" Dee Dee appealed to her.

Mandy had been sitting quietly in a corner of the den, wishing there was some way she could leave unobtrusively. Fond as she was of the young girl, this wasn't her business.

Connor cut in before she had to answer. "I'm the one who is responsible for you," he told his daughter. "I've made up my mind, and I don't want to discuss it any further."

That didn't deter Dee Dee, naturally. The argument raged on, with neither of them giving an inch. Unfortunately, it was an argument Dee Dee couldn't win.

If she'd been older, Mandy reflected, she would have known better than to provoke a direct confrontation—especially with a man like her father. Connor had stated his position so forcefully that he couldn't back down now even if he wanted to.

After the prolonged argument dragged on and on, Dee Dee was finally forced to give in. Connor had won, but it didn't make him happy.

"I know you think I'm being unfair, but someday, when you're a parent, I hope you'll understand."

"Yeah, sure," Dee Dee answered indifferently.

"You won't have to stay at that school for long, I promise you," he persisted. "I'll find someplace more acceptable and closer to San Francisco, so you can spend weekends at home when you like. Although I guess that's not much of an incentive right now," he said wryly.

"Yeah, it's cool." She stood. "I'm gonna go upstairs and pack."

Connor's expression was somber as he watched her leave the room. "You have no idea how much it hurts to have your daughter hate you."

"She doesn't hate you," Mandy said gently. "She's just a little upset right now. You both are."

He stuck his hands in his pockets and paced the floor. "I suppose you think I'm wrong."

"Not necessarily. You don't feel you have any other options," she said carefully.

"And you do?" Connor stopped pacing to face her. "If you have another solution, I'd like to hear it."

"Well, I was just wondering why you don't let her come home while you look for another school."

"I thought of that, but I don't want her to lose any more time. She's already been out of school for a week. By the time I find a better school and arrange to have her records transferred, she might be too far behind to catch up with the other students. Dee Dee will be better off in the long run if she can just stick it out for now. They won't discipline her. I intend to have a serious talk with the headmistress," Connor said grimly.

"I think that's a good idea. Cheer up." Mandy smiled at him. "Dee Dee will grow up, and you'll laugh about this someday."

"I hope you're right," he muttered.

Mandy stopped in the girl's room on the way to her own. Dee Dee's radio was blaring, and she was singing as she packed her suitcase.

"I'm glad to see you're not holding a grudge," Mandy said. "Your father feels badly enough about this."

Dee Dee scowled suddenly. "What's he got to feel bad about? He won, didn't he?"

"It isn't a question of scoring points. He loves you very much."

"I know." The young girl's expression softened. "He's not such a bad Joe."

"I'm glad you're being reasonable."

Dee Dee shrugged. "Dad says when life hands you a lemon, make lemonade. I learned a lot from him."

"Yes, he's a very unusual man."

Mandy was a little surprised by Dee Dee's acceptance of the situation. She would have expected more resentment than that one burst of temper. Dee Dee had sulked more when Connor refused to let her come to the cocktail party. No wonder he complained about gray hairs. Who could understand twelve-year-old girls?

Chapter Five

The ride to the airport the next morning was a lot more pleasant than Connor anticipated. He was delighted that Dee Dee wasn't sulking. He even had second thoughts about letting her come home, but it was too late by then.

Connor had coordinated their departure times as closely as possible. Dee Dee's flight took off for Switzerland half an hour before his and Mandy's plane left for San Francisco.

His voice was husky as he said goodbye to her. "Keep your chin up, sweetheart. I'll see you soon."

"No sweat, Dad," she answered cheerfully. "The time will go by like a flash."

When they had seen her board the plane and were walking to their own gate, Connor said to Mandy, "If someone will explain that child to me, I'll be forever grateful. Last night she was adamant about not returning to Switzerland, and this morning you'd think it was her idea."

"Just count your blessings." Mandy laughed.

* * *

Dee Dee waited five minutes and then calmly got off the plane. The flight attendants were so busy directing people to their seats and helping to stow luggage, that nobody stopped her or asked where she was going.

She walked over to her father's gate and waited unobtrusively behind a group of people until the announcement came that passengers could now board flight 402 for San Francisco.

Dee Dee watched as the long, straggly line of people inched forward, but she didn't join them. It wasn't until the waiting room was empty and they were about to close the gate that she made her move.

Dashing up to the gate, she shouted, "Wait! I have to get on!"

"Just a minute." An airline agent barred her way. "Do you have a ticket?"

"My father has it. He's already on the plane."

The man frowned. "He left you here and went on board without you?"

"No! We were already on the plane, but he was talking to somebody and I got off to get a candy bar. I thought there was plenty of time, only I got mixed up and went to the wrong gate. Please, you've got to let me on!"

A woman came over to join the man. "What's the problem?"

"This girl doesn't have a ticket. She says she boarded earlier and then got off the plane to buy candy. I don't know. It sounds fishy to me."

"You have to let me get on! The plane's gonna leave without me!" Dee Dee's voice rose. "I'll be all alone in a foreign country without any money or a place to stay. Who's gonna take care of me?" She was shouting now, and people walking by were stopping to listen.

"Calm down," the woman said.

"How can I calm down when I don't know what's gonna happen to me? I just want to go home!" Dee Dee couldn't squeeze out any tears, so she sobbed instead.

"You'd better let her on," the woman said to the man in a low voice. "It's just the kind of thing a kid would do."

"Yeah, and we don't want to be responsible for her," the man agreed.

Dee Dee made a dash down the long covered passageway to the airplane. As soon as she got on board, the door closed behind her.

The flight attendant came over to her. "You cut it kind of close, didn't you? Can I see your boarding pass?"

As Dee Dee rummaged in her large shoulder bag, the idling motors increased their tempo and the plane started to move slowly away from the docking area.

"You'll have to hurry," the flight attendant said. "We'll be taking off soon."

"I know I have it here somewhere." Dee Dee started to take items out of her bag, a comb, a wallet, a package of gum. As she dug out more items, a couple of them fell to the floor.

The attendant watched impatiently while the plane taxied down the runway, picking up speed. Then an announcement came over the intercom: "Flight attendants, please take your seats for departure."

The woman hustled Dee Dee over to some little jump seats near the door. "You'll have to sit here with me until we're airborne. I'll take you to your seat after the captain turns off the seat belt sign."

Dee Dee buckled up obediently, wearing a wide grin as the plane lifted off the ground and gained altitude. Timing was everything! The trick had been to board just as the plane was leaving, and then delay being found out until they were in the air. Otherwise her father would have dragged her off the plane and sent her back to Switzerland.

When they had reached cruising altitude the attendant said, "You can unbuckle your seat belt now. I'll get you settled as soon as you give me your boarding pass."

"I think there's something you should know," Dee Dee answered.

Connor and Mandy tilted their chairs back and stretched out their legs in the roomy comfort of the first-class section. There were only a dozen seats in the cabin, and they were all full.

He sighed contentedly. "This is the first chance I've had to relax all week."

"You deserve a rest," Mandy said. "Feel free to take a nap if you like. You don't have to entertain me."

Connor gave her a warm smile. "I'd be—" He paused as the flight attendant stopped beside him.

His expression changed after a few words from the woman. Mandy was aghast, too, but she couldn't help feeling sorry for Dee Dee. Connor's jaw was rigid, and his gray eyes were the color of a storm cloud.

"Where is she?" Each word was like a cube of ice.

Dee Dee was hovering in the entrance to the cabin. Her elation evaporated as she watched how her father took the news. It was replaced by apprehension she tried to hide.

Raising her hand, she said feebly, "Hi."

Connor unbuckled his seat belt and got up with great deliberation, clearly trying to keep a lid on his emotions. Mandy wanted to tell him to stay calm, but how restrained would any parent be under the circumstances?

Dee Dee came over slowly, hoping to enlist Mandy in her cause. "I know you're mad at me, Dad, but it was the only way I could think of to make you let me come home."

"This plane is going to San Francisco, but that's as close to home as you're going to get," he said ominously.

"You can't send me back!" she exclaimed in outrage. "That would be cruel and inhuman punishment!"

"You've never been punished in your life, that's the problem. But from now on things are going to be different."

"Okay, punish me if that'll make you feel better, but let me come home."

Mandy was conscious of the disapproving glances some of the other passengers were aiming at Connor. He couldn't have cared less, even if he'd been aware of them.

"You don't seem to get it," he told his daughter sternly. "This isn't minor mischief, like cutting a class or two. There might be serious penalties for sneaking on board an airplane without a ticket."

"Couldn't you pay for it?" she asked tentatively.

"I'll have to. The alternative is letting the authorities deal with you, which is very tempting. I can't continue to let you get away with these things with only a lecture. That doesn't do any good, anyway," he added. "I'm ready to admit I no longer know how to handle you."

"I promise I won't do stuff like this anymore."

"Until next time?" he asked wearily.

"No, honest, Dad! I'll go to class and get good grades. I just want to be with you."

"I wish I could believe that, but I can't trust you any longer," he said heavily.

Tears welled up in the young girl's eyes, and Mandy knew his words hurt more than any punishment. She was tempted to intervene, but the captain did it for her.

"Ladies and gentlemen, we're anticipating some turbulence. Will you please return to your seats and fasten your seat belts?"

The flight attendant approached. "I'll have to take your daughter to a seat, Mr. Winfield. We're full in here, but I can find a place for her in economy class."

A wintry smile eased Connor's tight mouth. "I hope she likes it, or she won't stay." He sat down and turned to Mandy as the attendant led Dee Dee to the back of the plane. "Do you still think I was wrong to send Dee Dee back to school—or, at least, attempt to?"

"I know how upset you must be over this," she answered evasively.

"Don't you think I have a right to be? Surely you're not excusing what she did?"

"No, of course not! I feel the same way you do. I can't help shuddering when I think what might have happened if she'd missed the plane."

"Exactly! A young girl all alone in Tangier. My God! It doesn't bear thinking about." A muscle pulsed in Connor's temple. "Dee Dee is sure my mission in life is to make her miserable. She doesn't realize how much I worry about her."

"Does any twelve-year-old?" Mandy smiled.

"The question now is, what do I do with her? I'm afraid to send her back to Switzerland. Their supervision was too lax—to put it charitably. But if I let her come home she'll think she can get away with anything."

"I don't believe this was a game to her, Connor, a way to one-up you," Mandy said thoughtfully. "I've watched you together this week, and you have a good relationship."

"I always thought we did," he said soberly.

"She loves you very much. It hurt when you told her you don't trust her anymore."

"You don't know how much it hurt me to say it."

"That's why I think this was more than a juvenile prank. Dee Dee took enormous risks, knowing you'd be furious with her. Maybe she felt it was the only way to show you how much she hates boarding school."

"You're suggesting I keep her at home? What happens if she gets into serious trouble? It wasn't just cutting classes. How do I know who she was running around with?"

"That's something you must insist on knowing. You should encourage her to bring her friends home."

"Dee Dee knows her friends are always welcome," Connor said uncertainly.

"That's not good enough. Make a point of meeting them."

"How? I'm at work all day."

"Then spend time with her on Saturdays or Sundays." Mandy didn't say what she was thinking, but Connor was aware of it.

"I did spend weekends with her. Contrary to what Dee Dee would have you believe, I didn't desert her to go off on my own with a bevy of beautiful blondes. We'd all go sailing or maybe horseback riding together, whatever I thought she'd like."

"Dee Dee doesn't need to meet *your* friends," Mandy said tartly. "You need to meet *hers*. Tell her to invite her girlfriends to go places with you."

"I suppose that would work," he said slowly. "But it doesn't solve the problem of her grades. Dee Dee has a good mind. I don't want her to slide through school without learning anything."

"I think she goofed off because she was bored. She needs more intellectual stimulation than she was getting. But the solution needn't be as drastic as sending her away. There are some excellent, academically enriched schools in the city. I read an article about one just a couple of weeks ago. It has open enrollment from anywhere in the city if a student can pass the entry exam. I'm sure Dee Dee could."

"If she wanted to," Connor drawled.

"Give her the option. I'll bet she'd jump at the chance."

"You might be right," he said slowly. "I suppose it's worth a try. I'm running out of alternatives."

Mandy hesitated, slanting a glance at him. "Have you thought of talking it over with Dee Dee's mother?"

"Lorna doesn't believe in dwelling on unpleasantness," he said curtly. "If things don't turn out as expected, her solution is to go on a shopping spree and find herself a new boyfriend."

Mandy thought that was remarkably unfeeling of him. "You sound as if the problem here is a broken fingernail. This is her daughter we're talking about! It's too bad they can't see more of each other," she couldn't help adding.

Connor's expression was grimly amused as he noted Mandy's disapproval. "You obviously think I got custody of Dee Dee because my slick attorneys took advantage of a poor mother who didn't have the resources to fight for her child."

That was exactly what Mandy thought, but she couldn't very well say so. "I'm sure you did what you thought was right," she said primly.

"No, you're not. It isn't important, but I'd like to set the record straight. I was awarded custody because Lorna didn't want Dee Dee."

"I can hardly believe that," Mandy protested.

"Believe it. Contrary to popular myth, all women aren't cut out to be mothers." Connor gazed out the window, remembering. "Lorna was a dancer when we met. She dreamed of starring in a big musical on Broadway, but the only work she got was in little revues, or as the foil for some third-rate comic or magician in a nightclub act. She was very beautiful—still is, for that matter."

When he was silent for a long moment, Mandy wondered if he was still carrying a torch for his ex-wife. "You must have been very young when you met her," she said tentatively.

"We both were. With the benefit of hindsight, I realize we had nothing in common except a strong sexual attraction. Lorna's only interest was show business, and I found most of her friends boring. She felt the same about mine."

"How could either of you consider marriage under those circumstances?"

"We each had something the other wanted." His smile was cynical. "She was very... alluring... and I had a rich father. Lorna liked the good life, but she didn't like living it in San Francisco.''

"Is that why your marriage broke up?"

"I suppose it was part of the reason. Although I doubt if any one man can give Lorna the attention she demands. I tried to tell myself her flirtations were harmless, but she got more and more restless. Finally she met a Hollywood director at a party. He had visions of Broadway, too, so they went back to New York together. She left me a note telling me to explain it to Dee Dee.''

"She moved out and left her child behind?" Mandy asked incredulously.

"Try explaining *that* to a ten-year-old! I was afraid of how the trauma might affect Dee Dee, although I softened the truth as much as possible. At first she did keep asking when her mother was coming back, but I made up excuses and spent a lot of time with her. When I couldn't be there, I arranged activities so she'd be kept busy. Gradually she accepted the fact that Lorna wasn't coming home.''

"You must have handled it incredibly well," Mandy exclaimed.

He shrugged. "I did what I had to. I'm just glad it worked. Dee Dee and her mother have a good relationship now. They talk on the phone like two teenagers—probably because they share the same sense of irresponsibility," he added ironically.

To a greater extent than he imagined! Mandy was sure Connor didn't know that Lorna discussed details of her relationships with her daughter. Such frankness would account for the fact that Dee Dee was so precocious.

"Perhaps now you understand why I don't consult with my ex-wife when I have to make decisions concerning Dee Dee. Lorna isn't a bad person, but she has difficulty focusing on anyone but herself.''

Mandy stole a look at him. He sounded so dispassionate. Was it an act to cover his true feelings for a woman he couldn't forget? Or was Connor incapable of love? Lorna's desertion would have hurt any man's pride, but was anything else involved? It was impossible to tell.

"You seem to understand Dee Dee better than I do," he continued. "That's why I've relied on your opinion."

"I'm no authority," Mandy warned.

"Is there such a thing?" His smile was almost natural.

"Only people on talk shows, who probably don't have children of their own." She returned his smile. "Would you mind if I went back to talk to Dee Dee? I hate to think of her all alone back there, worrying about what's going to happen to her."

"That isn't likely. You'll undoubtedly find her happily reading comic books and plotting her next escapade."

Connor was wrong. Dee Dee was a picture of dejection, huddled in a seat and staring bleakly out the window. She looked around apprehensively when Mandy took the seat next to her.

"I really goofed big-time, didn't I?" she commented.

"Did you expect your father to treat this as a huge joke?" Mandy asked.

"I knew he'd be mad, but not this mad. He doesn't like me anymore," Dee Dee said in a small voice.

Mandy resisted an urge to put her arms around the girl. Dee Dee had to understand her father's point of view. "What you did could have had serious consequences. Connor was terribly concerned, and when parents are upset they sometimes overreact. That doesn't mean he doesn't love you. It's *because* he loves you that he blew up."

"He said he doesn't trust me."

"Be honest. You haven't given him much reason to, have you?"

"I only wanted to come home," Dee Dee said wistfully. "I really meant it when I said I'd follow the rules if he gave me another chance."

"I gather you've promised that before."

"Yeah, but this time I really mean it. I'll even go back to Switzerland if that's what he wants." The young girl wiped her nose on her sleeve. "I want to prove to Dad that he can trust me again."

Mandy offered a handkerchief, concealing her own emotion. "It won't be easy after hitting him with a double whammy. But he's willing to give you another chance. Your father has decided to let you go to school in San Francisco. Now it's up to you to show him he made the right decision."

"You really mean it?" Dee Dee's face lit with incredulous joy. "I won't let him down, you'll see!"

"Show *him,* not me."

"You talked him into this, didn't you?"

"You know your father," Mandy answered evasively. "Nobody influences him."

"Except you. He never would have let me stay if you hadn't persuaded him. Thank you! Thank you! Thank you! You're the absolute greatest!" She threw her arms around Mandy's neck in an excess of gratitude. "I hope I can do something this super for you someday."

"You can. Just stay in school, get good grades and stop bugging your dad."

"You got it," Dee Dee said happily.

Connor's manner toward his daughter was austere when they met at the end of the trip, and Dee Dee was subdued. But Mandy was confident that neither attitude would last long.

A limo was waiting for Connor. By the time they'd claimed their luggage and were all settled in the car, relations had thawed considerably. On the ride from the airport, Dee Dee's head swiveled back and forth as she tried to see everything at once.

Her delight wasn't lost on Connor. He was touched, but he tried not to show it. "You haven't been gone that long," he remarked. "Nothing has changed."

"I've changed, Dad," she answered diffidently.

Mandy had a lump in her throat, watching Connor grip his daughter's hand tightly.

His voice was husky as he said, "It's good to have you home again, little one."

The limo dropped Mandy off at her apartment in the Marina district before taking Connor and Dee Dee to their apartment on Russian Hill. The young girl hugged her while the chauffeur was getting Mandy's luggage out of the trunk.

"Thanks again," Dee Dee whispered in her ear. "You're the best!"

"See that you are, too." Mandy smiled. She looked past her to Connor. "Well, goodbye and good luck. I hope you'll think of Jet Away the next time you have any travel requirements."

I sound like a television commercial, Mandy thought in disgust. But the easygoing friendship they'd shared all week had vanished now that they were back in San Francisco. Connor was once more the unapproachable tycoon he'd been when she first met him.

He gave her a brief smile. "I'll tell my staff what a good job you did."

That wasn't a commitment, Mandy thought as she let herself into her small apartment. She *had* done a good job—except for getting too involved in Connor's affairs.

He had revealed quite a lot about his private life. Would he regret being so frank when he had time to think about it? His reserve seemed to indicate he was already having second thoughts.

Mandy sighed as she carried her suitcases into the bedroom. She'd really blown it. Connor wouldn't want to be reminded that he'd acted human for once. Too bad Jet Away would suffer for it.

The telephone rang. "I've been calling every half hour!" Alexandra exclaimed. "You said you'd be home around six o'clock. Was your plane late?"

"No, it was on time, but you know how long it takes to get your luggage and drive home from the airport."

"How did everything go?"

"Just great!" Mandy's spirits lifted as she recalled the interesting week. "Tangier is fascinating, so exotic and different. We must recommend it to more people."

"What about the accommodations? You know how tourists are. They like local color—as long as it comes with a comfortable hotel room and a private bath."

They talked business for a while. Mandy gave her partner a rundown on the captivating souks and historic attractions she'd checked out personally.

"It sounds like you've been on vacation while I was slaving away here, holding down the fort," Alexandra complained.

"It wasn't all play," Mandy protested. "I arranged dinners and cocktail parties, and made sure there weren't any glitches."

"Poor baby! You must be exhausted from all that partying."

Mandy laughed. "It was a dirty job, but, hey, somebody had to do it."

"How was the terrible tycoon? Did he make your life miserable?"

"No, he . . . It wasn't too bad."

"You don't have to be polite with me. It must have been a downer, having to live in the same house with him. Did he make impossible demands? Men like that usually expect a lot."

Mandy had a vivid flashback to the night in the pool, when her body had been joined so tantalizingly with Connor's. He hadn't been the only one with expectations. She could still remember the sudden stab of desire that had made her want to reach out for him.

"It's a good thing he was in meetings all day," Alexandra persisted. "At least that gave you some breathing space."

"Connor isn't as bad as you're making out," Mandy objected. "He's a little forbidding until you get to know him, but he's really quite generous."

"That isn't difficult when you have money. But listen, I'm not complaining if *you* aren't. We made a bundle on this trip. I guess it's too much to ask for all of his business, but do you think we'll get some of it?"

"I wouldn't count on it," Mandy answered cautiously.

"Why not? You just said everything went great. Is there something you're not telling me?"

"No!" Mandy's answer was too quick and too explosive.

Alexandra knew her friend thoroughly. "Okay, now tell me the whole story. Did he make a pass at you? From all accounts, he's quite a ladies' man."

"You can't believe everything you read in those silly gossip columns. Connor is a very kind, sensitive man underneath that autocratic exterior. People only like to write about all the women he dates and his lavish life-style. They don't really know him."

"And you do, after one week? You're certainly singing a different tune," Alexandra said slowly. "It almost sounds as if you're falling in love with him."

"Don't be ridiculous! I'll admit my first impression wasn't exactly favorable, but I can be as wrong as anyone else. He's completely different when you get to know him."

After a slight pause, Alexandra asked, "Just how close did you get?"

"It was nothing like that! We spent a lot of time together, naturally, and I was able to help him out with a problem.'' Mandy told her about Dee Dee's escapades. ''Connor exploded when he found out, but it was only out of concern for her. When I watched them together and saw how much he cared about her, I realized what kind of man he really is under that imperious manner.''

Alexandra was unconvinced. ''His daughter sounds like the only female he truly loves. Those glamour girls he takes out last about as long as a carton of age-dated cottage cheese in the refrigerator section.''

''Maybe he's just looking for the right woman.''

Alexandra caught the wistful note in her friend's voice. ''Don't be a chump, Mandy. Do you know how many women have wound up with broken hearts because they thought they could convince some playboy that they were 'the right woman'?''

''I'm not interested in Connor. I merely think you're being unfair to him.''

''Okay, so I'm unfair. I just don't want to see you end up sadder and wiser.''

''I appreciate your concern, but it's misplaced. I doubt if we'll ever hear from Connor again. I thought we had a good shot at his business, but on the plane coming home he told me a lot of personal stuff about his first marriage. You know how it is when you tell somebody things you regret afterward. You avoid that person like the plague.''

''It isn't your fault he let his hair down. Winfield Enterprises would have been a lucrative account, but we got along without it. I'm just as glad you won't be seeing him anymore.''

Mandy sighed. ''I don't know how to convince you that Connor Winfield means nothing to me, so I won't even try. Tell me what's been happening while I was gone.''

''It's been a really busy week. I booked a charter group on a trip to the Greek Islands, and sent an older couple on a luxury cruise to celebrate their anniversary.''

"It looks like you did all right alone. Are you trying to tell me I'm not needed around here anymore?" Mandy joked.

After they hung up, Mandy unpacked, thinking about the new business they'd gotten, and some news Alexandra had told her about a friend. This was her normal life, not the exotic week in Tangier.

But when she came to the beaded dress in her suitcase, Mandy was unavoidably reminded of Connor. He was a real hunk, without any doubt. It wasn't just his ruggedly handsome face and superb physique. Connor had a rare charisma. He could vitalize a room just by entering it.

When Mandy realized she was hugging the dress to her body, she quickly hung it on a hanger. Naturally she found Connor stimulating to be with—eveyone did. But that didn't mean she was falling in love with him. Alexandra's accusation was ludicrous! This past week would be an exciting memory, nothing more. And so would Connor.

The next few days were busy ones for Mandy. A lot of paperwork had piled up in her absence as Alexandra couldn't do everything alone. Then there was the normal, everyday business to take care of.

By the time she got home at night, she was too tired to cook dinner. Her apartment seemed cramped, too, for the first time. Mandy knew it was because of the previous week's luxury. It had been a treat to have a large house to roam around in, and a staff of servants to prepare meals.

That was the way the rich lived. She'd had a glimpse, and now it was time to get back to reality, Mandy told herself. But she couldn't help wondering what Connor's Russian Hill apartment looked like, and how he and Dee Dee were getting along.

By Saturday she'd accepted the fact that the Winfields were out of her life for good. Connor hadn't phoned either her home or the office. She would always wonder if he'd taken her advice about Dee Dee, and if so, how it had worked out. But life was full of unfinished stories.

Mandy slept late on Saturday morning, which was a luxury after her hectic week. The rest of the day was free, too. She had a date that night, but nothing pressing to do until then.

She had eaten a late lunch and was lazily trying to decide if it was worth setting up the ironing board for just one blouse, or if she should wait until there were more. The telephone rang, making the decision for her. Dee Dee's voice couldn't have been more welcome.

"I've been thinking about you!" Mandy exclaimed. "How's everything going?"

"Just great! I took the entrance exam for Lafayette Middle School and I passed. They're going to let me start on Monday, even though it's the middle of the term."

"That's fantastic! Are you happy about it?"

"Do burgers and fries go together?" Dee Dee gave a bubbly laugh.

"How are you and your dad getting along?" Mandy asked casually.

"Pretty good, for the most part. But for a with-it guy, he has really weird taste."

"In what way?"

"Like clothes, for instance. Dad's way back in the Dark Ages! You should see some of the geeky things he wants me to wear."

"I've seen some of the things you chose on your own," Mandy remarked dryly.

"Okay, so maybe that one outfit I bought was a little far out. But no self-respecting kid would be caught dead in the stuff he wants me to wear. Will you talk to him, Mandy?"

Her heartbeat quickened, which was a good reason to refuse. "Your father wouldn't welcome any further advice from me. You're on your own now."

"I can't get anywhere with him. Do me this one more favor," Dee Dee wheedled. "He listens to you."

"Not anymore. I haven't spoken to him since he dropped me off a week ago. It's pretty clear that he doesn't need my help."

"He's been real busy at the office on account of being gone so long. I know he'd like to see you."

"I'm sorry, but I don't share your opinion."

Connor's voice was suddenly audible in the background. He sounded impatient. "Can't you make a simple phone call without turning it into an hour-long talk show? What did she say?"

"She says you don't want to see her," Dee Dee reported.

Mandy smothered a groan as Connor took over the phone. "What makes you think I don't want to see you?" he demanded.

"Dee Dee misunderstood," she answered carefully. "She said you were having a disagreement, and I said I didn't want to interfere."

"We *need* a referee. You wouldn't believe some of the things that child wanted me to buy her."

Mandy couldn't help laughing. "Yes, I would. Fortunately, you didn't see how she looked when she arrived in Tangier."

"It was a good week, wasn't it?" His voice had lost its edge.

"I certainly enjoyed it," she answered softly.

"You weren't alone. I—" He paused as Dee Dee interrupted, evidently at his elbow.

"Dad! You're the one who accused me of sitting on the phone, and now you're doing the same thing. The saleslady will put that skirt back in stock if we don't hurry up."

"I doubt if I could be that lucky," Connor answered ironically.

"You said you'd leave it up to Mandy. What did she say? Is she coming?"

"I don't know. I haven't asked her yet."

"Well, *ask* her!"

"I presume you heard that," he said to Mandy. "Will you come? We're at our usual impasse, and you're the only one who can mediate."

"Come where? I just assumed Dee Dee called from home."

"We're at Neiman-Marcus, in the junior department, trying unsuccessfully to buy her a school wardrobe. No school would let her in the door wearing some of the things she picked out. One of the skirts doesn't have enough material to make a hair ribbon."

Dee Dee could be heard making exaggerated retching sounds. "A hair ribbon! What do you think I am, a poodle?"

"You see what I mean?" Connor sighed.

Mandy laughed. "Hang on, Mandy the Miraculous will drive to the rescue. Can you avoid coming to blows for twenty minutes? I have to change."

"Don't ever change," he said deeply.

She got all warm and tingly, until she realized it was gratitude in his voice, not passion.

"I know I have no right to intrude on your weekend this way, but I'd be very grateful," he continued.

"It's okay, I have a couple of free hours," she answered dismissively, then hung up.

Mandy flew around the apartment, making excuses to herself as she changed into a gray pantsuit and a pink silk blouse. So what if she did make herself available as soon as he called? It wasn't as if she were doing anything important. Wouldn't it be foolish to stand on ceremony when she really wanted to see both of them again?

That's right, both of them, she told herself firmly. She missed Dee Dee as much as she missed Connor. Besides, it was nice to be needed—and they certainly needed her.

Mandy grinned, guessing what kind of clothes the young girl had picked out.

Connor and Dee Dee weren't any closer to an agreement when Mandy arrived twenty-five minutes later. He looked harried, and a saleswoman was trying hard to keep her professional smile. Only Dee Dee was having a good time. She was roaming the racks, choosing more things to add to the heap over her arm.

"Thank God!" Connor muttered when he caught sight of Mandy. "Am I glad to see you!"

She could have said the same thing. Connor had on a pale blue cashmere sweater over navy slacks and a white silk shirt. The casual outfit made him look like the athlete he was, emphasizing his virility. Mandy wanted to reach out and smooth the unruly lock of dark hair that fell across his wide forehead.

Instead, she smiled and said, "Okay, the marines have landed. What seems to be the problem?"

"A twelve-year-old girl who thinks good taste means a hot-fudge sundae," he answered.

Dee Dee rushed over when she saw Mandy. "Gee, it's good to see you again. You look great! I love that pantsuit."

Mandy laughed. "It won't do any good to butter me up. You're still too young for black leather miniskirts."

"How about this cat suit?" Dee Dee held up a slinky black garment.

"How about this?" Mandy countered, holding up a twin sweater set she took off a table stacked with them.

"You gotta be kidding!"

"Let's get real," Mandy said. "You won't get away with miniskirts or sequin halter tops, so I suggest we stop wasting time."

Connor's face registered amazement as she led his daughter around, selecting blouses, sweaters and skirts and offering them for the young girl's approval. Mandy didn't try to force anything on her. If Dee Dee didn't like something, it went back on the rack, but they agreed on the majority of her choices—even if grudgingly on Dee Dee's part.

The saleswoman brightened considerably. She followed them around, helping to find the right sizes. When she took Dee Dee into a dressing room, Mandy returned to Connor.

"That wasn't so hard. I don't know why you made such a big deal out of it," she teased.

"I could put together a million-dollar merger with less stress. Why is she so much more reasonable with you?"

"Because she knows I won't back her up if she wants something outrageous."

"I said I wouldn't buy it for her. How is that any different?"

Mandy smiled. "She figures maybe you'll change your mind if she wears you down long enough. You're putty in her hands."

Connor laughed unwillingly. "You can read me like a book, can't you? I'm glad I don't have to go up against you in a business deal. I'd lose my shirt."

"Not to me. I only know how you feel about your daughter. Other than that, I haven't a clue."

"I thought we got to know each other rather well last week."

"It takes longer than a week to really know someone."

"I'm not going anywhere." He smiled. "How about you?"

Mandy would have liked to believe that meant something, but she wasn't into self-deception. The truth was, Connor just couldn't help coming on to any reasonably attractive woman. If he was really interested in her, he would have called. She was only here today because of Dee Dee.

When she didn't answer immediately he said, "If you're not busy tomorrow, would you like to go sailing?"

"You're just feeling grateful because I got you off the hook with Dee Dee," she joked. "But you don't owe me anything. I'm very fond of her."

"I'm delighted. You're the kind of influence she needs. But I didn't ask you out for that reason. I'd really like you to come."

The urge to accept was so great that Mandy hesitated. "Don't you spend the weekends with Dee Dee?"

"She's going to a birthday party. That leaves you only two excuses. Either you're busy, or you can't take my company two days in a row."

"I wouldn't want you to get that impression, so I guess I'll have to accept."

His smile vanished. "I don't want to blackmail you into anything."

"Actually I'd like very much to go sailing with you." Why fight it? Mandy thought. She was dying to go.

"I was hoping you would. We spent a lot of time together last week. I've missed seeing you every day," he said in a honeyed voice.

That was too much for her to swallow, but she had to admit Connor was good. He even managed to sound sincere.

"You have a convenient memory," she said lightly. "There were times when you were very annoyed at me."

"Not really with you. It was Jacques who irritated me."

"Is his company part of the multinational corporation you put together?"

"Yes, he signed on as a member of the group. I expect it to be quite successful."

Connor didn't approve of Jacques's morals, but that didn't stop him from doing business with the man. Maybe that was how tycoons operated, she supposed. They would deal with the devil if it was advantageous. She studied his lean, intelligent face. How could he be so ruthless and yet so charming?

Connor's expression changed as he stared into her wide blue eyes. "It was a good week. You're my lucky charm."

"I'm glad I helped you make another million or two."

He frowned, catching the irony in her voice. "Is something bothering you, Mandy?"

"No, not a thing." She gave him a quick smile. "Dee Dee's been gone a long time. I'd better make sure she didn't sneak in something that will freak you out."

Connor's expression was unreadable as he watched her slender figure disappear into the entrance to the dressing rooms.

Chapter Six

Mandy returned home in a troubled mood after seeing Connor. She disapproved of almost everything about him, so why had she accepted his invitation? She was tempted to phone him with some excuse, like not remembering a previous date.

But that wouldn't be prudent. Connor was an important business connection. Besides, it was only one afternoon out of her life, she told herself, feeling a lot more cheerful.

Mandy had been looking forward to the party she was going to that Saturday night. It was being given by Alexandra's brother and his wife. Ralph was one of Mandy's favorite people, and Kim was just right for him. He had always been a happy-go-lucky kid, but in the few years they'd been married, Ralph had matured. He and Kim were talking about starting a family, now that the coffeehouse they'd opened in an upscale neighborhood had become profitable.

Mandy's date that evening was Carl Simpson, a man who periodically asked her to marry him, but was resigned to the fact that she wasn't going to.

His eyes lit up when she opened the door. "I know I'm early, but I couldn't wait to see you. You look fantastic! I've missed you."

She couldn't help remembering Connor making the same statement that afternoon. It was kind of ironic. Carl meant what he said, while Connor didn't. But Connor's husky voice and intimate manner made him the more believable of the two.

"I was only gone a week," she said.

"It seemed longer. It's great to have you back. Did you have a good time?"

"Yes, although I was there on business. Did you do anything interesting last week?" she asked, changing the subject.

They chatted about inconsequential things on the way to the party.

When they arrived, everybody was curious about Mandy's trip.

"Tell us all about Tangier," Larry said. He was a short, chubby man who was rarely serious. "Do they have visiting days at the harems?"

"I'd rather hear about Connor Winfield," his wife, Vivian, said, rolling her eyes. "I wouldn't mind going on a trip with him, myself. Is he as gorgeous as he looks in the newspaper?"

"He must be even handsomer," Kim said. "Newspaper photos don't do anybody justice."

"I can't see how you could improve on that beautiful bod." Vivian sighed.

"Big deal," Larry scoffed. "Name me one thing he has that I don't, outside of a few million dollars."

"Well, he's tall, broad-shouldered, and has a fantastic physique. He also has those eyes that kind of crinkle at the corners when he smiles, not to mention a mouth to die over.''

"I said *one* thing," Larry complained.

Mandy didn't join in the resulting laughter. She was thinking about all the qualities that weren't evident in a picture—Connor's ability to spellbind, his mind-spinning sexuality.

"Did I exaggerate?" Vivian appealed to her.

"A lot of blondes in this city seem to agree with you," she answered lightly. "Speaking of blondes," Mandy continued quickly, "has anybody heard from Rhoda since she moved to Sacramento?" The subject of Connor was dropped and the conversation moved to other topics, as she'd intended.

Later in the evening, Mandy carried some empty glasses into the kitchen. Ralph was in there alone, getting ice from the freezer. He greeted her with a smile, but she'd noticed the somber expression on his face when he thought he was alone.

"Great party, Ralphie," she said.

"I'm glad you're enjoying it."

"Everybody is." After a moment's pause, she added, "Are you?"

"Are you kidding? You're talking to the original party boy," he said, a little too heartily.

She looked at him uncertainly. "You always used to be."

"Still am. Don't be fooled, just because I run a business now instead of spending my nights sneaking into the girls' dorm."

"It's a wonder you made it through college without getting bounced," Mandy said fondly. "Who would ever think you'd wind up to be a solid citizen with your own business!"

"Yeah, a regular member of the establishment."

She caught the tinge of bitterness in his voice. Was Ralph chafing at the nine-to-five world? "We all have to grow up sometime," she said gently.

"True, but along with your diploma they ought to give you a stun gun to ward off the sharks."

Mandy gave him a puzzled look. "What kind of sharks?"

"Do you know of a good kind?" he asked lightly, evidently regretting his candor. "I'd better get the rest of this ice out of the freezer before Kim gives me a lecture on being a good host."

Mandy slanted a covert glance at him. Something was definitely bothering Ralph. She didn't like to pry, but she cared too much about him to just ignore it.

"How's business at the coffeehouse?" she asked. That seemed like a safe subject, since she knew he was doing well.

"It couldn't be better. We're packing them in every night." He banged an ice tray on the counter with unnecessary force.

"Then shouldn't you be celebrating instead of practicing karate chops on the kitchen sink?"

He turned to her with a mixture of irritation and wry amusement. "You always did have this urge to play 'Dear Abby' and solve everyone's problems."

"Only when it's somebody I care about a lot. What's wrong, Ralph?" she asked quietly.

"I didn't realize it was that obvious." He pulled out a kitchen chair and sank into it. "Oh, well, it won't be a secret much longer, so I might as well get it off my chest. I'm being squeezed out of business."

That was the last thing Mandy had expected. "But you said you're crowded every night."

"We are. I'm a victim of my own success. A big corporation called Global Ventures wants to buy me out. They already own a chain of coffeehouses like mine, along with God knows what else. Those big conglomerates are into everything. They're offering a good price, but I don't want to sell. I worked hard to make the Coffee Bean a success, and I figured this was just the beginning. Kim and I talked about owning our own chain someday."

"I don't see the problem. Just tell them you don't want to sell."

"It isn't that simple. They're using leverage on me. They said if I don't agree, they'll open a coffeehouse next door and undercut my prices. They can do it, too. Their other outlets can absorb the loss until I go bankrupt."

"That's terrible!"

"Tell me about it," he said morosely. "They've got me really boxed in. I have two options, either sell out or lose my whole investment."

"Your place is like a neighborhood club. Everybody knows everybody else. Surely your customers wouldn't leave you."

"Maybe not at first. But when they can get a cappuccino for half price right next door…well, you can't really blame them."

"Couldn't you threaten to sue this Global Ventures outfit?"

"On what grounds?"

"I don't know, but it seems as if everybody sues nowadays. At least it would tie them up in court."

"And wipe me out. Those guys keep lawyers on a yearly retainer. I'd just go broke a little sooner."

Mandy knew that was true. She'd recently had a weeklong lesson in how big fish swallow up little ones. "I'm so sorry, Ralph."

"Me, too." He smiled gamely. "Oh, well, I still have a month to conjure up a miracle. That's the amount of time they gave me to make up my mind. I guess they're too busy forcing some other poor jerk out of business to get around to me right away."

Kim pushed open the swinging door to the kitchen. "How long does it take to fill an ice bucket?" she asked her hus-

band. "You have a room full of guests holding warm
drinks."

"I told you I was going to catch it." Ralph grinned at
Mandy.

She felt deeply for Ralph. He'd worked so hard to become a success, only to see it snatched away. It wasn't fair,
but there was nothing anyone could do about it. She sighed
and went back to the party.

The next morning, Mandy awoke late and looked drowsily at the clock, then gasped and jumped out of bed. If only
she'd thought to set the alarm clock, so that she could have
dressed leisurely and appeared poised when Connor arrived.

The doorbell rang promptly at eleven o'clock, the time
he'd specified. It was too much to expect him to be late,
Mandy thought despairingly. She zipped up her skintight
white jeans, pulled a red T-shirt over her head and ran to the
door.

"Am I early?" Connor asked, gazing at her tousled hair
and bare feet.

"No, I overslept. I'm sorry." She tried ineffectually to
smooth her long hair.

"There's no hurry. Take your time."

She smiled ruefully. "Is that a polite way of saying I'll
need it to be presentable?"

"Not at all. You look great." His expression was admir-
ing as he looked her over, his gaze lingering on her rounded
hips. "I especially like those jeans." He grinned suddenly.
"Just out of curiosity, can you sit down in them?"

"I'll go and change."

He caught her hand. "Don't do that. I was only teasing
you. They're very becoming. You'll be the sexiest woman at
the yacht club."

She looked down at herself doubtfully. "That wasn't the
look I was aiming for."

"What's wrong with looking sexy? Marilyn Monroe was celebrated for it."

Another blonde! "I must be the only brunette you've ever taken out." Mandy tried to hide her irritation under a joking tone.

"I'm in trouble any way I answer that." He laughed. "Go put your shoes on. I'm getting hungry."

They drove over the Golden Gate Bridge in Connor's red Ferrari. It was a magnificent car, sleek and powerful, like its owner. The men they passed cast envious glances at the car, but the women were more interested in Connor's lean, relaxed body and handsome face.

It was a perfect day to be outdoors. The sun reflected off the blue waters of the bay, giving the surface a diamond sparkle. Small boats skipped across the choppy water like little children let out of school.

The yacht club parking lot was crowded, like the club itself. Several people waved to Connor as he and Mandy walked into the grill room, and others turned their heads out of curiosity. Everyone was very circumspect, but there were a lot of speculative glances cast at her.

"Do you have a table by the window, Ted?" Connor asked the waiter who came to seat them.

"Sure thing, Mr. Winfield. I saved one just for you."

When the man had given them menus and left to get coffee, Mandy remarked, "I must be the only outsider here."

"What makes you think that?"

"People are trying so hard not to stare. It's either the fact that I don't belong, or the tight jeans." She laughed. "I knew I should have changed."

"Why? You have a beautiful figure. What's wrong with showing it off to its best advantage?"

"That's not my style."

"Wearing a bikini didn't seem to bother you," he teased.

"It was a fairly modest one," she protested. "Besides, it was dark out."

"Not that dark," he murmured.

Mandy could tell he was picturing her body, seminude. She was glad the waiter returned to take their brunch order.

While they were eating, a beautiful blond woman came over and put her arm possessively around Connor's shoulders. "Hi, darling. Isn't it a perfect day for sailing?" She gave Mandy an insincere smile. "I'm glad to see you got someone to go with you."

Connor wasn't in the least embarrassed. "It's good of you to worry about me," he drawled, before introducing the woman as Brittany Lewis.

Mandy wondered what had happened to Barbara. Dee Dee didn't have to worry. Barbara was evidently history—as this one would be sooner or later.

The two women exchanged a couple of polite words, and then Brittany turned back to Connor. "Don't be late tonight, darling. It's a surprise party, remember. We want to make sure we get to Marian's before the birthday boy arrives."

"Dwight is too old to be having birthday parties, and I have yet to see anyone who was surprised by one of these archaic events."

"Don't spoil things, Connor," the blonde said, pouting.

"All right." He sighed. "I'll be on time."

"That's my love." She leaned down and kissed his cheek. Then, with an airy wave in Mandy's direction, she left.

A small silence fell when they were alone. Mandy concentrated on her eggs Benedict, aware of Connor's gaze.

"I didn't ask Brittany to go sailing today," he said finally. "You weren't second choice."

"It isn't important. I don't mind."

"That means you don't believe me. Why? Have I ever lied to you?"

"Not that I know of, and I'd prefer that you don't feel you have to start now. Your private life is your own. You don't owe me any explanations."

"No, I don't." He gave her a baffled look. "So why does it irritate me that you don't believe me?"

"Possibly because you're used to gullible women and I'm not one of them." She should have quit while she was ahead, but Mandy was angry that he hadn't reined in his tacky girlfriend. "You have a great line, but I've heard them all. It doesn't work with me."

Connor's puzzled expression turned to a smile that sent a little shiver up her spine. "Are you so sure, Mandy?" he asked softly. "I can be very persuasive."

As she stared into his smoky gray eyes, the waiter returned. "Can I get you anything else, Mr. Winfield?"

Connor looked inquiringly at Mandy. When she shook her head, he said, "Just the check, Ted."

Mandy realized her overactive imagination had played a trick on her. For just a moment, Connor's high cheekbones had seemed to sharpen, giving him the look of a predator, confident of his prey. There was no trace of anything like that now. He was lounging back in his chair, the picture of sophisticated urbanity.

"Are you ready to go sailing?" he asked.

"Whenever you are," she answered with a forced smile.

Connor's sailboat was relatively modest, surprising Mandy. Everything else about his life-style was so opulent that she'd been subconsciously expecting a yacht.

"This is the *Wind Star*," he said. "Come aboard, I'll show you around."

A narrow gangway led down to a compact galley. On either side of it were two small staterooms with bunk beds. Every inch of space had been utilized, making for close quarters.

When Mandy commented on the fact, Connor grinned. "It's a little cramped, but there are fringe benefits. People get to be very good friends."

Mandy couldn't help wondering how a man as big as Connor could fit into one of those narrow bunks—even without a companion. She was sure he didn't sleep alone very often.

It was perfect sailing weather, sunny but with a brisk wind blowing. When they were back on deck, the breeze whipped Mandy's long black hair around her face. Brushing it out of her eyes didn't help. The long tendrils blew right back.

Connor noticed the trouble she was having. "I should have told you to bring a hat, or at least a scarf."

"I guess I should have thought of it myself. That's what happens when you oversleep and have to rush." Mandy started to laugh. "Now I sound like my mother."

"We can fix your problem in a jiffy."

He opened a hinged wooden box on the deck, took out a yachting cap and handed it to her. After gathering her long hair in both hands, he twisted it into a loose knot on top of her head. Before reaching for the cap, he stared at her appraisingly.

"You look good with your hair pulled back. Have you ever worn it this way?"

Connor was standing within inches of her. So close that she could see the muscles shift in his powerful shoulders, underneath his cotton T-shirt. She moistened her lips, gazing past him rather than into his eyes. "It . . . uh . . . it always slips out of the pins and looks messy."

He drew in his breath sharply, suddenly as aware of her as she was of him. Her hair tumbled down when his hands lowered to cup her shoulders.

Mandy's lips parted as he drew her closer. Neither were aware of their surroundings, only of each other. As his head dipped slowly toward hers, a man's laughing voice called out.

"Hey, Connor, did you come down here to go sailing or to make out with your girl?"

Connor moved away without embarrassment. "Hi, Roger. Did anybody ever tell you that your timing is lousy?"

The two men joked together while Mandy turned away and tucked her hair inside the yachting cap. Connor was unaffected by what had almost happened, while she was filled with aching regret. It would only have been a kiss, she reminded herself. But would it have been? she wondered, thinking of the staterooms below. Was he demonstrating what he'd told her at brunch, that he could be very persuasive?

When he turned back to her, she said brightly, "Okay, I'm all tucked in. You can cast off now."

He gazed at her silently for a moment, revealing no emotion. Then he smiled. "All right, let's do it."

Mandy relaxed once they were out on the bay. It was exhilarating to skim over the waves, but it was chillier than she'd expected. When Connor noticed she was shivering, he tossed her a windbreaker from the same equipment box.

She put it on gratefully. "You're prepared for anything, aren't you?"

"Except unwelcome interruptions," he joked.

She concentrated on fastening her zipper. "Can I get you a jacket?"

"No, I'm not cold."

Didn't he have any of the weaknesses of other people? None that were visible. Except for the jeans and T-shirt, Connor could have been one of those epic athletes sculpted by the ancient Greeks. He would look magnificent in the nude, no doubt about it.

Connor looked over as she turned away abruptly. "Where are you going?"

"To see the view from the port side," she mumbled.

"Watch out!"

He snaked an arm around her waist and pulled her close. Before Mandy could react, the sailboat heeled sharply in the wake of a speeding motorboat. She lost her balance and leaned heavily against Connor.

"Those damn hotdogs think they own the bay!" He tilted her chin up. "Sorry, I didn't mean to manhandle you, but I saw it coming."

"It's all right," she said breathlessly, achingly conscious of their joined bodies. Connor's hipbone was digging into her soft flesh, and her breasts were crushed against his broad chest.

His embrace tightened as he stared into her eyes. "We might as well find out what it would be like," he muttered.

His head lowered swiftly, and his mouth covered hers. Mandy never considered resisting. Her lips parted willingly, and she clasped her arms around his neck. Connor's arms tightened at her response, and his kiss deepened. She could scarcely breathe, but she didn't want him to let go.

"Beautiful, adorable Mandy," he groaned, when he finally dragged his mouth away. "I've wanted to do that for such a long time."

Mandy didn't doubt it. She could tell Connor was attracted to her. But he was attracted to a lot of women. She couldn't attach too much importance to one kiss—which was as far as she could go without getting her heart broken. Mandy had to face the fact that she could easily fall in love with Connor.

He curled his hand around the nape of her neck and kissed the corner of her mouth. "It was bound to happen. The only question was when."

She couldn't pretend she hadn't felt the same burning curiosity. All she could do was try to downplay the effect. Moving away, she said lightly, "I must say, you live up to your reputation."

"You're not too shabby yourself, angel face. Shall we head back and have some champagne to celebrate the start of a beautiful friendship?"

"I thought we were already friends."

"There's always room for improvement." He grinned as he tacked the sails.

Mandy didn't know how to tell him his expectations were misplaced. Her response had been all too evident, so how did she explain why she didn't want a personal relationship? The truth would scare him off, she thought cynically. That she was already halfway in love with him. Connor wasn't interested in permanency. But she didn't want to expose her vulnerability by telling him the truth. It would be too easy for him to take advantage of it.

Connor hadn't overestimated his persuasiveness.

The bar was crowded by the time Mandy and Connor got back. They found a small table in the middle of the room, but people kept stopping by to chat. Private conversation was impossible, which was all right with Mandy.

They'd been alone for a few moments when a heavyset man came up to the table. His face was flushed and his jaw was thrust out pugnaciously. Connor greeted him pleasantly enough, but he was obviously not a friend. The man didn't lose any time in confirming the fact.

"I've been trying to get in touch with you, Winfield. This time you can't weasel out of talking to me."

"I'll be happy to talk to you, Franklin—in my office," Connor said evenly. "Call for an appointment."

"What do you think I've been doing? I'm tired of getting the runaround from all your high-priced yes-men. You'll talk to me right now, you lousy crook!"

"You're drunk." Connor's voice was edged with contempt. "Go home and sober up."

"You'd love to shut me up, wouldn't you?" The man gave a nasty laugh. "What's the matter, are you afraid your friends will find out you're nothing but a common thief?"

Connor's eyes were steely, but his voice remained calm. "You're out of line, Phelps."

"Because I won't roll over meekly and let you raid my company? My grandfather built that company! I'm not going to sit still for a hostile takeover." The man placed his palms on the table and leaned on them heavily, thrusting his face into Connor's. "You won't get away with this, Winfield. I'll fight you, and by God I'll win!"

Mandy was horribly embarrassed, along with the other people in the bar. The nasty argument was too loud to ignore, although they all pretended to.

Finally a man approached their table. "Is everything all right, Mr. Winfield?"

"Everything's fine," Connor answered smoothly. "Mr. Phelps has just had a little too much to drink. Perhaps you can put him in a cab and send him home."

"Certainly, sir."

Franklin Phelps jerked his arm away. "Take your hands off me, damn it! I'll leave when I'm good and ready."

"You're creating a disturbance, sir," the man said firmly. He was evidently an official of the yacht club.

"Too damn bad! Do you know what he's doing to *me*? Trying to ruin me, that's what!"

The official had been joined by two waiters, who gently urged the man toward the door.

Franklin realized he was outnumbered, but as they propelled him from the room, he loosed one last tirade over his shoulder. "How do you sleep at night, Winfield? Don't you have any conscience at all? I just hope that someday you find out what it's like to lose everything you care about."

It was very quiet at the table after he left. Mandy avoided looking at Connor.

"I'm sorry you had to sit through that," he said finally.

"Drunks are always unpleasant," she remarked.

"Yes." After a pause he asked, "Would you like another drink?"

"No, thanks. I'd like to leave, if you don't mind."

"I understand. I'm sorry if Phelps upset you."

Mandy looked at him searchingly. "Didn't anything he said bother you?"

Connor frowned. "In what way?"

"His company is the object of one of your hostile take-overs. He doesn't want to sell. Doesn't it bother you to force a man out of a business that's been in his family for generations?"

"I see," Connor said tonelessly. He raised a hand and called to a nearby waiter, "Check please, Danny."

Did he feel it wasn't necessary to defend himself? Mandy wondered. Although what could he say? Franklin Phelps was drunk, but his pain had come through, nonetheless. Didn't Connor have even a spark of compassion? Evidently not, judging by his set face.

They walked out of the bar and across the parking lot without speaking. The silence between them continued until they were inside the Ferrari. Instead of starting the motor, Connor turned to face her.

"You've evidently decided I'm a black-hearted villain who goes around foreclosing on widows and orphans—or their equivalent in the business world."

"I didn't say that."

"You didn't have to. It's written all over your face."

"All right, I couldn't help feeling sorry for that man," she said defensively. "He was rude and abusive, but you could tell he was suffering over the loss of his business. To you, it's just another company. You swallow them up all the time. But it was that man's heritage."

"Let me tell you about Franklin Phelps," Connor said impassively. "His grandfather founded the company, and his father built it into a thriving business. Then Franklin took over and ran it into the ground. He siphoned off the profits to pay for an extravagant life-style, leaving the company to founder because they didn't have the capital to replace old equipment, or even cover their bills. They've been on the verge of bankruptcy for a year."

"Did he know that?" Mandy asked uncertainly. "I mean, maybe his managers didn't tell him how bad things were."

"It's the responsibility of a competent CEO to know what's going on in every sector of his company. Franklin's managers told him the creditors were closing in, but he was too stupid and arrogant to believe them. They tried everything they could think of to keep the company afloat, and then they came to me."

She gave him a startled look. "It wasn't the other way around? You didn't initiate the deal?"

"No, Franklin's management team approached me. They were concerned about all the workers that would lose their jobs if the company went under. Some of them have been there as long as twenty years. They thought they had security, that Franklin was the man his father and grandfather were. In reality, he doesn't give a damn about the people who work for him—or the company, for that matter."

"But he seemed so angry."

"Because he's losing his own private treasury. He's damn lucky I thought the company was worth salvaging, otherwise he'd be out on his fat...ear." Connor substituted for the word he wanted to use.

"I didn't realize," Mandy murmured.

He looked at her without emotion. "But you decided I was robbing a man of his birthright."

"Anyone might have jumped to that conclusion," she said uncomfortably. "He did say the business had been in his family for generations."

"There are always two sides to a story. However, you didn't wait to hear mine. That tells me what you think of me."

"You're not being fair, Connor. I know you're a superb businessman, but I can't pretend to approve of all of your methods."

"It's a tough world out there, but I've never taken unfair advantage of anyone. Do you know of an instance where I've acted unethically?"

"Maybe not, but you're willing to bend your ethics if it's to your advantage."

"Can you be more specific?"

"I was thinking of Jacques," she said. "You disapprove of everything about him, yet you're willing to overlook the fact if it's profitable to do business with him."

"Tell me something, Mandy. Are all of your clients the kind of people you'd care to invite to your home for dinner?"

"You know they aren't, and it isn't the same thing," she protested.

"Why not? You enter into a business agreement with them, it's profitable for you. Maybe they're demanding and obnoxious. Socially you wouldn't give them five minutes of your time, but you don't get to choose your ideal associates in the business world. All you can do is keep your own principles intact."

Mandy wanted to dispute the point, but how could she? What Connor said was true. Everybody made compromises of one kind or another. His deals involved more money than hers, but she'd worked with people she really wanted to throw out the door.

Connor's face softened momentarily. "You weren't crazy about *me* at our first meeting. It didn't stop you from accepting my company as a client."

She smiled ruefully. "I guess I have a bad habit of being too judgmental."

His eyes cooled. "It isn't important. I just wanted to set the record straight." He turned the key in the ignition. "I'll take you home now."

Connor drove fast but competently, keeping his eyes on the road. Mandy stole a look at his chiseled profile, searching for some hint of the passion he'd displayed earlier. She might have thought she'd imagined it, if her mouth didn't still tingle at the memory of his deep, intoxicating kiss.

Connor wasn't thinking about that, obviously. His only interest was in getting her home as soon as possible. Mandy tried to tell herself it was for the best. A man could be ethical in business, yet still consider women fair game. It was a guy thing. A prudent woman avoided men like that.

After a few moments, Connor made a casual remark about the traffic on the freeway. Cars had slowed at the approach to the bridge.

"A Ferrari is so fast, it must be especially frustrating," Mandy answered with equal poise.

"Yes, it's an impractical choice for city driving."

They chatted politely, like two guests at a cocktail party who were stuck with each other. The trip home seemed endless. Mandy breathed a sigh of relief when Connor pulled up in front of her apartment house.

She had her hand on the door handle and her speech all ready. "Thanks for a lovely day. I enjoyed it."

"So did I." It was a conventional answer, at odds with the dissatisfied look he gave her.

When he unfastened his seat belt, she opened her door quickly. "You don't have to walk me to the door."

"Whatever you say." He continued to watch her, this time with an unreadable expression.

"Well...uh...thanks again," she mumbled.

"Goodbye, Mandy." He put the car in gear and drove away.

It had such a final note to it. Connor wasn't about to forgive her for misjudging him. She'd hurt his pride, a cardinal sin with any man. She would have thought Connor was more secure than lesser men, but she obviously didn't really know him.

Mandy was depressed all evening. She wandered around her apartment, trying not to think about Connor, out on a date with the bubblehead, Brittany. That was the way he liked his women, dumb and compliant, she thought with annoyance. Which was the reason there could never be anything between herself and Connor.

Mandy preferred not to remember how compliant *she* had been. But she couldn't forget his stirring kiss, or the feeling of his hard body straining against hers.

A week went by without any word from Connor. Mandy didn't really expect to hear from him, but she answered every call with breathless anticipation. For the first few days, anyway. Then she faced reality.

One day she received a phone call from Dee Dee. The young girl chattered on about how great school was, and told her what good grades she was getting.

"I really aced a history test this week," she bragged.

"That must have made your father happy," Mandy remarked casually.

"I guess so, although it's hard to tell. He's so grumpy lately."

"He's in a very high-pressure business. He probably has a lot on his mind."

"You can make excuses because you don't have to live with him," Dee Dee complained. "Dad is so unreasonable! Whenever I ask for the tiniest thing, he says no."

"Come on, Dee Dee, aren't you exaggerating? Your father might have his faults like everybody else, but he's more than generous, especially to you."

"Okay, so he buys me things," the girl conceded. "That's cool. But when is he gonna realize I'm grown-up?"

"Twelve isn't considered grown-up, except perhaps in a few underdeveloped countries."

"Exactly! In some places in the world I'd be old enough to get married, but Dad won't even let me date."

"Is that what this is all about?"

"It isn't like I asked him to let me go out with a high school kid, or anything like that. All I want to do is go to a party. Do you see anything wrong in that?"

"Where is the party?" Mandy asked cautiously.

"Bettina, one of the new kids I met at school, is having it at her house."

"Will her parents be there?"

"I guess her mother will. Bettina doesn't have a father. I mean, everybody has a father, but her parents are divorced. Her mother has a cool boyfriend who might be there, too. Bettina says he's a real hunk."

Mandy could see why Connor had refused permission. Bettina's mother might be a wonderful, caring parent, but Connor couldn't tell that without meeting her.

"Don't you think Dad should let me go?" Dee Dee persisted.

"It isn't up to me to say."

"Come on, Mandy, you know you agree with me! Talk to Dad," she coaxed. "You can convince him."

"You happen to be wrong about your father and me," Mandy said evenly. "I have no influence over him, and he wouldn't welcome my interference."

"He might argue at first. That's just his way. But you could talk him into it. He really likes you."

Not anymore, Mandy could have told her. "Believe me, Dee Dee, it wouldn't do any good. The only thing I can do for you is give you some advice. Let your father get to know your friends. Do you ever bring them home?"

"A couple of times, but he isn't here in the afternoon. How's he supposed to get to know them?"

"Why don't you give a party?"

"Oh, sure, that would be some great party, with my father patrolling the room!"

"I have news for you. He wouldn't enjoy it any more than you would," Mandy said dryly. "I wasn't suggesting you ask him to the party, just that you introduce your friends to him. Then, when somebody who isn't a perfect stranger invites you, he'll be more apt to say yes."

"That doesn't help me with this weekend," Dee Dee grumbled.

"No, it doesn't. But there are a lot more weekends coming up."

"And I'll probably spend all of them watching TV," Dee Dee said gloomily.

"Count your blessings. You could be in Switzerland right now."

"Okay, I get the message. When are we gonna have lunch together and go shopping? You said we would."

Mandy hesitated. "Maybe you'd better check with your father first."

"Why should I do that? He'll be pleased to be off the hook. Dad thinks he has to spend every weekend with me if I don't have plans. It must really louse up his love life." Dee Dee laughed.

"I'm sure he works it out somehow," Mandy commented.

"Evidently. He has a new girlfriend. This one is named Carole."

That surprised Mandy. "What happened to Brittany?"

"I never heard of that one."

Connor's attention span was getting shorter by the hour, Mandy thought cynically. She listened unwillingly as Dee Dee talked about her father. Finally Mandy managed to change the subject. She also avoided making a definite lunch date with the girl, not knowing if Connor would approve. Dee Dee was a darling youngster, but maybe a clean break was better all around.

Connor's phone call Saturday morning came as a complete surprise. Mandy had just gotten out of the shower and

gone into the bedroom to get dressed. When she heard
Connor's voice, she sank down on the bed abruptly.

He sounded distant, the same as he had the last time she'd
seen him. "Dee Dee said you told her to ask if it was all right
if she had lunch with you," he began without preamble.
"What's that all about?"

"I just wanted to be sure you didn't have any objections," Mandy answered carefully.

"Why should I?"

"Because we both know I'm not your favorite person."

"I'd say it was the other way around," he replied sardonically.

She sighed. "I don't want to argue with you, Connor. I'm
sorry for the misunderstanding between us. I learned a
valuable lesson about not judging people. I'm just sorry it
was at the expense of our friendship."

After a moment's silence his voice warmed. "That's a
handsome apology."

"I already apologized. *That* was an explanation."

"Okay, I accept both."

"I'm glad." There didn't seem to be anything else to say.
"Well . . ."

"Now that that's settled, I'd like to talk to you about Dee
Dee, if you have a minute," he said quickly.

Mandy hesitated. "Can you hang on for a second? I had
just gotten out of the shower when the phone rang."

"Are you standing there without any clothes on?"

"Sitting, actually." Her legs had given way when she
heard Connor's voice. "On the edge of the bed."

"By all means, go and put some clothes on. I'll wait."
Laughter edged his voice. "The thought of carrying on a
conversation with a naked woman is unsettling."

Suddenly Mandy wasn't cold any longer. Her entire body
heated at the thought of Connor picturing her nude. It
wasn't that much more difficult to imagine his hands gliding over her body.

She put the receiver down and made a quick dash to the closet. After pulling on a robe and belting it tightly around her narrow waist, she returned. "All right, I'm back. What about Dee Dee?"

"Are you dressed now?"

"I have on a robe—a heavy terry-cloth one," she added crisply, in case he was picturing something seductive in chiffon and lace. "What was it you wanted to talk to me about? I don't mean to be rude, but I'm in rather a hurry."

"I understand, and I'll try to be brief. It's about a party Dee Dee wants to give. She says you suggested it."

Mandy was immediately on the defensive. "I don't think it's such a bad idea. What better way to find out who her friends are? You wouldn't worry about her so much if you knew who she's running around with."

"I agree with you completely."

"Oh." Mandy was thrown off stride, having been expecting an argument. "Then what did you want to talk about?"

"The party idea is excellent, but that's about the only thing Dee Dee and I agree on. For instance, is it unreasonable of me to set a time limit?"

"Not at all. Tell her you're not just being arbitrary, their parents have to know when to pick them up."

"Good thinking," Connor said approvingly.

"What else do you disagree on?"

"Too many things to go into when you're so pressed for time. I feel as if I'm imposing."

"It's all right, I can spare a few more minutes." After claiming to be in a hurry, Mandy couldn't very well admit she had nothing planned.

"I have a better idea. Why don't you come over here for brunch tomorrow? The three of us can sit down together and hammer out all the details."

"Well . . ." She knew it was a bad idea. So why didn't she just say no?

"It would be a lot easier than having one or the other of us calling you constantly," he coaxed. "I could pick you up tomorrow around ten-thirty, if that's convenient."

"No, I have my own car."

"All right, if you'd rather. I know this is an imposition, but I really appreciate it. I'll look forward to seeing you tomorrow."

Mandy cradled the receiver slowly, wondering how she'd let herself be maneuvered so blatantly. It was clear that she was no match for Connor when he wanted something.

But the realization didn't bother her greatly.

Chapter Seven

Connor lived in a high-rise apartment building on top of Russian Hill. The large courtyard in front made it convenient for guests to drive up to the front door, where parking attendants were waiting to take their cars.

Mandy left her small compact with one of them, then gave her name to a doorman who had been told to expect her. She walked across a lobby so plushly carpeted that her footsteps didn't even make a whisper. An equally silent elevator carried her to the top floor.

Dee Dee was waiting for her when the elevator doors opened. "Hi, Mandy. Boy, am I glad to see you!" she exclaimed. "You gotta tell Dad he's way off base."

"You might let her get inside the door first." Connor appeared in back of his daughter. "Hello, Mandy, I'm glad you're here, too." He smiled. "As you can see, we need you."

"I only hope your confidence isn't misplaced," she

laughed. Her eyes widened as she walked inside. "What a magnificent apartment!"

Floor-to-ceiling windows in the living room and dining room gave a stunning view of the city and both bridges, the Golden Gate on the left and the Bay Bridge on the right. A terrace outside the windows held outdoor furniture with gaily colored cushions, and there were trees in big pots. It was like a garden high in the sky.

Mandy could barely tear her fascinated gaze from the view, but the apartment itself was equally eye-catching. The elegant living room was furnished in neutral tones of beige and white, with splashes of color provided by large paintings on the walls. A variety of collectibles were displayed casually on the tables around the room.

"I'll give you the grand tour after brunch," Connor said as her head continued to swivel in an attempt to look at everything. "I hope you don't mind eating in the kitchen."

"Not at all," Mandy answered, concealing her surprise. She would have thought Connor was the type who ate in the dining room, served by a uniformed maid, even though he was dressed informally in jeans and a black turtleneck that clung to his broad chest.

The kitchen was a large, sunny room with every modern appliance. In one corner was a round glass table and four chairs. The table was set for three, but there was no cook presiding over the stove, as Mandy expected.

"Sit down and drink your orange juice while I start the pancakes," Connor said.

Mandy's eyebrows climbed. "*You're* going to make them?"

"Why the surprise? I happen to be a very good cook."

"Get real, Dad! Pancakes are the only thing he knows how to make," Dee Dee explained. "He learned how on account of Ivy."

"I see," Mandy said, visualizing one of Connor's willowy blondes.

He grinned, as if reading her mind. "Ivy was the love of my life. I would have done anything for her."

"She was Dad's bullterrier. Grandma said she wasn't making pancakes for a dog, so that's why he had to learn how."

Mandy looked at Connor curiously. "You're full of surprises. I've never heard you mention having a dog *or* a mother."

"Which one surprises you the most?" He chuckled.

"Grandma is really great," Dee Dee said. "Only she isn't around very much. After Grandpa died, she started to travel a lot. When is she coming home, Dad?"

"In a couple of weeks. She phoned yesterday from Bali." He brought a heaping platter of pancakes to the table. "Eat them while they're hot. I have more in the skillet."

It was a very relaxed meal. Mandy could hardly believe this was the same man who'd said goodbye so decisively the last time they were together. Of course, he needed her assistance now, she thought cynically.

Mandy didn't really mind. She enjoyed helping to plan Dee Dee's party. They sat around the kitchen table, setting various conditions, with Mandy acting as mediator when Connor and his daughter reached an impasse.

"I think we've covered everything," Mandy said finally. "It should be a really great party. You'll have to phone me the next day and tell me all about it."

"Aren't you going to be here?" Dee Dee asked.

"You don't need me."

"Yes, I do! Who's gonna keep Dad company?"

"What she really means is, who's going to keep me from keeping an eye on *them*?" he said ironically.

Dee Dee didn't bother to deny it. "Please, Mandy, you just gotta come!"

"Would you consider it?" Connor looked at her appealingly. "There's absolutely no reason for you to give up a Friday night, but I'd be most grateful."

Mandy smiled. "It's flattering to be in such demand. I'd be happy to come."

"Yay!" Dee Dee jumped up to give her a hug. "You're the most! What did we ever do without her, Dad?"

"Argued a lot," he answered dryly.

"You can say that again! You know what would be great? If you and Mandy got married. Then she could move in here and settle all our fights."

As Mandy stared at her speechlessly, Connor laughed. "You're too young yet to understand that men and women rarely get married for that reason."

"I know all about sex and stuff like that. I'm not a little kid."

"You're talking like one," Mandy said tartly. "People don't get married solely because of sex, either. Don't you talk to your daughter about these things?" she asked Connor.

His eyes danced with merriment. "Are you suggesting tell her sex isn't important? How much credibility would have?"

Mandy was disappointed, but not surprised. Connor obviously didn't know the difference between sex and love, any more than his twelve-year-old did. It was what she'd suspected all along.

"You're plenty sexy, and so is Dad," Dee Dee said "You'd be great together."

"Out of the mouths of babes," he murmured.

"You'll have to do your matchmaking somewhere else," Mandy told the girl firmly. "I'm not looking for a husband."

"Don't you want me to demonstrate my capabilities before you make up your mind?" he teased.

"No, and I can see why your daughter is so precocious." Mandy stood and picked up some plates. "Let's do the dishes."

"Dee Dee can put them in the dishwasher. Would you like the tour I promised you?"

Mandy was still annoyed with him, but it was an offer she couldn't refuse. She'd never seen an apartment so luxurious outside of the movies. It was a duplex penthouse with a spiral staircase. On the upper floor were several bedrooms besides the master suite, which was almost as big as a small apartment.

It had every comfort. The marble bathroom had a huge tub with a built-in Jacuzzi, the dressing room was spacious, with shelves and drawers behind mirrored doors, and the bedroom had a marble-faced fireplace on the wall opposite the king-size bed.

"You live like a pasha!" Mandy exclaimed.

"Hardly." Connor smiled. "I don't have a harem."

"I'm sure you would if it wasn't against the law," she remarked, walking over to the window, where a telescope on a tripod was trained on the waterfront. She squinted into it. "I can't see anything. How do I adjust this gadget?"

"You don't have to. The angle is wrong for you, that's all." He put an arm around her shoulders and tilted the telescope. "Is that better?"

"Oh, yes! This is fantastic! I can see the seals off pier 39. Aren't they adorable?"

"From a distance. Up close they're noisy and they smell fishy."

"How can you say that? Look at their sweet little faces. They're beautiful."

"Very beautiful," he murmured.

Something in his husky voice alerted her, and she turned her head. Their faces were only inches apart. His hand tightened on her shoulder, and Mandy could feel her heartbeat quicken. When his head dipped slowly toward hers, she was mesmerized by the sultry intensity of his compelling gray eyes. As he drew her closer, Dee Dee's voice came from the hall.

"Hey, where are you guys?"

Connor moved away unhurriedly. "We're in here. Are you finished with the dishes?"

Dee Dee appeared in the doorway. "All done. What are we gonna do now?"

"Whatever you ladies choose."

Mandy envied his poise. She was still vibrating from their latest encounter. But seduction was a way of life with Connor, she reminded herself. It didn't mean anything.

Dee Dee was unaware of any undercurrent. "Let's go to the movies," she suggested. "There's like this real cool flick I want to see, *Scream In The Dark*."

"Isn't that R-rated?" Connor asked. "It sounds as if it should be."

"Those ratings don't mean anything," she said dismissively. "They're just stuck on by a bunch of old geezers who don't want kids to have any fun. Tell him, Mandy."

"You're asking the wrong person," she said. "Some of those R-rated movies turn *my* stomach."

Dee Dee looked at her reproachfully. "I didn't think you'd side with Dad."

Connor gave Mandy a slow smile. "Believe it or not, there are some things we agree on."

It turned out to be a relaxed afternoon, in spite of the earlier incident. The three of them went to a family movie and ate popcorn. Afterward they strolled through the neighborhood shopping district, dropping into the stores that were open.

In one shop Connor bought Dee Dee a T-shirt with a funny saying on the front. In another he bought her a watch with a cartoon character on the face and some plastic junk jewelry she liked.

Mandy disapproved, but she didn't say anything until Dee Dee darted off to look at some cashmere sweaters. "Do you really think you should buy her everything she asks for?"

Connor shrugged. "Why not?"

"Because it doesn't prepare her for the realities of life— you can't always have everything you want."

"She'll learn that soon enough. Besides, aren't you the one who's always telling me to lighten up with her?"

"I didn't mean you should spoil her. I realize you're in a position to give her everything she could possibly want, but that won't make a difference in her feelings toward you. You can't buy love."

His mouth curved sardonically. "A diamond bracelet buys a reasonable facsimile."

"If you find that acceptable, I feel sorry for you."

His face sobered. "I was only joking. The truth is, I enjoy doing things for the people I love."

It was surprising to hear that word from Connor. Mandy had wondered if he was capable of love. But, of course, love for his daughter was a different thing.

"I guess I can understand that," she said. "But if I were you, I'd try to curb my impulses a little."

"That's always been difficult for me." He squeezed her hand and grinned. "I'm like warm taffy in the hands of a beguiling female."

Gazing at his strong face, Mandy couldn't imagine Connor being vulnerable to anyone, certainly not a woman. He was the elusive dream that many women had chased and never captured. Instead of debating the point, she changed the subject.

Connor had expected to call for Mandy on the night of Dee Dee's party, but she was detained at the office on Friday. She phoned to tell him she'd take her own car.

Some of the guests had already arrived by the time Mandy got there. Loud music was coming from the living room, and refreshments were set out in the adjoining dining room.

Connor was making small talk in the den with some of the parents who had accompanied their children upstairs out of curiosity to see the apartment. He greeted Mandy gratefully, which amused her. For all his sophistication, Connor was anxious about presenting the right image in front of Dee Dee's friends and their families. It wasn't something he'd ever had to work at. She could have told him to relax. They looked dazzled by his charm.

Mandy was especially interested in meeting Sharon, the single mother with the hunk for a boyfriend. Roger was indeed handsome, but he was also thoroughly nice. And Sharon was delightful.

"I'm so happy to meet both of you tonight," she told Mandy. "Single working parents don't have much opportunity to get to know their children's friends. Bettina talks about Dee Dee all the time, and now that I've met you and Connor, I feel comfortable about their friendship. I can tell that you supervise her as closely as I keep tabs on Bettina."

"Well, yes, Connor does," Mandy answered uncomfortably. "I'm not Dee Dee's mother."

"We have something in common." Roger smiled. "You and I are the support system, when the going gets too tough for one person."

"I'm sure Sharon feels the way I do." Connor put his arm around Mandy's shoulders and smiled fondly at her. "We'd be lost without you."

After the current crop of parents had left, and before more arrived, Mandy chided Connor. "You shouldn't have given Sharon and Roger the idea that our relationship is like theirs."

"Aren't you jumping to conclusions? Perhaps they're just friends."

Mandy shook her head. "No way. Did you notice how they looked at each other?"

Connor's eyes shone with amusement. "That's not proof I look at you that way, and how much good has it done me?"

The doorbell rang, saving her the necessity of a reply.

Finally all the parents had dropped off their children and left. Some had lingered for a drink, others had introduced themselves, exchanged a few words with Connor and taken off.

He breathed a sigh of relief when he and Mandy were alone. "The things you do for your kids! I've never worked this hard at getting people to like me. How did I do?"

"You were a big hit with the women." Mandy grinned.

"You think I came on too strong?" He frowned. "I was only trying to be friendly."

"Relax, it wasn't anything you did. You just can't help being a very sexy fellow when there are women around," she teased.

He gave her a sultry look. "Why doesn't it work with you?"

"Because I've seen your dark side." Mandy meant it as a joke, but it was too close to the truth. "I'll flip you to see which one of us walks through the living room to remind the kids that we're here," she said quickly.

"You'd better go. I have a bad habit of intimidating people," he drawled.

Mandy left without comment, hoping Connor wouldn't dwell on her unthinking remark. The evening had been going so well up to now. It had been fun to be mistaken for Connor's wife, she admitted to herself, although the idea was ludicrous. They'd be lucky if they got through the night without arguing.

Dee Dee and her friends were having a wonderful time. Some were dancing, others were playing the games Mandy had placed on tables around the room. The rest of the kids were clustered around the dining room table where food and soft drinks were in plentiful supply.

Dee Dee raced up to Mandy excitedly. "It's a really cool party. Everybody's having a neat time. You're the best!"

"Thank your father, not me. I'm just the designated party police." Mandy laughed. "And since nobody's throwing food or making out on the couch, I'll leave you alone."

"How long until your next round? Pete Wilkerson's been coming on to me." Dee Dee giggled.

"Tell him to grow up first," Mandy advised with a smile as she left the room.

Connor had switched on the television set in the den. He got up to turn it off when Mandy returned, but she stopped him.

"Leave it on, I love football."

"You're not just being polite?"

"No, I'm a big fan." She sat on the couch next to him, facing the TV. "I didn't know *you* liked it."

"We don't really know much about each other, do we?" he asked slowly. "Outside of the fact that we're attracted to each other."

She put the focus on him instead of herself. "You're attracted to a lot of women. It doesn't mean anything."

"How about you, Mandy? Do you find a lot of men attractive?"

"I guess you could say I'm normal," she answered evasively.

"Normal, perhaps, but certainly not average," he said in a deepened voice.

"Don't go getting seductive on me," she joked. "We're chaperoning a kid's party, remember?"

"It won't last all night," he murmured, tracing the shape of her lower lip in an erotic caress.

"Neither will I, after the long day I put in at the office," she answered lightly, starting to rise.

"Don't go." He took her hand.

Mandy was caught off balance. Her feet tangled with his and she stumbled forward, sprawling across Connor. His arms closed around her, cradling her against his body. Her head was pillowed against his shoulder, and his face was so close she could feel his warm breath feathering her lips.

For a long, tantalizing moment, Mandy was unable to move. She knew Connor was going to kiss her, and she'd never wanted anything more in her life. She ached to put her arms around his neck and curl up closer to him.

"Beautiful...adorable...Mandy..." He punctuated the words with a kiss at each corner of her mouth and a nip of her lower lip. "What have you done to me? I've never felt this way about any woman before."

She was too spellbound to care that it was only a line. Reaching up tentatively, she anchored her fingers in his thick, dark hair. "Connor..."

"Yes, darling." He kissed her gently—a lover's kiss, with carefully repressed passion. "What do you want, my little love?"

"I..."

She was on the verge of telling him when suddenly there was a loud crash from the living room, followed by several female shrieks. They looked at each other in disbelief at this intrusion into their private world.

Then sanity returned and Mandy jumped up. Without looking at Connor, she mumbled, "I'll go see what happened."

"We'd both better go," he said.

Before they reached the door, Dee Dee appeared. "It's nothing humongous," she told them hurriedly. "Pete was juggling some oranges, and one of them sort of got away from him and knocked over a lamp. It didn't break, though, only the bulb. That's what made the loud noise."

"I'll take care of it," Connor said.

"It was just a little accident. You're not gonna yell at him, are you?" Dee Dee asked anxiously.

"No, I'm going to make sure nobody gets cut on the shards."

Mandy remained in the den, trying to recover her poise. How did she get herself into these situations over and over again? It was just a game to Connor, but she was beginning to suspect *her* feelings were becoming all too serious.

He returned with a reassuring smile. "You'd have been proud of me. I acted like a father, not a tycoon."

She managed to return his smile. "You didn't fire anyone or dock anybody's pay?"

"I was the soul of understanding, even though I felt like wringing Pete's scrawny little neck." He smoothed her long hair. "I only hope his timing improves with age."

"Yes, well..." She picked up her purse. "The party's almost over. You don't need me any longer."

"Running away won't solve anything, Mandy," Connor said quietly. "We have to talk about this."

"There's nothing to talk about," she murmured.

He cupped his hand around her chin and tilted her face up to his. "You can pretend that's true, or we can discuss it and decide where to go from here."

Her long lashes swept down to fan her flushed cheeks. "I'll admit there's a strong sexual attraction between us, but that's really all we share. In every other way, we're poles apart."

"Not really. We've had our misunderstandings, but we've also had a lot of fun together. It's only when I touch you that you panic. What are you afraid of, Mandy?"

"Nothing," she said quickly. "I just don't want to get involved with you. It's as simple as that."

"Why not? I'd try very hard to see that you weren't disappointed," he said softly.

She turned away. "You just don't get it, Connor. I want more from a relationship than sex, no matter how fantastic it is."

He put his hands on her shoulders. "We're making progress. At least you admit I could satisfy you."

"I've never doubted that." She sighed. "Sex is a way of life for you, but I don't believe in meaningless affairs."

"I can't believe any relationship with you could be meaningless," he said in a husky voice, kissing the back of her neck. "But I know you don't trust me, so we'll take it slow and easy." He turned her in his arms. "Is that what you want?"

She summoned a wry smile. "I think it would be safer if we just remained friends."

"You're too young to play it safe. Take a chance, honey. You never know what might happen."

Mandy could imagine, and the picture was graphic enough to make her pulse race. As they gazed at each other, the doorbell rang.

Connor frowned. "Who the devil could that be? It's a little early for the parents to be picking up their kids—although I'd gladly drive them all home myself. Stay here, I'll see who it is."

His frown turned to a look of surprise when he opened the door. "Mother! I didn't expect you back for another week."

"I got tired of strange beds and stranger food, so I decided to come home," Louise Winfield said calmly. She was a stunning woman, tall and imposing like her son, with his penetrating gray eyes. She turned her head as a blast of laughter came from the living room. "What on earth is going on in there? Did I interrupt an orgy?"

"No such luck." Connor smiled and kissed her cheek. "Dee Dee is having a party. Come into the den, it's relatively quiet in there." As they walked down the hall, he said, "Why didn't you let me know you were coming? I would have picked you up."

"It was just as easy to take a taxi. I will accept your hospitality for the night, however. I'll have to contact the staff and have them prepare the house."

"Of course, you're welcome to stay as long as you like. This is Mandy Richardson," he said when they reached the den. "You see, I really do have a mother," he told Mandy.

"Did you doubt it, my dear?" the older woman asked her.

"He's so autocratic. I couldn't imagine anyone telling Connor what to do." Mandy smiled.

"The Winfield men are quite a handful. You have to stand up to them early in your relationship."

"Thanks a lot, Mother." Connor chuckled. "I'm having enough trouble with our relationship already."

"Connor said you were in Bali," Mandy said hastily. "It must have been fascinating."

"It's quite romantic—beautiful beaches and swaying palm trees," Louise said. "If you can pry my son away from his megadeals, you should get him to take you there."

"I'm afraid I can't get away, either. I'm a working woman."

"Really? What do you do?"

"My partner and I have a travel agency. That's how I met Connor. We handled some of his company's travel arrangements."

"I see." The older woman looked at her thoughtfully, reassessing her relationship to Connor, as Mandy wanted her to. "Perhaps you can plan some trips for me."

"I'd be happy to."

"Where are you off to next?" Connor asked. "Mother never stays in one place for long," he explained to Mandy.

"I thought I might go on an African safari. When is the best time of year?"

"December and January are peak travel seasons," Mandy said. "It's warm, but not oppressively hot yet. We have some very deluxe tours if you're interested."

"It would be an ideal time. Why don't you and Dee Dee join me?" Louise asked her son. "She'll be out of school for the holidays."

"I promised to take Dee Dee to New York for Christmas. You're welcome to join us. New York is very festive at holiday time. We can have a family Christmas."

"Does family include Lorna?"

"She *is* Dee Dee's mother," Connor said quietly.

"Too bad that means more to you than it ever did to her," Louise commented tartly. "Thanks, but I'd rather take my chances with the lions."

Dee Dee popped her head in the door unexpectedly. Whatever she'd come for was forgotten when she saw the older woman. "Grandma! What are you doing here?"

"I got lonesome for you, pet." Louise opened her arms, and Dee Dee rushed into them to give her grandmother a big hug and a kiss.

"I missed you, too. I have all kinds of things to tell you. I was in Tangier for a week, and I'm going to school here in San Francisco now."

"That's sensible. I never approved of sending you all the way to Switzerland, of all places!"

"Mandy didn't, either. She convinced Dad to let me come home."

"Really?" Louise looked at Mandy with renewed interest.

"It was only a suggestion," Mandy said carefully. "Connor was the one who made the decision."

"After the two of them ganged up on me." He grinned. "One man is no match for two determined females."

Dee Dee was torn between joy at seeing her grandmother and a desire to return to the party. Louise noticed the girl's dilemma. "Go back to your guests, darling. We'll have plenty of time to visit tomorrow."

"Thanks, Gram." Dee Dee kissed her again. "I'll call you first thing in the morning."

"Your grandmother is staying here tonight," Connor said.

"Super! We'll have breakfast together, and then maybe we can go shopping."

"Whatever you like, pet." Louise looked her over. "I must say, your taste in clothes is improving. You used to dress like a ragamuffin."

"I still like far-out stuff, but Mandy always talks me out of it." Dee Dee grinned. "Dad has her brainwashed on that one point. Outside of that she's totally cool."

After Dee Dee had returned to her party, Louise remarked, "She certainly seems happier than the last time I saw her. If you're responsible, my son and I owe you a debt of gratitude."

"Dee Dee is a darling girl," Mandy said, without taking any credit. "We hit it off right away."

"That's putting it mildly." Connor chuckled. "Dee Dee suggested that Mandy and I get married."

"Is this your way of telling me something?" Louise asked.

"It was just a joke." Mandy answered before he could. "If Connor ever got married, it would devastate the female population of San Francisco."

"Do you know Lorna, his ex-wife?" Louise asked.

"No, I've never met her."

"If you had, you'd understand his reluctance to make another mistake."

Connor tried to cover his annoyance with a slight laugh. "As you can see, my mother has a tendency to carry a grudge."

"And you, my dear son, are much too forgiving. You've never been able to admit that woman is morally bankrupt."

Mandy began to revise her opinion of Connor as a carefree playboy. Did he go from one woman to another because he couldn't have the one he wanted? Was his former wife the only love of his life?

"I doubt if Mandy is interested in an in-depth discussion of a person she's never met." Connor's smile didn't soften the steel in his voice. "Why don't you tell us more about your trip, Mother?"

Mandy stood. "I know you two have a lot to talk about, so I'll run along."

"You don't have to go, my dear," Louise protested. "I didn't mean to intrude on your date."

"It wasn't really a date. I was just helping Connor chaperon the kids. Everything's under control, though, and the party is almost over. It was lovely meeting you, Mrs. Winfield."

"I enjoyed it, also. I'll phone you in a few days, after I get settled. Perhaps you can give me more details about a safari. I'm definitely interested."

"I'd be happy to help in any way I can." Mandy turned to Connor. "Hang in there. The parents should be arriving soon."

"I'll walk you to the door," he said.

"Your mother is very nice," Mandy remarked politely as they walked down the hall.

"She really is, although she sounded like a harridan tonight." He sighed. "You know how mothers are. Their children can do no wrong. It has to be the other partner's fault."

"Yes, they're fiercely partisan." Mandy stopped by the door. "Tell Dee Dee I'm glad the party turned out so well."

"I'm sure she'll phone you for a blow-by-blow discussion. When am I going to see you again?" he asked.

"Call me," she answered evasively. "You'll be busy with your mother for a while."

"She'll probably only stay overnight. I know she's anxious to get back to her own house."

"I'm sure she wants to spend some time with you and Dee Dee. I can tell how close the three of you are."

"You're right. When can I see you?" Connor cut through the chitchat. "How about dinner Sunday night?"

Mandy was curiously reluctant, now that she suspected he was still in love with his ex-wife. It had been bad enough when she thought he was avoiding commitments—it would be worse if he'd already made one.

"Or Monday night, if you're busy on Sunday," Connor persisted.

"You don't have to repay me every time I help out with Dee Dee."

"You know that's not the reason. I thought we agreed to be friends."

"I don't think you're going to be satisfied with that," she answered frankly.

"Try me and see." He smiled. "I promise not to have a tantrum if we have different interpretations. I'm a big boy."

That was the understatement of the year! Connor was a magnificent example of a virile male in his prime. His body promised rewards that any normal woman would find hard to refuse. And Mandy was very normal.

"I guess I could make it Sunday night," she said hesitantly.

He laughed. "Not the most enthusiastic acceptance I've ever had, but I'll take it. Good night, honey. Thanks for coming." He cupped her face in his palms and kissed her lightly.

Mandy responded like a flower to the sun. Her lips parted, and she made a tiny sound of satisfaction. Connor was clearly surprised, but he reacted instantly, drawing her close and deepening the kiss. They clung together for an electrifying instant, oblivious of the children's voices coming from the living room.

He was the first to become aware of them. Drawing away reluctantly, he said in a wry voice, "You pick the damnedest times to be cooperative."

Mandy pulled herself together swiftly. "Timing is everything, I always say." She gave him a bright smile. "Good night, Connor."

He stood there for a long moment after she left, then went back to the den.

"She's a beautiful girl," his mother observed. "Quite different from your usual companions."

"Meaning I normally date dogs?" he asked sardonically.

"Not at all. They're usually stunning but vapid blondes who resemble Lorna."

"Perhaps I feel the need to keep reminding myself not to get involved again."

"That's nonsense! Anyone can make a mistake—especially at twenty-two, when judgment is overruled by hormones."

Connor shrugged. "Okay, then maybe I'm just attracted to vapid blondes."

"Where does Mandy fit into that picture?"

"She's in a different category. We're just friends."

"Oh, please, Connor! I may be getting old, but I still have all of my faculties. One would have to be blind not to see the chemistry between you. It was so intense I felt like a voyeur."

"You're exaggerating. Naturally I'm attracted to her. What man wouldn't be? As you so astutely pointed out, she's very beautiful." He stuck his hands into his pockets and strolled over to look out the window. "She's also intelligent and completely down-to-earth. My money means nothing to her. If anything, it's a drawback."

"And you find those qualities repugnant?" Louise asked dryly.

"You don't understand. We've only known each other a short time. We haven't ever.... I mean, we've had some misunderstandings," Connor corrected himself carefully. "Sometimes I think I should leave her alone. She seems so vulnerable. I don't want to hurt her."

"Then by all means stop seeing her." Louise watched her son with an enigmatic expression.

"That's the hell of it!" Connor paced the floor. "I can't stop thinking about her. We argue and I tell myself it's for the best. Then something comes up with Dee Dee and I find myself calling her. She's very good with Dee Dee." He paused and stared at a vase reflectively. "That's part of her attraction. If it weren't for Dee Dee, Mandy would be just another pretty face."

"If that's what you choose to believe, go right ahead."

Connor flung himself into a chair and stretched out his long legs. "You're right, I'm just kidding myself. Mandy is the first woman I've ever been this attracted to—or ever felt this protective toward. I don't want to talk her into something she'll regret, but it's difficult not to try when I'm with her."

"She seems like a very levelheaded young woman. I think you owe her the courtesy of letting her make up her own mind about whether she wants to become romantically involved with you. Unless, of course, you're only intrigued because she won't sleep with you."

"Mother!"

"Don't look so shocked, darling. Your generation didn't invent sex."

"Perhaps not, but it's a little embarrassing for a grown man to discuss his sex life with his mother."

Louise gave him an impish smile. "From what you tell me, there's nothing to discuss. In any case, I'm not asking for details. I'm simply advising you not to let Mandy get away. She's the first one of your many women that I've ever approved of."

"You haven't met all of them." He grinned.

"Because you lose interest so rapidly. But it's your life, my dear. You have to do what you think is best."

"For whom?" he asked soberly.

"For everyone concerned. I have faith in you, Connor. You're a man of integrity—and that isn't the mother in me speaking. You've never hurt anyone knowingly, and you won't start with someone you care about." She rose as the doorbell rang. "I'll go to my room now and leave you to deal with the hordes of invading parents."

Connor looked at her affectionately. "Thanks for the vote of confidence."

She returned his gaze lovingly. "If you can't count on your mother, it's a sorry state of affairs. Go and answer the door, darling, before they wear out the bell."

[faint offset text from facing page, illegible]

Chapter Eight

Mandy could hardly wait for her date with Connor that Sunday night. She'd made up her mind once and for all. He was right about taking chances. Playing it safe was cowardly, something she'd never been. Maybe a meaningful relationship would develop between them, or maybe it wouldn't, but at least she wouldn't have regrets, wondering about what might have been.

She was all dressed when Alexandra phoned. Her partner's voice wasn't as upbeat as usual. "Can you handle things tomorrow if I don't come in until noon?"

"Sure," Mandy said. "What's up?"

"I want to help Ralph and Kim take inventory. He's decided to sell out to that corporation, Global Ventures."

"Oh, Alex, what a shame!"

"Yes, Ralph is really upset about it. They worked so hard to make the place a success."

"Can't he tough it out?"

"David wouldn't win against Goliath in real life. Ralph might be okay in the beginning, but business would fall off little by little and he'd wind up with nothing. This way, at least he'll salvage his original investment. Maybe he can find another location and start over."

"With no assurance that the same thing won't happen all over again if he's successful. That's pretty discouraging."

"I know." Alexandra sighed. "A small businessman is helpless against those heartless conglomerates."

The doorbell rang, and Mandy walked to the door carrying her cordless phone.

"Am I early?" Connor asked.

"No, I'll be right with you," she said.

"Your date is there, I won't keep you," Alexandra said.

"I do have to go, but don't worry about tomorrow. Take the whole day if you need to. And tell Ralphie I'm so awfully sorry."

"Problems?" Connor asked after she set the phone down.

"It's my partner's brother. He's having business troubles."

"Tell me about it," he said as they walked out to the car.

"You wouldn't be interested. He's just a small businessman, not in your league."

Connor turned his head to look at her before putting the car in gear. "I'm back to being the indifferent tycoon?"

"I didn't mean it that way. You just wouldn't understand, especially since Ralph is up against one of those conglomerates like the ones you put together."

"They're mounting a hostile takeover of his company?"

"Nothing that grand. It's a small coffeehouse with only a few employees, but it's Ralph's dream. He started from scratch and built a thriving business. Now a big consortium wants to add it to its chain."

"If he doesn't want to sell, why doesn't he say so?"

"You, of all people, know how conglomerates work. They told Ralph he could either sell out to them or they'd open a place next door and charge half what he does. What choice does he have?"

Connor frowned. "They can't cut prices in only one store. Your friend could force them to offer the same prices in all their outlets. I doubt if they'd be willing to do that simply to acquire one small coffee shop."

"How could Ralph force them to do anything?"

"By taking them to court. What they threatened is illegal."

The hope drained out of Mandy's face. "He couldn't afford a long-drawn-out court battle, which is what it would probably turn into. Those big companies have attorneys on yearly retainers. Their job is to sue."

"True, but I guarantee Ralph would win."

"It wouldn't be much of a victory. He'd be wiped out."

"That's too bad. What's the name of the conglomerate?" Connor asked casually.

"It's called Global Ventures. Ralph says they're into all kinds of businesses besides coffeehouses. Do you know the company?"

"I've heard of them." Connor seemed to lose interest in the subject. "I made a reservation at the Château. I hope that's all right with you."

"I'm delighted." It was a new, very expensive restaurant that had just opened. Mandy hadn't been there yet.

A parking attendant took Connor's car in front of an elegant building that looked like a castle, high on a hill.

The dining room was softly lit by candles on every table and crystal chandeliers overhead. They were shown to a table by a big picture window that overlooked the glittering lights of the city.

"This is a treat for me, but it's old hat to you," Mandy remarked. "You have a view out of every window in your apartment."

"I don't have a view like this," he answered, looking at her with a smile.

"You're very gallant," she said lightly.

"I'm on my good behavior." He grinned. "I don't turn into a tiger until after dinner."

"Is that a warning?"

"I was hoping you'd take it as a promise," he said softly.

The wine steward arrived with a bottle of wine that he opened with a flourish. He then went through the ritual of pouring a small amount in Connor's glass and waiting for his approval. By the time he had filled both their glasses and left, the seductive mood had dissipated.

They talked about the weekend and Dee Dee's party as the waiter served dinner.

"Is your mother still staying with you?" Mandy asked.

"No, she rounded up her household staff and went home. I don't know why she doesn't move to a condominium, since she travels so much, but she refuses to give up the old homestead."

"A lot of older people resist change."

"Not my mother. She's a thoroughly modern woman, except for this one quirk and an unexpected streak of sentimentality. She keeps the family albums prominently displayed, including the ones with embarrassing pictures of me as an adolescent." He smiled.

"I can't imagine you as anything but poised, even as a teenager."

"It's hard not to be self-conscious when you're a head taller than all the other kids."

"I'll bet you excelled at sports."

Connor shrugged. "I played a little football." He gazed at her admiringly. "What did you excel at, Mandy—besides boys? You must have been adorable, with those big blue eyes and that ravishing mouth. I'll bet your parents had to sweep the boys off your doorstep."

She smiled reminiscingly. "I wasn't as poised as you suppose. I tried to act grown-up, but I was so innocent. I remember the first time a boy kissed me. His name was Freddy Westover. We bumped noses and our teeth clicked together, but it was wonderful. You never forget your first kiss."

Connor covered her hand with his and gazed into her eyes. "I wish I'd been the one to give you your first kiss. I'd like to occupy that special place in your heart."

Mandy always melted when Connor was this tender. It was the side of him most people didn't know about.

As she leaned toward him, the ever-efficient waiter appeared to take away their plates. While he was clearing the table, they made idle conversation.

"How is Mr. Kleinhold?" Mandy asked. He was one of Connor's vice presidents, the man she'd arranged a cruise for.

"He's no longer with the company," Connor said in a clipped voice.

"That's too bad, he was a nice man. You must have been sorry to see him go."

"Scarcely. I fired him."

"Why? What did he do?"

"He was stupid and greedy, two things I won't put up with."

"He seemed so pleasant."

Connor's face set in hard lines. "I hire people for their ability and integrity, not their personality."

"What did he do that was so terrible?"

"He used information about one of our mergers to buy up stock before it was offered to the public. That's called insider trading, and it's illegal, besides being unethical. Kleinhold made an excellent salary, in addition to large bonuses. There was no reason to step over the line."

"Maybe he needed the money for something you don't know about," Mandy said slowly.

"White-collar crime isn't any more acceptable than any other kind. If anything, it's more reprehensible, because the perpetrator has other avenues to turn to. If Kleinhold had needed money, he could have come to me. It was greed, not need."

The waiter returned with dessert menus, but Mandy shook her head. "Just coffee for me, please."

After the waiter had left, Connor said, "Where would you like to go from here? Shall we look in at the disco on top of the St. Francis?"

He had dismissed the unpleasant subject of John Kleinhold, but she couldn't. It wasn't a question of the man's guilt or motivation. Mandy was chilled by the hard streak that surfaced so easily in Connor. How could he be so tender and charming one minute, and so coldly autocratic the next? Was the charm just an act that covered the real man?

She realized he was waiting for an answer. "Do you mind if we skip the disco tonight? I have to be at the office early in the morning. It's going to be a heavy day without Alexandra."

"Of course, I understand. We'll do it another time."

When Connor walked Mandy to her door a little later, she asked if he'd like to come in. It was still fairly early, so it seemed the polite thing to do. She didn't honestly know whether she wanted him to accept or not.

He hesitated for a moment. "Perhaps I'd better not."

Mandy felt a small pang of disappointment, but she knew it was for the best. Things had a way of getting out of hand between them, even when she was confused about her feelings for him. Like now.

"Thank you for a lovely dinner," she said formally.

"The pleasure was all mine." He smiled and dipped his head to kiss her briefly.

The chemistry that was always present between them ignited when his mouth touched hers. Mandy's lips parted, and she moved closer. Connor's arms circled her instantly, and he drew her against his taut body.

Her own body seemed to liquify and reform until it molded perfectly to his. When his tongue explored the moist recess of her mouth, little tongues of flame licked at her midsection and she made a tiny sound of pleasure.

"Darling Mandy, you're so enchanting." His words were muffled against her hair as he tightened his embrace. "I can't seem to stay away from you."

"I don't want you to," she whispered.

"My little love!" One hand cupped her bottom, urging her against the juncture of his loins.

Their bodies were tightly clasped together, but still it wasn't close enough. She wanted to be part of him, to have him fill her with more joy than she'd ever known. She was in love with Connor, Mandy admitted to herself. It was useless to keep denying it.

She lifted her face, looking at him with a dazzled expression. For a moment, Connor's eyes glowed with a fierce intensity. Then his fingers bit into her shoulders as he put distance between them.

"Go inside, Mandy," he said hoarsely. "Now!"

"I don't understand. I thought you wanted . . ." She faltered to a stop.

"I do." He lifted one hand to stroke her cheek tenderly. "I've never wanted any woman more, but it has to be what you want, too."

As the hot tide of passion slowly receded, Mandy's cheeks paled. Could Connor tell she was in love with him? Was that why he backed off, because for him it would only be sex?

He dropped his hand and looked at her with a wry expression. "I'm afraid I can be quite convincing. I wouldn't want you to have any regrets."

She nodded wordlessly and turned toward the door.

"Good night, sweetheart." He stroked her hair briefly. "I'll call you tomorrow."

* * *

When she was alone in her bedroom Mandy got undressed slowly, trying to be grateful that Connor was an honorable man. It was difficult when her body was still throbbing from his touch.

The sensible thing would be to stop seeing him, but she knew she wasn't going to be sensible. The thought of never being with Connor again was intolerable, in spite of her doubts about some aspects of his character. Love didn't have to be blind to persist.

He'd told her they should take it nice and easy and see what developed. Well, maybe something would. It wasn't inconceivable for him to fall in love with her.

Mandy got into bed, trying to be optimistic in the face of daunting odds.

Connor phoned Mandy at the office the next day, as he'd said he would. "I know you're swamped, and I won't keep you," he said. "I just wanted to tell you what a good time I had last night." His voice was warm and friendly, without a hint of what had—or rather had not—happened the night before.

That eased any embarrassment Mandy might have felt. "I had a nice time, too."

"I'm glad. We'll have to do it again soon."

Connor hung up without making another date, but Mandy told herself not to be paranoid. He knew she was busy, and he probably was, too. If he didn't feel something for her, he wouldn't have bothered to call at all.

A couple of days later, Alexandra received a phone call from her brother that brought whoops of joy.

"What was that all about?" Mandy asked after her partner had hung up.

"Global Ventures backed off. They're not after Ralph's business anymore. Can you believe it?"

"That's fantastic! What made them change their minds?"

"Who knows? They said they'd reconsidered the desirability of his operation and decided it wouldn't be economically viable to pursue it at this time. You know, standard doublespeak. The important thing is, they aren't going to force him out. Isn't that wonderful?"

"I hope so. Do you think there's a chance that they intend to open their own coffeehouse, instead of going to the expense of buying him out?"

"He thought of that, but they said they're planning to expand in another location instead. I think they realized it was Ralph's personality that made the place a success. Without him, they've got just another coffeehouse."

"You may be right," Mandy said thoughtfully. But, she told herself, they must have taken that into consideration when they made the offer. Could Connor have had anything to do with this turn of events? She'd mentioned Ralph's dilemma to him on Sunday night. At that time it had appeared to be a done deal, yet barely three days later Global Ventures had changed their minds. It seemed like quite a coincidence. Why would Connor intervene, though? This was the kind of business deal he did all the time. Mandy didn't know the answers to the questions running through her mind, but she intended to find out.

She had to go through quite a few secretaries and spend a lot of time listening to canned music before she finally reached Connor.

"This is a nice surprise," he said.

"It is to me, too. Nobody wanted to let me talk to you."

"I'm sorry, honey. I'll give you my private number so you can call me directly next time. What can I do for you?"

"I want to talk to you about Ralph, my partner's brother, who was being pressured to sell out. I just heard the conglomerate changed its mind."

"That's good news, isn't it?"

"Very good. What I want to know is, did you have anything to do with it?"

After an imperceptible pause, Connor said, "What gave you that idea?"

"That's no answer. Did you, or didn't you?"

"I just happened to mention it to one of our attorneys. It was no big deal."

"It was to Ralph. That's the most generous thing I ever heard of, Connor. I don't know how to thank you."

"You don't have to." Laughter colored his voice. "I'm one of those heartless tycoons who keep a stable of attorneys on a yearly retainer. It was time they did a little work for their money."

"For a complete stranger? I can't believe you went to all that trouble for somebody you don't even know."

"If he's a friend of yours, he must be somebody special," Connor said fondly. "I hate to cut you short, honey, but I'm due in a meeting. Can I call you later?"

"Better than that, will you let me cook dinner for you tonight? I want to do something tangible to show my gratitude."

"You don't have to go to all that bother, but I'd love to have dinner with you. We can go out."

"I'd really like to cook for you. Will eight o'clock be all right?"

"Perfect, I'll see you tonight."

Mandy planned a simple dinner, since she didn't have a lot of time to prepare it. She left the office early to go marketing for steaks, baking potatoes and salad ingredients. A stop at the bakery rounded out the menu with rolls and lemon tarts for dessert.

After scrubbing the potatoes and putting them in the oven to bake, she washed the salad greens and set the table. Candles in her grandmother's silver candlesticks and a small pot of African violets made the table look festive.

When she'd done as much as she could beforehand, there was still time for a quick shower. By a quarter to eight, her face was freshly made-up and she was dressed in lavender silk pants and a matching silk cable-knit sweater.

Mandy had agonized long and hard over what to wear. She didn't want to look too sexy and give him the wrong impression, but what woman wouldn't want to look attractive for a man like Connor? She hoped her outfit struck a happy balance.

At eight o'clock, when he rang the doorbell, soft music was playing in the apartment, the ice bucket was filled and Mandy's blue eyes were sparkling with anticipation.

Connor handed her a box of long-stemmed red roses and a bottle of wine. Gazing admiringly at her, he said, "I can't believe you worked all day, made dinner and still managed to look this incredible."

"You don't know what you're getting for dinner," she joked. "These roses are gorgeous. I'll put them in water."

Connor followed her into the kitchen. "Can I do anything to help?"

"No, thanks, everything's under control. Besides, I thought you only knew how to make pancakes," she teased.

"I had in mind something like fixing drinks." He smiled.

"That would be lovely. I'm going to broil steaks, so we can eat whenever we feel like it."

After showing Connor where the liquor and glasses were kept, Mandy took a plate of raw vegetables and a bowl of sun-dried tomato dip out of the refrigerator.

When they were seated on the couch in the living room, she said, "I told Alexandra what you did for Ralph. She was as bowled over as I was."

"I honestly don't deserve this outpouring of gratitude. All I did was turn the matter over to my attorneys. It didn't take any effort on my part."

"You're being much too modest." Mandy looked at him curiously. "I must admit I'm puzzled. You take over companies all the time. I should think your sympathies would be with the conglomerate, not Ralph.''

He smiled mirthlessly. ''I'll never convince you that I'm not a modern-day Attila the Hun, will I? Listen to me, Mandy, it's true that some of my acquisitions are hostile—not all of them—but the companies I target have the opportunity and means to fight back. Your friend Ralph didn't. To me, that's immoral. I don't believe in standing by while somebody destroys a little guy's dreams. So, you see, I really don't deserve any credit. I would do the same for anybody in a similar situation.''

''How can you say you don't deserve the credit? You're a . . . a knight on a white charger!''

''Hardly, but it's nice not to be the villain for a change.''

''I've jumped to all the wrong conclusions about you since the day we met.'' She sighed. ''I don't know why you bother with me.''

''Have you looked in a mirror lately?'' He chuckled.

''That can't be it. You know women a lot more glamorous than I.''

''I can't think of any,'' he said in a husky voice.

''That's nice, but you almost have to say that,'' she said wistfully.

''You're back to not trusting me,'' he teased.

''No, I'll never doubt you again. You're the nicest, kindest, most honorable man I know.''

''You wouldn't say that if you knew the fantasies I have about you.''

''If you don't act them out, it doesn't count,'' she said lightly.

''That's what I keep telling myself.'' He rose and picked up his glass. ''Can I fix you another drink?''

''No, I'm fine, but make one for yourself.''

''I think that's a good idea,'' he muttered, walking toward the kitchen.

Mandy followed him, knowing what she was about to do was foolish, but unable to stop herself. "What's so different about me, Connor?"

He turned his head to smile at her. "Besides the fact that you're gorgeous and sexy?"

"I don't want compliments, I want the truth. Do you usually have platonic relationships with women?"

"It's been known to happen."

"Even when you're attracted to them? You can't pretend we're indifferent to each other."

A muscle twitched in his jaw. "Let it be, Mandy. You're getting into dangerous territory."

His harsh voice and hard expression reinforced the rejection. Mandy turned away. Why couldn't she accept the fact that Connor didn't want to get involved with her, not after he'd found out she was in love with him? Of course he knew. He was too experienced not to recognize the signs.

"I'll put the steaks on," she said dully.

"Mandy, sweetheart." He put his hands on her shoulders. "I'm sorry if I sounded curt. You mean a great deal to me. Tonight I thought I'd finally convinced you that I'm not such a bad guy. I don't want anything to spoil that."

"I understand." She avoided looking at him by reaching for the broiler pan.

He took it out of her hand and tilted her chin up. "I don't think you do. This is about Sunday night, isn't it? You didn't believe my reason for not making love to you. It's even more valid tonight. If I was curt, it's because I want you so much. You're making it difficult for me to restrain myself, but I can't make love to you just because you feel grateful to me."

She gave him a startled look. "Is that what you think?"

"What other reason could possibly stop me?"

"You needn't pretend you don't know I'm in love with you. I didn't want it to happen any more than you did, but sometimes you don't get a choice." She sighed.

Connor was staring at her in amazement. "Is this some kind of joke? A good part of the time we've known each other, I didn't think you even *liked* me."

"I wasn't so sure myself. But even when I thought you were cold and heartless, it didn't change my feelings. You don't have to worry, though, I'm sure I'll get over it."

"I certainly hope not." A smile lit up his face like sunshine. "Why didn't you tell me? No, that's stupid. Why didn't I know?" He put his arms around her waist and swung her around, laughing exultantly. "What difference does it make? I love you, angel face!"

Mandy was dazed by the way things were turning out. "You don't really mean that," she said tentatively.

"Does this tell you how serious I am?"

He gathered her in his arms and kissed her with great tenderness. It was the kiss of a lover, and it brought tears to Mandy's eyes. Incredibly, all of her dreams had come true.

She clasped her arms around his neck and gazed up at him, starry-eyed. "Tell me again that you love me."

"I'd rather show you." He swung her into his arms and carried her into the bedroom.

A single lamp lit the room softly. Connor set her on her feet, and they gazed at each other for a long moment, anticipation building in both of them.

His hands circled her waist, then slipped under her sweater to caress her bare back. She quivered as he unhooked her bra and removed it, along with her sweater.

He drew back to look at her while he stroked her breasts erotically. "I've done this a thousand times in my dreams, but it was never like this. You're so gloriously alive."

"You're the one who brings me to life," she whispered. "I was just going through the motions until I met you."

"My darling love, I want to make you so happy."

"You do," she breathed as Connor strung a line of kisses over the slopes of her breasts. "Oh, yes, you do."

His mouth closed over one aching nipple, and Mandy anchored her fingers in his thick hair. While his tongue curled around the rosy little bud, he eased the silken pants over her hips. She stepped out of them, holding on to Connor, in part because her legs were trembling.

He lifted his head to look at her with blazing eyes. "You're so exquisite. I need to touch you everywhere."

He stroked her naked body with the tips of his fingers, trailing paths of fire from her shoulders to her thighs. She drew in her breath sharply when he lingered at the damp curls that indicated her mounting desire, then parted them to penetrate her throbbing secret.

She reached for him, uttering a broken little plea. "Please Connor," she moaned. "Oh, please."

"Yes, sweetheart, I want to bring you more pleasure than you've ever known."

His intimate touch fed the flames that were consuming her. As they grew in intensity, turning her molten inside, she flung her arms around his neck and kissed him passionately.

"I need you so much, darling," she pleaded.

He reacted instantly, carrying her to the bed. After discarding his clothes in a blur of motion, he returned and covered her body with his. The sensation was incendiary. Their nude bodies moved against each other, sensually at first, then with increasing urgency as their passion mounted.

"I can't wait any longer," he said hoarsely. "I have to have you."

Connor's entry filled Mandy with ecstasy. They held each other close, moving to a wild rhythm that drove them to unbelievable heights. Wave after wave of sensation thundered through their bodies, growing in intensity until the final implosion released them. Their taut muscles relaxed, and they clung to each other, completely satisfied.

Connor finally stirred enough to stroke her damp hair languidly. "I knew it would be like this."

"I didn't know it could be," she said.

They kissed tenderly for a while and murmured words of love, curled up together in utter contentment. When Mandy rubbed her cheek against his chest with a sigh of pure pleasure, Connor smiled lazily.

"I told you we'd be good together," he said.

"I guess I should be glad you're so experienced."

"Does it bother you, angel?"

"Maybe a little," she admitted. "I don't like to think of all the women you've been with."

"I can't deny knowing other women. I'm a man, honey, not a boy. But there haven't been as many as you imagine, and none of them meant what you do."

"You must have thought they did at the time," she said wistfully.

"No, we had mutual needs. I've never taken unfair advantage, though. I never made promises I didn't intend to keep."

He hadn't made any promises to her, either, Mandy reflected. Did that mean he didn't intend to? She banished the disquieting thought. Why worry about it now? She'd made her decision and she was supremely happy—no matter what happened somewhere down the road.

"It's a good thing I didn't wait for you to stop being noble," she said mischievously. "We wouldn't be here now."

"Maybe not tonight, but very soon." He chuckled. "I was finding it increasingly difficult to keep my hands off you."

"There's no reason to anymore," she murmured.

He stroked her bottom sensuously. "You mean I can do this whenever I like?"

"Only in appropriate places."

He slid his hand between her thighs. "Is this an appropriate place?"

"You know what I meant." She laughed. "And yes, that's one of the places I would have chosen."

"I'm glad we think alike."

He leaned over her and traced the shape of her mouth with the tip of his tongue. Mandy's lips parted and her tongue twined with his. As Connor deepened the kiss, his hand moved erotically over her body, awakening sated passions.

She stroked him in the same way, tracing the supple muscles under his smooth skin. He groaned with pleasure, and when her fingers closed around his rigid manhood, he cried out hoarsely.

"Mandy, darling, I want to make love to you the way you deserve, but I'm not made of steel."

She smiled seductively. "I like you this way." It gave her a sense of power to make this experienced man lose control.

"All right, you little devil. Two can play that game."

He straddled her hips and lowered his head to string a line of kisses down to her navel—and beyond. Mandy twisted restlessly as he lifted her leg and slid his mouth slowly over the soft skin of her inner thigh. Then he reached his goal.

"You win," she gasped, reaching for him.

He moved up her body to cover her face with kisses. "You're a prize a man would do anything for."

Their lovemaking wasn't as frantic this time. They moved voluptuously against each other, trying to give as much pleasure as each was receiving. It was love, not merely sex. An expression of deep feelings.

The tempo escalated inevitably as their need increased. Torrents of molten passion throbbed through their fused bodies, bringing shared rapture that crested when it couldn't go any higher.

Afterward, Mandy nestled her cheek in the curve of Connor's neck. "I thought it couldn't get any better, but it did," she said softly.

He kissed the top of her head. "And this is only the beginning."

She gave him an impish look. "You mean, I can expect a return engagement?"

"Can you give me a little time to recharge my batteries?" he asked plaintively.

"Poor baby. You didn't even get the dinner I promised you."

"I got something much better." He pulled her closer.

Mandy sat up abruptly. "The potatoes! I forgot to turn off the oven."

"I hope it was because you had something more important on your mind," he teased.

"That's pretty obvious." She laughed. "The potatoes are ruined, but I can still broil the steaks and make a salad."

"Don't bother, unless you're hungry."

"My hunger has been satisfied," she answered softly.

"Mine never will be," he said, kissing her tenderly.

They talked quietly, clasped in each other's arms. After a while they were content to just lie there. Words weren't necessary, only their close contact.

When Connor's breathing slowed, Mandy shook him gently. "You can't fall asleep. You have to get up and go home."

He looked at her drowsily. "Why?"

"Because you can't stay here all night. What will Dee Dee think?"

"She'll think I got up early and went to work."

"Are you sure? I wouldn't want her to get the wrong idea."

"You mean you don't want her to get the *right* idea." He grinned.

"Yes. She's too young to understand."

"That's true, although Dee Dee approves highly of you. Which is a first," he added dryly.

"That's your fault for only dating dizzy blondes."

"I couldn't turn into a recluse while I was waiting for you to come along," he teased. "After all, you weren't sitting home alone."

"Maybe not, but at least I dated men with intelligence," Mandy replied tartly.

"Which probably accounts for the fact that you never married." He laughed.

Did he think she didn't have opportunities? "It has nothing to do with the caliber of my dates. I'm single by choice," she said coolly.

"I never doubted it." Connor looked at her searchingly. "Don't you want to get married?"

It was a far cry from a proposal. He merely sounded curious. But it was really too soon to expect him to take such a big step.

Mandy didn't want to scare him off, so she said, "I have nothing against marriage, but I'm not in any hurry. There's plenty of time."

"That's true, you're young yet." His face was expressionless in the indistinct light.

"I'd better turn off the oven," she said.

While she was in the kitchen Mandy put away the vegetables and the dip, and washed their glasses. By the time she returned to the bedroom, Connor's eyes were closed and his breathing was regular.

She slid into bed quietly, so as not to waken him. He stirred and put his arms around her when she curled up next to him, but it was in his sleep. She was content to lie there quietly, filled to the brim with happiness.

This was what marriage must be like, Mandy thought poignantly. Someone to share everything with. If only Connor felt the same way. She couldn't bear to lose him now. A smile replaced her sober expression as she remembered his inspired lovemaking. What was she worried about? They both wanted the same thing. He just didn't know it yet.

* * *

The next morning Connor eased out of bed, trying not to disturb Mandy. She was instantly awake, however. The knowledge that someone was in the room startled her—until memories of the previous night came flooding back.

"I'm sorry, darling," he said. "I didn't mean to wake you."

"It's all right." She smiled in blissful remembrance. "I have to get up and go to work, anyway."

Connor slid back into bed. "It's still early," he murmured, nibbling on her ear.

"Not early enough for what you have in mind."

"Can you think of something you'd rather do?"

She smoothed his rumpled hair and kissed him lovingly. "If I could do whatever I liked, I'd choose to spend the day in bed. But we both have businesses to run."

"The world won't stop spinning on its axis if we take a day off. I think it's a fantastic idea."

"I have an appointment at ten with a travel wholesaler," Mandy said reluctantly. "He can throw a lot of business our way."

Connor curved his hand around her breast and slid his mouth across her bare shoulder. "Are you sure I can't change your mind?"

"That's the whole trouble. You can convince me of anything."

"Is that a problem?" He raised his head to look at her closely. "Are you having second thoughts about last night?"

She smiled enchantingly. "I expect to think about it constantly. It was the most wonderful night of my life."

His tension vanished. "That's what I needed to hear."

"Darling Connor, you didn't seduce me. If anything, it was the other way around." She grinned.

"Feel free at any time to do it again."

"How about tonight?"

"I did have a date with a dizzy blonde," he teased. "But for you, I'll break it."

Mandy suspected he might be telling the truth. It hurt to be reminded that there were other women in his life, but she tried to hide the fact. "I keep forgetting what a busy social life you lead," she remarked lightly. "Call me when you have some free time." Without waiting for an answer, she walked into the bathroom and turned on the shower.

Connor followed her. "It was a joke, sweetheart. When will you believe I meant it when I said I love you?"

"I want to believe it," she said slowly.

"I don't know of any other way to show you."

He looked so concerned that her heart lifted. "I'm sorry, darling. Everything happened so fast. One minute we were on the verge of another argument, and this morning I woke up in bed next to you. I'm almost afraid to be this happy. It's like a dream I don't want to wake up from."

"If I have anything to do with it, the dream will never end," he said huskily. "Now get in the shower before I drag you back to bed."

She put her arms around his neck. "You were right. We still have a little time left."

"A good executive uses time efficiently." He gave her a sultry smile, taking her hand and drawing her into the shower.

"This is what I call real service," Mandy said as he soaped her back.

"I haven't displayed all of my talents yet." He made circular motions over her bottom, then slipped his hand between her legs.

She turned to face him, taking the washcloth from him and soaping his chest. "I have a few talents of my own."

Mandy lingered over his flat nipples, then moved down to his taut stomach. Connor's slick skin felt unbelievably erotic. She could have caressed him for hours. But when she stroked the rigid proof of his power, he arched his body with a hoarse cry and entered her.

The warm water showered them gently, adding to the sensuality without extinguishing the fierce heat inside them. Mandy met Connor's driving force with equal passion. Her hands gripped his buttocks, holding him tightly while he filled her delight.

At the end, they clung together as spasms of completion shuddered through their bodies, leaving them limp, but totally content.

Connor held her closely for long minutes. "I talked you into something again, didn't I? I suppose I should say I'm sorry, but it wouldn't be true."

"Obviously I didn't mind," she answered fondly. "It's going to cost you, though. I intended to make you a big breakfast, but there isn't time now."

"I'd make a trade like that any day! I'll take you out to breakfast, instead. Get dressed, and don't dawdle," he ordered. After turning off the shower he wrapped her in a bath towel and dried her briskly. "I'll give you fifteen minutes."

"Oh, *now* you're in a hurry." She laughed. "I can be dressed in ten minutes, but it will take longer than that to put on my makeup."

"You don't need any." He framed her face between his palms and gazed into her eyes. "You're a natural beauty."

They each took their own car to a coffee shop near Mandy's house, where they ordered a huge breakfast. While they waited for their food, she glanced at the headlines of the paper he'd bought, and Connor jotted down some notes for the day ahead.

When their food came, they talked quietly about business and the coming weekend. Mandy reminded him to include Dee Dee in part of it, and they discussed where to take her. They finished breakfast with just time enough to get to their respective offices.

Connor walked her to her car and gave her a kiss on the cheek. "I'll see you tonight. Have a good day, honey."

"You, too."

Mandy drove away with a feeling of euphoria. This was the way it was going to be when they got married—passion, but also warm companionship. Could life get any better?

Chapter Nine

The next couple of weeks were unbelievably happy. Mandy and Connor saw each other as often as possible during the week and spent every weekend together. On Saturdays and Sundays they took Dee Dee sailing, or shopping, or to one of the museums, but the evenings belonged to them alone. Mandy enjoyed being with Dee Dee, although nothing could compare with her time alone with Connor. He had become so important to her that it was almost scary.

She was especially gratified to be invited to his mother's house. She liked Louise, but it also dignified her own relationship to Connor.

The Winfield family home was an imposing three-story mansion with a scenic view of the ocean. It was located in an exclusive residential area of similarly luxurious houses.

"Your home is lovely!" Mandy exclaimed on her first visit.

"I'm glad you like it, my dear," Louise said. "Connor

wants me to move to an apartment, but I'd hate living in a little box. He can't seem to understand that."

"I wouldn't describe my apartment as a 'little box,'" he said. "You could get something that size."

"It still wouldn't be large enough for all my things." She waved a hand around the treasure-filled living room. Besides the profusion of couches and chairs, there were cabinets and tables filled with exquisite art objects. "What would I do with the rest of them?"

"You'd use what you could, and call in Butterfield's to auction off the rest."

"Men have no sentiment," Louise told Mandy. "How does one auction off a lifetime of keepsakes? He'd probably toss in the family albums."

"Oh, no!" he groaned. "You're not going to drag those out again?"

"Shame on you," Mandy said. "I'd love to see them."

"I knew you were a woman of taste the first time I met you." Louise patted the place next to her on the couch and took a leather album from a cluster of books on the lower shelf of the coffee table.

"This is Connor's father." She pointed to a picture of a distinguished-looking man wearing a golf sweater.

"He's very handsome," Mandy commented truthfully. Connor resembled his father.

"This is one of my favorite snapshots of him." Louise gazed wistfully at the small photo. "Phillip could be quite imposing if you didn't know him, but he was actually a very kind man."

"His son takes after him," Mandy said softly.

"Yes, I'm a fortunate woman. Connor is very like his father." Louise turned the page, and her reflective expression changed to a smile. "This was taken when Connor was just a toddler. Isn't he precious?"

"Simply adorable," Mandy agreed. "Look at those chubby little legs."

"And that round little bottom," Louise pointed out.

"I hope you ladies know this is damned embarrassing," Connor said plaintively.

Dee Dee came in from outdoors. "What are you guys doing?"

"I'm showing Mandy my picture albums," her grandmother said.

"Neat!" Dee Dee went over to take a seat next to Mandy. "Show her the ones of Dad when he was a big football star." She flipped some pages forward. "This is when he was in high school."

Connor was already tall, but his rangy body hadn't filled out to its present mature perfection. He had the same obvious charm, however. His generous mouth was curved in a smile, and he had his arm around a pretty blonde.

"Who's the girl?" Mandy asked.

"One of his girlfriends," Dee Dee said dismissively. "He had lots of them."

"I don't doubt it," Mandy murmured.

"One of his girlfriends was homecoming queen. I'll show you." Dee Dee flipped some more pages.

"Surely there are pictures of other people in there," Connor said with annoyance. "Show her some of those."

"Do you want to see my baby pictures?" Dee Dee asked.

"Yes, I'd love to," Mandy said.

"They're in a different book." Dee Dee pulled a white leather album from the pile. "The first part is all pictures of Mom and Dad."

"She wouldn't be interested in those," Louise said smoothly. "Show her the ones of you on the pony rides."

Mandy was dying to see a picture of Lorna, but she made dutiful comments about Dee Dee on a pony, in a swimming pool, at a birthday party. Eventually her patience was rewarded. One of the snaps showed Dee Dee holding the hands of her mother and father in a lovely garden.

"That's Mom, the day we went out to see Aunt Harriet in Hillsboro," Dee Dee said. "She isn't a real aunt, but I call her that."

Mandy barely heard her. She was staring at the small photo.

Lorna Winfield was a stunningly beautiful woman with long blond hair that floated glamorously over her slender shoulders. She had perfect features and her skin was a pale golden tan. Most of it was exposed by the skimpy bikini she wore. A tiny scrap of cloth covered her full breasts, and another scrap rode low on her hips. Only someone with a flawless figure could wear a suit like that. From the confident look on Lorna's face, she was well aware of it.

No wonder Connor couldn't forget her, Mandy thought desolately. She'd known his ex-wife must be beautiful, but who could compete against perfection?

"It's my turn now," Louise said, after a glance at Mandy's expression. "I want to show Mandy my pictures of Bali."

"Did you get them back?" Dee Dee asked. "I want to see them, too."

They looked at photos of exotic temples, and women washing clothes on rocks in a river. Even Connor came over for a look while his mother gave them a running commentary.

"Where are you going next, Gram?" Dee Dee asked when they'd seen everything.

"I'm considering an African safari."

"Wow, cool! That's what *I'd* like to do, see all those wild animals and stuff. Can you wait until school's out so I can go along?"

"You mean summer vacation? I believe that's the rainy season in Africa. I was planning to go over Christmas and New Year's." Louise slanted a glance at Connor. "You and your father could both come with me if you weren't going to New York."

Dee Dee turned to her father with an eager expression. "Maybe we could go to New York over Easter, Dad."

"It's too late to change our plans now. Your mother is expecting you."

Louise sniffed. "If she remembers you're coming."

Connor's mouth thinned. "I've asked you not to talk about Lorna that way."

"You're right, my dear. I'll try to restrain myself in the future."

He stood, giving his mother a moody look. "I'm going for a walk along the beach. Do you want to come?" he asked Mandy.

"Take Dee Dee. I'll stay here and keep your mother company." She had a feeling Connor really wanted to be alone.

"I was already down there," Dee Dee said. "It's too cold. I'm gonna coax Gram into making me some hot chocolate."

"You know that won't be difficult." Her grandmother smiled.

"That leaves you with nothing to do," Connor told Mandy. "There are some warm jackets in the hall closet. Put one on."

She did as he said, since anything else was liable to provoke an argument. Connor seemed to be wound tightly. Was the picture of his ex-wife responsible? Had seeing her again released all his pent-up longing? Mandy's heart plunged like a stone when she thought about her competition. How could she fight an obsession?

They walked silently along the deserted beach. The wind and fog had chased everyone else away. Mandy put her hands in her pockets and burrowed her chin into the collar of her coat.

Connor turned his head to look at her. "Is it too cold for you? Do you want to go back?"

"No, I'm all right."

He hesitated for a moment. "I'm sorry for being out of sorts. Mother does that to me sometimes."

Mandy managed a little laugh. "Everybody's mother does."

"I suppose so. She really shouldn't talk about Lorna in front of Dee Dee, though. Lorna *is* the child's mother."

There was no answer to that, so Mandy didn't make one.

"Mother never cared for Lorna, although she tried to conceal the fact while we were married, I'll give her that. But when Lorna took off in the way she did, Mother felt free to speak her mind, which she does regularly. It puts me in an awkward position, because I told Dee Dee the divorce was nobody's fault. She doesn't blame her mother for leaving."

"You both must have been very convincing. How did Lorna explain it to her?"

"With a lot of double-talk about needing her own space. She did have the good sense to tell Dee Dee she loves her. And maybe she does—in her own way. I'm only hoping someday she'll realize it and be a real mother to Dee Dee."

Mandy stooped to pick up a rock, afraid the expression on her face might reveal her inner turmoil. Connor clearly hadn't given up hope of getting Lorna back.

Skipping the rock over the water so she wouldn't have to look at him, she said, "Maybe when you're all together this Christmas, she'll realize what she's missing."

"I'm not counting on it." He brushed a strand of hair out of Mandy's eyes. "I hate being away from you for the holidays. I'd ask you to come with us, but I'm afraid it wouldn't be much fun for you."

"I couldn't go, anyway. I have all sorts of plans."

"What are you going to do?"

"Lots of things. We have a big office party for all our clients, and I'm invited to some other parties, too."

"Are you bringing a date?"

"You wouldn't want people to think I couldn't get one, would you?" she joked lamely.

"Men are probably lining up already." He turned her to face him. "I just want you to know I'm jealous as hell."

"You shouldn't be," she murmured. "You'll be with a beautiful woman."

"I'm going to be with my ex-wife, who just happens to be attractive." He opened his jacket and drew Mandy against his body for warmth. "But I'll be thinking about you."

She wanted desperately to believe him. They had something wonderful together, if only he could let go of the past.

"Don't you have some kind of errand you have to do?" he asked in a smoky voice. "We could leave Dee Dee here and go back to your place for a couple of hours."

"You know we can't do that. Your mother expects us to spend the day here."

"But not the night." He parted her lips and moved against her suggestively. "We're leaving right after dinner."

"You won't get any argument from me." She smiled.

They held hands walking back to the house, and the roller coaster of Mandy's emotions climbed back up to the top. Lorna was just a distant dream—this was reality.

The rest of the day was relaxing. Dee Dee and Mandy worked on a giant jigsaw puzzle in front of the fireplace while Connor leafed idly through the Sunday newspaper.

Louise surveyed the domestic scene with great satisfaction. After a short time she said to her son, "Could you help me with something in the other room?"

"Certainly." He put the paper aside and followed her into his father's former study at the back of the house.

"Sit down." Louise indicated a large wing chair and took the one facing it.

"This sounds serious." Connor smiled. "Dad used to call me in here for a good talking-to when I'd done something wrong. What did I do this time?"

"It's nothing like that. I just wanted to have a talk with you about Mandy. She's a lovely girl."

"Yes, she is," he answered noncommittally.

"Dee Dee adores her, and with good reason. Mandy is wonderful with her. You can tell she genuinely likes the child. It isn't an act."

"Where are you going with this, Mother?" Connor asked quietly. "I presume you're making a point, but frankly, I don't know what it is."

"I was merely expressing pleasure that you've finally found someone so suitable, although it took courage to mention it. A mother's approval is usually the kiss of death."

"You've never been shy about expressing your opinion," he answered dryly. "And I value your judgment. Is that what you brought me in here to tell me?"

"Not entirely. I went to my safety-deposit box recently to get some legal documents, and I happened to notice your grandmother's diamond engagement ring. It's a shame for it to just lie there, but I have no use for it. Your father was so generous about giving me jewelry. I thought you might like to take it and have it reset for Mandy," Louise said casually.

"You're being a little premature. I haven't asked her to marry me."

"What are you waiting for? It's obvious that you two are in love."

"Love and marriage don't always go together, in spite of what the songwriters would have you believe."

"That's nonsense! Do you expect to remain single all your life because of one youthful mistake?"

His mouth curved mockingly. "You make it sound as if I chose the wrong tie. It was a major error in judgment."

Louise looked at him uncertainly. "Perhaps I jumped to conclusions. If you're not sure of your feelings for Mandy, then you're wise to wait."

"My feelings aren't the problem, hers are. We had a discussion recently, and Mandy told me in so many words that she didn't want to get married."

"I can hardly believe that. I've seen the way she looks at you."

"There's a reason for that, but it isn't one you discuss with your mother."

"Don't patronize me, Connor," she said impatiently. "I remember the joys of sex. I also can recognize the look on a woman's face when it's accompanied by love."

"It doesn't mean she wants to get married. Times have changed."

"Not that much. If you were living together, it would be different. You're right about the changing times. Couples who live together don't see the need for a piece of paper."

"Are you suggesting I ask Mandy to move in with me—and Dee Dee?"

"Of course not! I'm merely suggesting you ask her to marry you. She might surprise you by accepting."

"Or she might be frightened off and decide to stop seeing me. I don't intend to take that chance."

"I think you're wrong, but I'm not infallible," Louise said slowly. "I suppose you have to do what you think is best."

"I'm trying, anyway." He sighed and got to his feet. "Come on, Mother, it's cocktail time. I'll make us all a drink."

Mandy and Connor were completely happy together. She was as much a part of his household as if she lived there, but the time they spent alone were the golden moments. They avoided displays of affection in front of Dee Dee, so the young girl looked on Mandy as a family friend. It was an almost ideal life.

One night the telephone rang as Mandy was getting ready for a date with Connor. "I just wanted to tell you I'll be a little late." He sounded stressed.

"That's okay, I can use the extra time. Is everything all right?"

"More or less. I'll tell you about it when I get there." He hung up without giving her a chance to ask questions.

Connor was usually so unflappable that Mandy was worried. Nothing ever caused him more than a momentary irritation. What could be wrong? She fretted over it until he got there.

"What happened?" she asked, the minute he walked in the door. "You sounded upset on the phone."

"It's Dee Dee." He sighed. "That kid is a loose cannon. I never know what she'll do next."

Mandy relaxed. "Let me guess," she said with a smile. "She wants to dye her hair or have her nose pierced."

"Something almost as bad. You know how much time she spends on that computer I bought her? I was so pleased that she was getting interested in something besides clothes and talking on the phone for hours. That was before I found out what she was actually doing."

"I don't understand. What's wrong with playing on a computer?"

"The kind of games she was playing," he answered tersely. "She wanted to go on-line, so I had her hooked up to the Internet. That means she can communicate with people all over the country."

"Yes, I'm familiar with the way it works."

"Do you also know there are programs where people meet and exchange intimate details about themselves?"

Mandy gave him a startled look. "But those are for adults."

"I don't have to tell you that Dee Dee considers herself an adult. She's been on-line with a twenty-one-year-old man from Boston."

"That's terrible!"

"You bet it is," Connor said grimly. "I don't know what messages she sent him, but his were pretty graphic. I went through the roof when I saw one."

"What did Dee Dee say?"

"She thinks it's a big joke. She told him she's the same age he is, and she's delighted that he believed her. Which explains his explicit messages."

"Not necessarily. There are all kinds of sick predators out there. I hope you told her that."

"I told her a lot of things, including the fact that she's grounded for two weeks."

"That's all?"

"She's too old to spank. Besides, that's called child abuse these days." Connor smiled. He was feeling better after unburdening himself.

Mandy wasn't. "I don't think you're taking this seriously enough. There have been cases in the newspaper about young girls who were persuaded to run away from home and go live with some creep."

"Dee Dee has too much sense for that."

"You hope! It certainly isn't worth taking a chance."

"I had a long talk with her. At this age she's starting to get interested in sex, like all kids. But it isn't a priority yet. She just thought she was doing something daring."

"I still think she needs more punishment than merely being grounded for two weeks and taken off the Internet."

"I didn't disconnect her."

"You have to be joking! Why not?"

"Because she promised she wouldn't do it again. If I took away her access, it would look as if I don't trust her."

"Ordinarily I'd agree with you, but this is a special case. You could tell her it's part of her punishment."

"I can't suddenly tack on another penalty."

Mandy was alarmed enough to try to change his mind. They argued back and forth without getting anywhere.

Finally Connor said, "I appreciate your concern, but I believe you're overreacting. Since we obviously don't agree, I think it would be better if we didn't talk about it anymore."

Mandy's temper snapped. "Okay, fine! She's your child, not mine, thank heaven. I'm glad she *isn't* my responsibility. I wouldn't want to have to deal with her when she's a full-fledged teenager."

His face became expressionless. "There's no reason why you should. Shall we go to dinner now?"

That was the last thing Mandy wanted, but if she refused, it would look as if she were sulking. "I'll get my purse," she said stiffly.

Conversation was strained in the car, and at the restaurant when they got there. For the first time since they'd known each other, neither had anything to say. They'd always been able to talk about Dee Dee, if nothing else, but that subject was off-limits.

"I got some brochures on Africa for your mother," Mandy remarked as they ate their salads.

"That will please her, but I'm rather worried that the trip will be too hard for her."

"You needn't be concerned, this is a luxury safari. Guests are housed either at country clubs or in private tents complete with their own facilities."

"I thought a safari meant roughing it in the bush," he commented.

"There are those kind of trips, but the one I'm suggesting to your mother is first-class all the way."

After they'd discussed Africa in more detail than either of them wished, they struggled to find something else to talk about. Both were relieved when dinner was over.

Connor said good-night at Mandy's door. They both knew he wasn't coming in. He kissed her chastely and said, "I'll call you tomorrow."

She merely nodded.

Mandy had an older couple in her office when Connor phoned the next day. She wanted to patch things up with him, but under the circumstances she had to appear businesslike.

"You sound rushed," he said tentatively.

"I'm with some clients. Can I call you back?"

"I'll be in a meeting. I just wanted to tell you I won't be able to see you for a few days."

"Oh?" She managed to keep the desolation out of her voice. If Connor wanted to let their quarrel escalate into something major, that was his decision.

"I have people coming in from Japan this afternoon. They'll be here for several days, and I'll have to be with them. I'm sorry."

"Don't worry about it," she said coolly. "I'll manage to keep busy without you."

"It's nice to know I'm not indispensable," he drawled.

"My sentiments exactly. You'll have to excuse me now, I have people waiting."

It was an effort to pin a smile on her face and keep her mind on business, but she managed. After her clients had gone, Mandy slumped in her chair.

Alexandra looked over at her. "Something wrong?"

"Just about everything." Mandy sighed. "Connor and I had our first major fight last night."

"It was bound to happen sooner or later. You'll make up."

"I'm not sure he wants to."

"Don't get paranoid. He's probably worried about the same thing. You'll kiss and make up tonight."

"If we were going to be together, that is. He just called to say he couldn't see me for a few days."

"Well, that's probably a good idea," Alexandra said. "It will give you both a chance to cool off."

"He's the one who's carrying a grudge." Mandy's chin set. "Well, if that's the way he wants it, it's fine with me."

"Yes, I can see how happy you are," Alexandra remarked dryly.

Mandy's eyes turned somber. "It's scary to have somebody mean this much to you. I don't know what I'd do without Connor."

"I'm sure he feels the same about you."

"Then why doesn't he ask me to marry him?"

Alexandra shrugged. "You were getting along so well that he might have decided there wasn't any necessity. Maybe this will give him the nudge he needs."

"I wish he'd get the urge before Christmas," Mandy said wistfully.

"You'd like a Christmas wedding?"

"It isn't that. Connor is taking Dee Dee to New York for the holidays. He'll be spending a lot of time with his ex-wife, and I'm not sure all the embers are dead. If she wants him back, I might lose him."

"You don't intend to just sit back and let her have him, do you? That isn't like you. You've always been a fighter. Go to New York with him," Alexandra urged.

"You have to be asked first." Mandy's smile was humorless. "Connor said it wouldn't be any fun for me. What good would it do, anyway? Lorna has more ammunition than I do. She's Dee Dee's mother. The three of them will be spending time together as a nostalgic family group. I'd be on the outside looking in."

"He won't be with her every minute. You could keep busy going to the theater and museums, not to mention the wonderful shopping in New York. Even if you only saw Connor for a couple of hours now and then, he'd be reminded of how important you are to him."

Mandy briefly considered the idea, then rejected it. "No, I don't want to try and influence him. What kind of marriage would it be if he's still in love with Lorna?"

"They've been divorced for a couple of years. Why should he suddenly want her back?"

"It's the other way around. She left *him*. If she's changed her mind, there's nothing I can do about it. I might as well find out now rather than later." As Alexandra started to protest, the telephone rang. Mandy reached for it, saying, "All I can do is hope for the best."

It was difficult to keep hope alive when the days passed without any word from Connor. Mandy steadfastly refused to call him, as Alexandra urged. All she had left was her pride. He couldn't take that away from her.

Connor's mother phoned when Mandy was at a low point. "I received the brochures you sent, and I'm quite excited. The trip sounds stimulating."

"Yes, I think you'll like it. It's a unique way to spend the holidays, especially if you can't be with your family. They have a lot of festivities planned, like parties and entertainment on Christmas and New Year's."

"One thing that bothers me is being restricted to a single duffel bag for the flight into the bush. I could fill that with my cosmetics alone." Louise chuckled. "As you get older, it takes a lot of creams and lotions before you're prepared to face the world."

"Lions and leopards aren't as judgmental as humans." Mandy laughed. "I've never been on this trip, but I understand the duffel bag they provide is quite roomy. You won't need fancy outfits, anyway. The activities in the bush are very informal, so I think it will be adequate."

"I should have called you earlier. I have a million more questions, but I'm due at a charity board meeting. Why don't you and Connor come over for dinner tonight, when we'll both have more time?"

"Connor has some business associates here from Japan," Mandy said without elaborating.

"I suppose I can wait until the weekend. Are you free on Saturday or Sunday? Cook has Sunday off this week, but we can always go out to a restaurant."

"I think you'd better check with your son," Mandy answered carefully.

"Surely you can make an appointment without Connor's approval. You mustn't let him dominate you. He's a dear boy, but he's just like his father. Phillip liked to take charge, too."

"It's possible that Connor has other plans. I think you should talk to him first."

"I see." Louise didn't sound as if she did. "Well, if that's what you'd prefer."

After saying goodbye and hanging up, Louise called her son immediately. Without telling him she'd talked to Mandy, she repeated her invitation to dinner that night.

"Sorry, Mother, but I've had businesspeople here from Japan for the last few days. I'll be tied up with them until tomorrow afternoon."

"So it's true!" she exclaimed in relief.

"Of course it's true. Why would I lie about it?"

"I just thought perhaps... Well, never mind. It isn't important."

Connor frowned. "What's going on? I get the feeling you had some other reason for calling me."

"You're imagining things."

"I don't think so. You already knew I was busy tonight, didn't you? Why would you call to confirm it?"

Louise lost patience with diplomacy. She was used to speaking her mind. "If you must know, I wondered if you told Mandy the truth."

Connor's jaw tightened. "She thought I was lying?"

"I didn't say that. I was the one who wondered about it."

"Don't you think this is a matter that should be left to Mandy and me?"

"You mean, I should mind my own business?"

"I wouldn't have put it that bluntly, but I would appreciate it."

"You must realize I'm not simply being meddlesome. You're my son, I have your best interests at heart."

"I know." He suppressed a sigh. "But I'm a grown man, Mother, and Mandy is an adult woman. We don't need someone to tell us to be good little children and play nice together."

"So, you did have an argument."

"It was a difference of opinion," Connor answered cautiously. "Nothing major."

"Yet you haven't made any future plans to see her."

He swore under his breath. "Do you also know what I had for breakfast this morning? Your surveillance system is better than the CIA's."

"It didn't take a rocket scientist to figure out you two had an argument and stopped seeing each other."

"Only temporarily."

"In the meantime, you've left that poor girl dangling."

"What makes you think she cares?" Connor's eyes were bleak. "Mandy doesn't need me to make her happy. She told me so."

Louise uttered a small sound of disgust. "I'm sure you said some things you didn't mean, either. Now both of you are miserable and neither of you will admit it. Why don't you phone her and straighten out this silly misunderstanding before it becomes serious?"

"I intend to call her."

"When?"

"You want the exact time?" he asked in annoyance. "I'll call her this evening. Will that make you happy?"

"What's more important, I believe it will make *you* happy. Why don't you simply admit you're lost without her and marry the girl?"

"We've been through all that. I told you, Mandy doesn't want to marry me."

"I still maintain that you're wrong. She sounded so unhappy on the phone. A woman doesn't mope around after a quarrel if she's indifferent to the man. This would be the perfect time to propose."

"Catch her in a weak moment?" Connor asked sardonically. "I hate to rewrite your perfect ending, Mother, but you're laboring under a delusion. It isn't only that Mandy doesn't want to get married, she doesn't want to marry *me*. However hard you find that to believe."

"Wherever did you get a bizarre notion like that?"

"She told me so when we were having our quarrel, or misunderstanding, or whatever you choose to call it. Actually, the argument was over Dee Dee. Mandy doesn't want to take on a ready-made family, and you can't really blame her. Dee Dee is a handful."

"That's the silliest thing I ever heard! Mandy is so sweet with her, and the child adores her. They already seem like mother and daughter."

"I'm not saying Mandy doesn't care about Dee Dee. She does. But that doesn't mean she wants to be responsible for her on a day-to-day basis. Mandy has never been married. If or when that day ever comes, she wants to start out with just a husband to contend with. I'm a package deal, no matter how I feel about her."

"I can't believe Mandy indicated any of this to you," Louise protested.

"I could quote you her exact words, but I'd rather not," Connor said heavily. "Just take my word for it, there was no room for misunderstanding."

"But she loves you." Louise sounded bewildered. "I know I'm not mistaken about that."

"And I love her. That's why I'm not going to risk losing her by trying to pressure her into anything. I'd rather have our present relationship than nothing at all. This argument will blow over and, hopefully, we'll go on the way we were."

"It seems such a waste." Louise sighed.

Connor tried to sound cheerful. "Well, who knows? Maybe Mandy will change her mind when Dee Dee gets older. I'm willing to wait."

"I only hope Mandy is, too."

"So do I," he answered soberly.

Connor was still sitting at his desk, staring at the telephone, when it rang unexpectedly. It was his private line, the one only a few people had access to. His dejected manner vanished as he reached for the phone.

"Hi, Dad, are you too busy to talk?" Dee Dee sounded uncharacteristically subdued.

Connor's eagerness fled when he heard his daughter's voice instead of Mandy's, as he'd hoped he would. Forcing down his disappointment, he answered her in a normal tone. "No, you caught me at a good time. What's up?"

"Are you still mad at me?" she asked in a small voice. "I haven't seen you in days."

"I told you I had people in from out of town. It has nothing to do with you, honey. They've kept me busy every night."

"Are you sure that's why you don't come home anymore?" She sounded doubtful.

"I seem to have a credibility problem," he commented ironically. "That's the reason, I assure you. Our meetings end tomorrow, and they'll be leaving right afterward. Things should get back to normal after that. I'll be home to have dinner with you tomorrow night."

"Could we have it at Grandma's house? She called just now and said she was lonesome, and could I come for dinner and spend the night. I know I'm grounded, but that doesn't include Grandma, does it? She sounded really bummed out."

A smile started in Connor's eyes and spread over his entire face. "I wouldn't worry about your grandmother, she keeps very busy. I happen to know she's hard at work right now on a big project."

"What's her project?"

"I'll let her tell you about it." His mouth curved in a mischievous smile. Let his mother explain that!

"So, I can tell her we'll come?"

"I don't think she's expecting me, and I have something to do. You can go, though."

"Thanks, Dad." Dee Dee hesitated for a moment. "I love you."

"I love you, too, baby," he answered huskily.

Minutes later Connor dialed his mother's number. "I hear I'm invited to your house for dinner tomorrow night."

After a moment's pause, Louise said, "Certainly, if you'd like to come. You know I'm always glad to see you."

"Some times more than others." He laughed. "If you don't mind, I'll take a rain check."

"You have another date?"

"Not yet, but I hope to. I thought I'd ask Mandy to dinner."

"Well, I certainly can't compete with that. Have a lovely time."

"I'm sure I will. You and Dee Dee enjoy yourselves, too." Before she could answer, he added, "By the way, Mother, have you decided what restaurant I should take Mandy to? And did you make the reservation in my name or yours?"

Instead of acting defensive, she answered calmly, "Neither. I thought a nice dinner at home would be cozy. I know it's your housekeeper's night off, so I'll send my cook over to prepare it at your apartment. Kate is very efficient. She'll leave your kitchen spotless and be out of there right after dinner."

"You're a very wicked woman, Mother." Connor chuckled.

"I know. At my age, it's the only fun I get."

Chapter Ten

Connor's telephone call was as unexpected as it was welcome. Mandy was too ecstatic to act distant. "I didn't expect to hear from you," she said breathlessly.

"Never again?" he teased.

"Well, it's been almost a week."

"I know, darling, and I'm sorry. Those people from Japan are tireless. We've been having meetings all day, and then we talk business over dinner until late at night."

"You didn't even have time for a phone call?" Mandy didn't want to start another argument, but she couldn't help expressing her hurt.

"I wasn't sure you wanted to hear from me."

"Oh, Connor, you should have known better than that. I missed you terribly!"

"Not even half as much as I missed you, sweetheart. Will you have dinner with me tomorrow night?"

"Anything you want," she said joyously.

"I'll remind you of that," he answered in a throaty voice.

* * *

Mandy was waiting impatiently for Connor the following night. As soon as she opened the door, they went into each other's arms. Several minutes were spent kissing hungrily and murmuring little endearments and words of remorse over the argument.

Their hands moved restlessly over each other, as though they needed to refresh their memories, although nothing could ever erase them.

Finally Connor drew back, reluctantly. "At this rate we'll never make it to dinner."

"I can think of things I'd rather do," she murmured.

"So can I, angel, but I have a special evening planned. Trust me, it will be worth the wait—besides fulfilling one of my fantasies."

She was filled with curiosity, but he refused to answer any of her questions as he led her to his car.

Mandy felt slightly let down when Connor drove up to the entrance of his building. Fond as she was of Dee Dee, she'd looked forward to this night alone with Connor. It was a touchy subject, however, since his daughter had been the source of their quarrel. Mandy didn't let her disappointment show when he led her to the elevator.

Soft music was playing in the apartment, and a bottle of white wine was chilling in a silver ice bucket on the cocktail table in the living room. It was a glamorous setting, with the lights of the city forming a backdrop to the softly lit room.

"This looks like the seduction scene in a French movie." Mandy laughed. "You didn't have to go to all this trouble. I'm in a very cooperative mood."

"That's what I was counting on." He gave her a mischievous grin.

"I hope you'll practice restraint in front of your daughter. Where is Dee Dee? I want to say hello to her before we leave."

"She's spending the night at her grandmother's. I thought we'd have dinner here tonight."

"Pancakes?" Mandy teased. "Or do you expect me to cook dinner? Not that I'd mind."

"Would I ask you to do that? My mother sent her cook over. You won't have to lift a finger."

Mandy suddenly realized what Connor had planned. Dee Dee would be gone for the entire night. They had the apartment to themselves. She put her arms around his waist and they exchanged a meaningful glance.

As his head descended toward hers, an older woman in a neat uniform entered the room, carrying a plate of hors d'oeuvres.

"I made your favorite crab puffs, Mr. Connor," she said.

"Thank you, Kate, they look delicious." After she went back to the kitchen, he remarked wryly, "No plan is perfect."

"This one is. I love being here with you." She could pretend they were married. Then they'd spend every night like this—but of course Mandy didn't say that.

"Anywhere you are is where I want to be." Picking up the plate he offered it to her. "Have a crab puff, before I start something I can't finish. At least, not right now," he added in a voice like plush velvet.

Anticipation of the night ahead lent an extra fillip of excitement to the evening. The delicious dinner was incidental to their pure joy at being together again.

While Kate served dinner unobtrusively, they talked about what had gone on during the week. Mandy discussed a collections problem she was having, and Connor told her about the deal he'd been working on. The only thing they didn't talk about was Dee Dee, which wasn't normal. Always before, they'd laughed over the latest fad she was into, or Connor had asked for advice on how to handle some problem, usually a minor one.

Mandy knew they had to discuss their quarrel before it became an awkward barrier between them. Dee Dee was too much a part of both their lives to pretend she didn't exist.

"About the argument we had," Mandy began hesitantly.

"You were right and I was wrong," he conceded promptly.

"It isn't a question of who was right. The very anonymity of the Internet makes adolescents vulnerable. I was worried about Dee Dee's safety. I still am."

"Don't be. I had her disconnected, as you suggested—or should I say demanded?" He grinned.

"I'm really relieved. Did it cause a problem between you?"

"No, I told her that on further reflection, I didn't think her punishment had been severe enough. In addition to being grounded for two weeks, I gave her the choice between giving up her trip to New York over the holidays or going off-line. That way it didn't look as if I'd lost faith in her."

"She chose to be disconnected?"

"Fortunately for me." Connor laughed. "I'd really have been stymied if she'd chosen to give up the trip."

"I think you made a pretty safe bet. She's really looking forward to going to New York."

"I am, too. We don't get to spend enough family time together. I'm going to enjoy taking her skating in Rockefeller Center and to matinees and museums—although I might have to drag her to those." He chuckled.

"Maybe not. Dee Dee has a lively interest in everything."

Connor reached over and squeezed Mandy's hand. "I wish you were coming along."

"You'll be too busy to even miss me," she answered brightly.

"That day will never come."

Mandy was careful to mask her melancholy, but the thought of Connor spending the holidays with his wife was painful. His *ex*-wife, she reminded herself, trying to believe the title would remain permanent.

They had coffee in the living room while Kate cleaned up the kitchen, and Mandy's mood gradually dissipated, as it always did when she was with Connor. It was unthinkable to imagine they wouldn't always be together. His behavior certainly indicated they would.

When Kate finished clearing the table and turned off the lights in the dining room, he gave Mandy a sultry smile. "The first act is over and the second is about to begin."

"How many acts are there in this play?" she murmured.

"As many as you like, sweetheart. I expect it to last all night."

The cook appeared briefly in the doorway, wearing her coat. "I'm all finished, Mr. Connor. I put the leftovers in the refrigerator. There's enough for you and the child tomorrow night."

"That was very thoughtful of you, Kate. I'm sure Dee Dee will enjoy it as much as we did."

"Yes, everything was delicious," Mandy agreed.

After the woman had said good-night and left, Connor and Mandy gazed into each other's eyes.

"I don't think I could have waited much longer," he said. "Is there any law that says we can't go to bed at nine o'clock?"

"None that I can think of."

"Good." He held out his hand to her. They walked up the stairs together, feeling the same thrill of anticipation.

The lamps weren't lit in Connor's bedroom, but the drapes were open and moonlight bathed the room in a silvery glow. He took her in his arms and kissed her with slow deliberation. Desire spread through Mandy like a flowering vine, reaching full blossom in her taut breasts and aching loins.

"I've dreamed about making love to you in my bed," he said huskily. "I can't believe it's really going to happen."

"I can't, either." She unbuttoned the middle buttons of his shirt and slipped her hands inside to caress his chest. "I need to touch you to make sure this isn't *my* dream."

"I always need to touch you."

After shrugging off his jacket and removing his tie, he unzipped her dress and gently urged it off her shoulders. It slid to the floor in a soft pool of silk, and Mandy stepped out of it. Heat throbbed in her veins as he unhooked her bra, leaving her clad only in sheer-to-the-waist panty hose. Connor's breathing quickened. In the muted light she appeared to be completely nude.

"You don't know how exquisite you look with moonbeams caught in your hair and stars in your eyes."

"You put them there," she whispered. "Only you could."

"Ah, darling, I love you so."

He stroked her tantalizingly, with little feathery touches that left her yearning for more. She reached for his belt with trembling fingers. Connor helped her, and in seconds he was splendidly naked. She ran her hands over the triangle of his torso, then clasped his lean hips and urged them toward her own. The heated contact told her what she'd already seen, that his passion equaled hers.

They clung together for a rapturous moment before he swung her into his arms and carried her to the bed. Her panty hose were stripped off in seconds, and then they experienced the ecstasy of their bare bodies touching at every point.

Mandy moved erotically against him, enhancing the sensation until Connor cried out hoarsely. He entered her swiftly, sealing their union and plunging deeply. They moved together with the certain knowledge of how to please. She called out his name over and over again, and he answered the way he knew she wanted.

They expressed the ultimate love between a man and a woman, and when their bodies were sated, they demonstrated it in a different way, with gentle kisses and tender, murmured words.

Mandy gazed up at him and stroked his cheek. "I was so miserable when I thought we might never be together again like this."

"You couldn't really have believed that." He held her closer. "Every couple argues sooner or later. We were just lucky it didn't happen sooner."

"I don't see anything lucky about it."

"Look at the fun we had making up." He grinned.

"I suppose you're right, but there are better ways to keep excitement in our relationship."

"Are you going to teach me a few things?" he teased. "You're the love guru."

"With only one disciple." He kissed the top of her head. "You're enough woman for any man, sweetheart."

"I hope so," she said wistfully.

"If you don't know, then I must be doing something wrong." He raised up on one elbow to look at her. "You don't still have any doubts about me, do you?"

She mustered a quick smile. "No, I just like to hear you say it."

Connor relaxed and scissored one leg over hers. "I'll say it more often then. I want to make you so happy you'll never leave me."

"I can't imagine anything that would make me even consider it."

After a companionable few minutes of silence he said, "It's going to be so fantastic to wake up next to you tomorrow morning."

"It won't be a new experience," she said mischievously.

"It will be to have you here in my own bed. I wish we could be together like this every night."

Mandy's heart started to beat rapidly. "I do, too, but we'd be setting a bad example for Dee Dee." Somehow she managed to keep her voice casual as she waited breathlessly for him to offer an alternative.

After a still moment, Connor said, "Yes, I guess living together is out."

It was difficult to hide her wrenching disappointment. Mandy needed some time alone. "I think I'll take a shower."

"I have a better idea. I'll turn on the Jacuzzi. I've always wanted to share it with somebody."

"I thought you'd been there, done that," she remarked in a brittle voice.

"You're forgetting that my daughter lives here, too." Connor got out of his side of the bed. "Start the water running. I'll be right back."

He returned with a cold bottle of champagne and two glasses.

"You don't have to ply me with champagne." Mandy smiled at him from the tub. "You've already had your way with me."

"I'm not that easily satisfied." He joined her in the tub and wound his legs around her waist.

They kissed, playfully at first. He nibbled on her ear, then explored its inner contours with the tip of his tongue. When his hand curved around her breast and he rotated his thumb over the taut nipple, she pulled his head down for a deep, urgent kiss.

It was an incredible experience. Connor's intimate caresses and the churning water ignited Mandy's passion. She felt as if he were not only inside of her, but all around her. The waves they generated were symbolic of the inner turbulence that surged to a crescendo.

When it was over, they remained clasped in each other's arms. Connor finally opened his eyes and smiled tenderly at her.

"I think that deserves some champagne, don't you?"

"Plus confetti and a brass marching band," she agreed, kissing the hollow in his throat.

"Forget the band." He chuckled, reaching for the bottle. "I want you all to myself."

Mandy was so idyllically happy that she refused to worry about Christmas, which was approaching rapidly. Connor loved her—there was no doubt about that. Their brief separation had brought them even closer together.

She hung on to that belief when Dee Dee called, as she did frequently. The young girl was bubbling over with excitement about her upcoming trip.

"It's gonna be so cool! Mom is having a party for us, and Dad's gonna take us to that new musical on Broadway that nobody can get tickets to."

"It's nice that you'll get to see so much of your mother," Mandy remarked neutrally.

"Yeah, she's a blast. You can't help having a good time with her. Will you go shopping with me on Saturday, Mandy? I need some things for my trip."

"You can't need very much. Wouldn't you rather wait and go shopping with your mother?"

"No, I can't always count on her. Sometimes she gets her dates mixed up and she cancels out on me. I don't really mind, 'cause I know how she is, but I really want to check out the sweaters at Saks. Say you'll go with me," Dee Dee coaxed.

Sure, good old dependable Mandy. But she didn't really mind. A day with Dee Dee was always enjoyable or—as she would say—a blast.

On the night before he left for New York, Connor came over with an armload of packages to put under Mandy's tree.

"So many!" she exclaimed. "I didn't give you that much."

"You've made me happier than I ever hoped to be," he said tenderly. "That's a priceless gift."

They were both unhappy about even a brief separation. "I wish I didn't have to leave you." He sighed.

"You'll be back before you know it."

"I suppose so. What are your plans for the holidays?"

"I'm invited to quite a few parties, and I'm giving one of my own on Christmas Eve." She tried to sound excited about it, so he wouldn't feel guilty over leaving her.

After a passionate evening and a reluctant parting, Mandy's confidence was restored. Nobody could take Connor away from her.

Mandy's Christmas Eve party was a great success. The apartment was very festive, with mistletoe over a doorway, carols playing on the stereo and a tree with colorful ornaments and Christmas lights. Connor's elegantly wrapped presents under the tree attracted a lot of attention.

"Why don't you open them so we can all see what he gave you?" Alexandra urged. "If the packages are that gorgeous, I can't wait to see what's inside."

"I don't think I want Jenny to find out," Bob, one of the guests said with a laugh. "She'll throw rocks at my gift after seeing what Mandy got."

"I don't expect you to compete with a millionaire," his wife, Jenny, told him. "Just as long as you picked up on my hint about those gold earrings at Shreve's."

"Go ahead, open them, Mandy," several of the other guests coaxed.

"You're not supposed to open your presents until Christmas morning," she said.

Alexandra looked at her watch. "It's almost midnight. By the time we all get some more eggnog, it will be Christmas."

Mandy let herself be convinced. Alexandra sat on the floor next to her and handed over each gift for her to open. While the women exclaimed over the exquisite lingerie, expensive perfume and other extravagant things, the men groaned at the lavish display. Finally only one package remained, the largest of the lot.

Alexandra shook it tentatively. "I saved the biggest one for last. It must be something special, but it's awfully light. I can't imagine what it could be."

"Probably a ticket to fly around the world on the Concorde," her date, Norman, remarked. "It's the only thing he hasn't given her."

Mandy was equally mystified when she lifted the lid and began to remove layers and layers of tissue paper. Near the bottom was a small square box wrapped in silver paper and tied with a satin bow. Her heart started to beat rapidly when she tore away the paper and found a dark blue velvet jeweler's box.

"If you think we were in trouble before, guys, wait until she opens that box." Norman chuckled.

"We'd better leave now, while our wives are still talking to us," Bob joked.

Mandy barely heard them. Her fingers were trembling as she opened the box. While everyone crowded around to exclaim in admiration, her mouth drooped.

Pillowed on a bed of white satin was a sapphire pendant surrounded by a circle of large, sparkling diamonds. Only a woman who was hoping for an engagement ring could be disappointed. It was a magnificent piece, impressive yet tasteful.

After a bleak moment, Mandy managed to swallow her disappointment and count her blessings. Connor had put a lot of thought into her gifts. They were evidence of his love. Wasn't that what she really wanted?

The party lasted until the early hours, so Mandy slept late the next morning. She longed to talk to Connor, but by the time she phoned his hotel, he and Dee Dee were gone. Naturally they'd be out, she told herself. It was three hours later in New York. Still, why didn't he need to talk to *her?* a small voice asked. But Mandy refused to listen. Connor must have left early, and he hadn't wanted to wake her. He'd known she was having a Christmas Eve party and would get to bed late.

Mandy was invited to spend Christmas at Ralph and Kim's. A steady stream of people dropped by all day, and many stayed for a buffet dinner. Mandy smiled and pretended she was having a good time, but she missed Connor terribly. Just hearing his voice would have helped.

There were messages on her answering machine when she got home, and one of them was from Connor.

"Sorry I didn't catch you at home, darling. This time difference is the pits! I wanted to wish you a Merry Christmas and tell you how much I miss you. I hope you're having a happy holiday, my love. I'll try to get you tomorrow."

Mandy played the message over and over, then went to sleep with a smile on her face.

Connor phoned the next morning at eight-thirty. "I hope I didn't wake you. I was afraid if I waited any longer, you might go out again."

"It's all right." She settled more comfortably against the pillows. "I felt awful about missing your call. I went to Ralph and Kim's for Christmas. They had a big crowd over."

"It sounds like fun. How was your party?"

"Just great! I opened your gifts, and everybody thought they were fantastic, especially the pendant. It's just gorgeous, Connor!"

"I'm glad you liked it."

Mandy suddenly realized he was being very reserved. At first she thought it was because there were people around. She could hear voices and laughter in the background. Connor couldn't say the things he wanted to, she assured herself—that he loved her, and wished they could be together. She soon discovered it wasn't other people who were inhibiting him, it was one special person.

A woman's voice called out to him. "Will you help the bartender pour champagne, Connor darling? He's unbearably slow, and everybody is absolutely parched."

In case Mandy had any doubt that the woman was Lorna, Dee Dee grabbed the phone. "Hi, Mandy. We're having the coolest time ever! Mom had a Christmas party yesterday, and today we're at a champagne brunch she's giving in honor of Boxing Day. It's an English holiday, but she said there's no law that says we can't celebrate it in America. Dad told her she hasn't changed since the day he first met her.''

Connor wrenched the phone away from his daughter, ignoring her indignant cries that she wasn't finished yet. ''I'm sorry about that. Dee Dee will talk your ear off if you let her.''

''I found it very interesting,'' Mandy remarked evenly. ''It sounds as if you're both having a wonderful time.''

Connor hesitated. ''I should have waited until I got back to the hotel to call you. It's difficult to talk with everybody around.''

''I won't keep you, then. You're missing your party.''

''I don't give a damn about the party!'' he said with pent-up irritation. ''I wish I was back in San Francisco.''

Did he expect her to believe that? Mandy wondered indignantly. ''You will be, soon,'' she answered, as lightly as possible under the circumstances. ''Time flies when you're having fun.''

''Mandy, we have to talk. I—'' He stopped abruptly as Lorna apparently approached.

''Are you still on the phone, darling? You're not being a very gracious host.''

Mandy was suddenly freezing cold under the warm blanket. Her fears were valid. Connor and his wife had found each other again.

''I'll phone you later,'' he said. ''It's impossible to talk here. Will you be home this evening?''

''I—I'm not sure.'' She needed time to pull herself together before she spoke to him again.

''Well, I'll catch up with you sooner or later.''

After they said goodbye, Mandy remained in bed, staring at the sapphire pendant on the nightstand next to her. She'd thought it was a token of Connor's love. Maybe he'd thought the same thing when he picked it out, but that had been before he saw Lorna again.

Mandy dragged herself out of bed, wondering how long it would take for the pain to go away. Or if it ever would.

Connor was the love of her life. What was she going to do without him?

Connor phoned Mandy at the office the next day, but she was out doing an errand. She didn't return his call.

He phoned again when Alexandra was sitting at the next desk, so she couldn't speak freely. Although what was there to say? Connor was alone this time and under no restrictions. His voice was a lot warmer than it had been when he called from Lorna's.

"Thank God I finally have a chance to talk to you, sweetheart. I couldn't say any of the things I wanted to."

"I suppose it would have been rather awkward," Mandy answered, without inflection.

After a slight pause he said, "At least Dee Dee is having a great time. That was the general idea."

"Yes, she seems thrilled to be spending so much time with her mother. I'm happy for her." It was the one thing Mandy could be sincere about.

"They've been having a ball together. Probably because they're the same age emotionally," Connor said dryly.

"Some people never change. I guess that's part of their charm."

"If you say so."

Mandy didn't want to talk about Lorna anymore, so she said, "New York must be beautiful at this time of year, with snow on the ground and all the holiday decorations."

"What's wrong, Mandy?" he asked slowly. "We're talking like two strangers on an airplane. Are you angry because I didn't wake you to say Merry Christmas? I thought I was being considerate."

"I'm not angry," she said quickly, then couldn't help adding, "but I would rather have talked to you than gotten a few more hours of sleep."

"That's sweet, darling. I guess I just wasn't thinking straight."

Mandy could guess why, and the knowledge made her desolate. "I have to go, Connor," she said abruptly. "Some clients just walked in."

"It's always something, isn't it?" He sighed. "Okay, honey, I'll let you go."

Mandy hung up before he could say anything else.

It was a bad week. Connor called a couple of times more, but they couldn't establish their former rapport. Mandy thought she couldn't get any more miserable, but that was before he returned.

Dee Dee phoned her even before Connor did. She couldn't wait to tell Mandy how great New York had been, and to describe all the things she'd done. And then she dropped her bombshell.

"Remember how I said you and Dad should get married, but you said he wasn't your type? Well, it's a good thing, because I think he and Mom might get back together again. They spent lots of time talking, and she even said maybe they should give it another try."

Mandy forced her voice to remain steady. "That sounds promising. I'm happy for all three of you."

"It isn't a done deal yet. I don't know where we'd live. Dad doesn't want to leave San Francisco, and Mom wouldn't move out here."

"Things can be worked out if two people love each other," Mandy said stoically.

"I guess so, but I don't want to leave here, either." Dee Dee abruptly lost interest. "Wait till I tell you what I got at a street fair in Greenwich Village."

Mandy was devastated after talking to Dee Dee. Under different circumstances, she would have fought for the man she loved, but she was powerless against an obsession that had lasted this long. Connor had never stopped loving Lorna.

There was another reason for stepping aside. Dee Dee. The young girl was so excited about being with her mother again. How could Mandy deny her a normal family life with two parents who cared for each other?

By the time Connor got in touch with her, Mandy had decided to end their relationship with as little trauma as possible, no confrontation, no recriminations. Connor was a decent man. She didn't doubt that he still loved her—in a special kind of way. He would apologize and offer excuses, which would be painful for both of them. The kindest thing all around would be to pretend that things were moving too fast between them and they needed a cooling-off period.

Connor didn't make it easy for her.

"What do you mean, you can't see me tonight?" he demanded when he phoned to make a date. "I've been gone for ten days!"

"I guess I forgot to write down exactly when you were coming home."

"You had to make a note in order to remember? That's very flattering," he said sarcastically.

"You weren't exactly sitting around a hotel room thinking about *me*," she snapped, unable to help herself.

"Oh, so that's what this is all about. You think I was having such a ball that I didn't have time to call you."

"Well, you must admit you didn't make the telephone company rich." This was the sort of scene Mandy had wanted to avoid, but Connor was pushing her to the limit.

"Aren't you being a little childish?" he asked coldly.

"You're the one who's sulking because I didn't spend my nights sitting by the fire, waiting breathlessly for your return."

"You didn't even remember when that was. Perhaps you no longer have time for me in your busy schedule."

He'd given her the perfect opening. All she had to do was give her little speech about breathing room. She hesitated, looking for the right words.

But Connor didn't wait. "If you have to think about it, I get the picture. So long, Mandy. Call me if you have some free time in six months or so."

* * *

Mandy tried to keep up appearances, but Alexandra could tell something was wrong. She finally coaxed the story out of her.

"That's really heavy, although not conclusive." Alexandra was concerned, but she tried to put the best spin on the situation. "Did you ever consider that Dee Dee might have gotten the wrong impression? Connor and Lorna would naturally have a lot to talk about. After all, they have a daughter in common. But that doesn't necessarily mean they want to try again."

"What's the use in kidding myself? All the evidence is there. It isn't just that he practically forgot I existed once he saw Lorna again. Connor moved right back into her life, playing host at her party, telling her she hasn't changed in all these years. She's still the girl he fell in love with—and never got over."

"Then why did he want to see you when he got back?"

"Connor would never end our relationship by just breaking off all contact. He isn't that kind of man."

Alexandra tried to sound positive. It was all she could do for her friend. "You could be overreacting. I've seen you and Connor together. He's crazy about you. He'll probably phone tomorrow, wanting to make up, and you'll have put yourself through all this for nothing."

But Connor didn't phone, not the next day or the days that followed. Mandy avoided mentioning his name, but she couldn't hide her misery. It colored her whole life. All she did was go to work and come home again, too lethargic to want to see anyone.

By the end of the week, Alexandra decided something had to be done to lighten Mandy's mood. A slight case of the sniffles gave her an idea. After getting her date's cooperation, she pretended to feel much sicker than she actually was.

"I don't know how I can go to the ballet tonight," she told Mandy. "I hate to disappoint Norman after he paid such a fortune for the tickets, but I feel really rotten."

"You shouldn't have come in today," Mandy scolded. "You ought to be home in bed."

"That's where I'd like to be, but I can't do that to Norman."

"He can get somebody else to go with him. This performance has been sold out for weeks. A lot of people would jump at the chance."

"Of course! Why didn't I think of it? You can take my place."

Mandy gave her a startled look. "I didn't mean me."

"Why not? You and Norman are good friends, and at least I know you won't try to take him away from me." Alexandra smiled.

Mandy tried to get out of it, but Alexandra was adamant. If Mandy wouldn't go, she'd have to go herself. Finally Mandy gave in, out of concern for her friend.

Although she hadn't wanted to go, Mandy's spirits lifted as she got dressed that evening. Norman was always fun to be with, and she desperately needed to laugh.

The red silk dress she chose was one of her favorites, but it emphasized her pallor. After looking critically at herself, Mandy applied more makeup than she usually wore. Blush to erase her wan appearance, blue eye shadow and mascara to detract from the circles under her eyes.

Norman was very complimentary. "Why didn't I ever notice you were this gorgeous? Alexandra must have been crazy to fix us up."

"She knew she could trust both of us." Mandy smiled.

"That's the curse of being an honorable man," he joked. "You can't hit on beautiful women."

"You already have the best." Mandy started back to the bedroom. "I'll get my coat and be right with you."

The doorbell rang as she went to the closet. "Will you answer the door for me?" she called.

Connor's smile faded and his expression turned grim when he saw Norman. Before either man could say anything, Mandy appeared in the doorway.

"Who is it? I'm not expecting—" She stopped abruptly.

Connor looked her over, from her glamorous makeup to her festive outfit. "It seems I've come at an inopportune moment."

"I... We're going to the ballet." Mandy stared at him hungrily. It had been so long. She was too dazed to explain the situation, or even to introduce the two men.

"I see. Well, at least now I know why you've been unavailable," he remarked coldly.

"No, you don't understand...." she began.

"I'll admit I didn't before," he drawled. "Don't let me keep you from the ballet."

"It can wait. We have to talk."

"That's what I thought, but I was mistaken. What I came here to say isn't important, anyway. I foolishly thought I owed you an apology, but it's obvious that you didn't give our little argument a second thought."

"Can I say something?" Norman had been shifting uncomfortably. "This isn't what it looks like. Mandy and I are just—"

Connor cut him off. "You don't owe me an explanation." His expressionless gaze swung back to her. "It might have been nice if you'd simply told me you didn't want to see me again instead of precipitating an argument. It would have saved me from feeling guilty over nothing." Without waiting for a reply, he turned and left.

"I'm sorry." Norman broke the small silence that fell when he and Mandy were alone. "I tried to tell him we were just friends."

"It isn't your fault," she said dully. "He didn't want to listen."

"I could call him tomorrow, after he's cooled off."

Mandy squared her shoulders, unable to bear the pity on Norman's face. "Don't worry about it. Connor has a quick temper, but he always gets over it."

"If you say so." Norman clearly had his doubts.

Mandy spent a sleepless night deciding what to say to Connor. Because she had to make him listen to her explanation. It was unthinkable to allow him to believe she'd been dating behind his back.

She waited to call him at his office the next morning, so there'd be no chance of Dee Dee being around.

Connor's curtness became more pronounced when he heard her voice. "I'm very busy, Mandy. Whatever it is, will you please make it brief?"

"I just wanted to correct the impression you got last night. I didn't have a date with Norman."

"We must have a different definition of the word," he commented sarcastically.

"Okay, I guess, strictly speaking, it was a date, but not the way you think. Norman doesn't mean anything to me."

"I'm beginning to wonder if any man does. You can be really convincing, though, I'll give you that. I honestly thought we had something together."

"That's a rather vague description, but it pretty much sums up our relationship," she said bitterly.

"Whose fault is that?" he demanded. "You're the one who didn't want a commitment."

Mandy gasped at the injustice of such an accusation. "That's a convenient excuse for your own indifference. I couldn't have meant very much to you if you forgot about me for ten days."

"When are you going to get over the fact that I didn't phone often enough?" he asked impatiently. "It's no excuse for lying to me."

"I've never lied to you!"

"I suppose that's true." Connor's anger was replaced by cool indifference. "You told me you were too busy to see me. I was just too stupid to realize why."

"Norman wasn't the reason," she protested.

"I'm sure there were others, but I'd prefer not to hear about them. You're free to date whomever you please. There are a lot of men out there. Maybe you'll find what you're looking for. If you'll excuse me now, I have to get back to work."

Mandy couldn't believe it had ended like this, not with such bitterness and distrust. Surely Connor didn't want that, either. He would call, and they'd patch things up so they could at least part friends.

But time passed and Connor didn't phone. One day Mandy discovered why. She saw his picture in the newspaper with one of his generic blondes clinging to his arm at a museum opening. Connor's attention span had run its course. He was looking for new challenges.

Chapter Eleven

Alexandra tried to console Mandy. "Look on the bright side. Connor got over his obsession with Lorna. She was more of a threat than his string of dumb blondes."

"What difference does it make now?" Mandy asked bleakly. "Everything is over between us."

"I can't believe that. You know how stubborn men are when their pride is involved. Now that he's had time to cool off, why don't you call him again and tell him how you happened to go out with Norman?"

"It wouldn't do any good and it would be embarrassing for both of us. I'm beginning to think Connor used Norman as an excuse to break up with me. He wouldn't let either of us explain."

"Because he was angry at the time. If Connor was getting itchy feet, he wouldn't have given you all those gorgeous Christmas gifts."

"He's a very generous man and he has plenty of money." Mandy's mouth twisted wryly. "Maybe they were going-away presents—something to remember him by."

"Damn decent of him!" Alexandra's eyes sparkled angrily. "I've been trying to give him the benefit of a doubt, but if you want my real opinion, I don't think he's worth it. No man is if he makes you this miserable. There are plenty of guys out there who would turn cartwheels to make you happy. Forget about Connor. He doesn't deserve you."

Mandy tried to take Alexandra's advice, but it was impossible. Everything reminded her of him, including his daughter. Dee Dee phoned regularly, unconsciously rubbing salt in the wound.

"Why don't I ever see you anymore?" she complained. "You don't come over, and we haven't gone shopping in ages."

"I'm sorry, honey, I guess I've been busy," Mandy said.

"On the weekends, too? How about this Sunday? We'll go sailing or something, and then get Dad to take us someplace fab for dinner."

"It sounds great, but I'm tied up this weekend."

"You're no fun at all anymore," Dee Dee grumbled. "Okay, then, how about next Sunday?"

It took all of Mandy's ingenuity to get out of making a date. Connor must not have told his daughter they weren't seeing each other any longer, but Dee Dee should start getting a clue as time went on. It couldn't be soon enough for Mandy.

As the days turned into weeks, Mandy tried to put her life back together. She worked long hours at the office and went out almost every night. Once it became known that she was back in circulation, she didn't lack for dates.

On the surface, Mandy had bounced back from her unhappy love affair. She never mentioned Connor, and if one of her friends did, she looked disinterested. It was too soon for her memories of Connor to fade, but they might have subsided to a dull ache if it hadn't been for the dreams that tormented her.

He came to her in the night and awakened her body as only he could. She whispered his name over and over while he caressed her sensuously during deep, drugging kisses that turned her liquid with desire. In the dreams, Connor told her he loved her as their passion flared and he urged her against his hardened loins.

Mandy would wake with a start, her body aching and unfulfilled. It took a moment to realize it had only been a dream. She would get out of bed and stare out at the darkness, unable to go back to sleep.

Mandy was so adept at hiding her feelings that Alexandra thought the circles under her eyes were caused by too much partying.

"I'm glad you took my advice about getting back into the swing of things, but maybe you're overdoing it." Alexandra stared at her critically. "You should stay home now and then and get a good night's sleep."

"That's boring," Mandy answered lightly. "I have better things to do."

"Who are you going out with tonight? Anybody I know?"

"I don't think so. His name is Stan Bigby. I met him at a party at the Melvilles. You weren't there that night."

"What's he like? Is he a keeper?"

Mandy shrugged. "None of them are, but what's the alternative?"

Alexandra slanted a worried glance at her. "You aren't still thinking about—" She paused, unwilling to mention Connor's name.

Mandy forced herself to do it. "About Connor? Heavens, no, he's history."

"I hope so." Alexandra continued to look at her soberly. "I'd hate to think you were still carrying a torch."

"Does it look like it? You just told me I'm dating too much."

"Maybe you are. I'd rather see you narrow the field down to someone you really cared about."

"Been there, done that." Mandy meant to sound ironic. When Alexandra looked concerned, she added hastily, "What I meant was, after coming off a heavy-duty affair, I prefer to play the field for a while. It's a nice change to go out with lots of different men, more interesting. You don't run out of things to talk about."

"What does Stan do?"

"He's a stockbroker. Maybe I'll learn how to manage my portfolio—if I ever have one."

"Sounds like a fun evening," Alexandra commented dryly. "Where is he taking you?"

"We're going to Plaza One. It's that new place that just opened downtown. Very trendy."

"Yes, I heard you have to make reservations weeks in advance. And even then they keep you waiting for a table. Norman goes ballistic when that happens."

"I'll let you know if it's worth it or not."

The restaurant was jammed when Mandy and Stan got there later that evening. Even the cocktail lounge was crowded. All the tables in the bar area were taken, and people were standing in the foyer, waiting for their names to be called.

"What a mob scene!" Stan exclaimed. "You'd think it was the only restaurant in town."

"You know how it is when a place first opens," Mandy said. "Everybody wants to say they've been there."

"True. A month from now they'll be happy to honor a reservation. The restaurant business is a high-stakes gamble. You'd be amazed at the percentage that close during the first year. I have the figures in the office. It's as risky as IPO's in the stock market. That stands for initial public offerings."

"How interesting," Mandy murmured. "Perhaps you'd better go to the desk and tell the maître d' we're here."

"Good thinking, and then I'll fight my way to the bar and get us a drink. We'll never find a waiter to take our order."

When she was alone, Mandy sighed. Stan wasn't exactly stimulating company. He'd seemed like more fun at the party where they met. She glanced with more interest at the crowd of people around her, listening to snatches of conversation and looking at the women's outfits.

As she idly scanned the room, her heart caught in her throat. Connor was standing not far away, staring intently at her. He was with a redhead for a change, but she was as glamorous as all of his other girlfriends—the same sexy figure, the same model-perfect features. They were chatting with a group of people. After saying a few words to his date, Connor started toward Mandy.

The unexpected sight of him was unnerving. Why did he have to look as handsome and virile as she remembered? Because she did remember everything about him—the high cheekbones that gave his face a patrician look, the changeable color of his gray eyes. They always darkened with passion. Her fingernails bit into her damp palms as he approached.

"It's nice to see you again." He glanced around. "Surely you're not alone?"

"No, my date went to try and get us a drink. It's terribly crowded, isn't it?"

"Yes," he answered absently. His gaze was fixed on her face.

"Stan and I were discussing how these trendy restaurants don't always survive." Mandy made nervous small talk because Connor's close scrutiny was unsettling.

"You've lost weight," he said abruptly. "Are you all right?"

Did he think she was pining away after him? She raised her chin. "I've never been better."

"You have dark shadows under your eyes." He reached up, as if to touch her face, then dropped his hand to his side.

"Too many late nights," she said lightly. "You're used to going without sleep, but I don't have your stamina."

"I can remember when you stayed up all night and still looked glowing in the morning," he said softly.

Mandy glanced away. Why was he tormenting her with memories that couldn't mean anything to him? She'd never known Connor to be vindictive. Was avenging his hurt pride that important to him?

"I'm sorry," he drawled when she didn't answer. "Perhaps you'd prefer to forget about those nights."

"I try not to dwell on the past," she said in a low voice.

"That's commendable. There's nothing more pathetic than trying to hang on to something that's over."

"Hadn't you better get back to your date?" Mandy asked pointedly.

"She's being taken care of. I don't like to leave you here all alone."

"Stan will be back any minute. Besides, I don't mind being alone."

"It must be a novelty for you," he remarked ironically. "So many men, so little time. Does Stan know you're not interested in long relationships?"

"You can ask him yourself. Here he comes now."

Stan was weaving his way through the crowd, trying not to spill the two drinks he was carrying.

"I deserve a combat badge for getting these." He handed Mandy one of the glasses. "You wouldn't believe the crush at the bar."

"I hope you're properly impressed," Connor told her.

Stan suddenly realized that Connor wasn't merely a stranger standing next to her. "Did you pick up some other guy because you thought I wasn't coming back?" He laughed.

"It's been known to happen." Connor's smile was sardonic. "You can't take your eyes off her for a minute."

Stan was looking at him curiously. "Don't I know you? You look familiar."

"We may have met," Connor said politely. "The name is Connor Winfield."

"Of course!" Stan put out his hand and supplied his own name. "I saw your picture in the business section. You just put through that merger between Tritex and Solo-Systems. Some of my customers think I'm a genius because I touted them onto Tritex a few months ago. I'm a stockbroker."

"Your clients were very fortunate to own shares before the merger."

"I like to think they benefited from my good advice." Stan grinned. "At least that's what I tell them."

"Yes, well, that's what a stockbroker is for," Connor said vaguely.

"What I'd really like to do is branch out into your field, where the serious money is. You might be interested in an analysis our office just did of undervalued companies. Maybe we can have lunch and discuss a possible deal."

"We have a department that looks into those things, but you're welcome to talk to them." Connor glanced at Mandy with a hint of amusement.

Her cheeks flushed with embarrassment. She knew what he was thinking. How could she date such a nerd? Stan didn't even realize he'd gotten a polite brush-off. He was preparing to pursue the subject when, fortunately, Connor's date came over to join them.

Linking her arm with his, the redhead pouted. "I thought you'd deserted me."

"No man would be foolish enough to do that." He gave her a sultry look before introducing the woman as Marilee Conroy.

"We've been standing around for ages," she complained, still simmering over his neglect. "Why don't we go somewhere else?"

He shrugged. "Everyplace is going to be crowded at this hour."

"Not like this," Mandy said, hoping he'd be persuaded to leave.

"Why don't the four of us look for another restaurant?" Stan suggested.

"I'm sure our table will be ready soon," Mandy said swiftly. "And they're here with other people."

"Those were simply acquaintances we happened to run across." Connor was secretly amused at her attempt to get rid of him. "Marilee and I are just a twosome."

"Well, great!" Stan said. "Why don't you join Mandy and me? One table will be easier to get than two. I'll go talk to the maître d'." He hurried off before Mandy could stop him.

Marilee wasn't any more pleased than Mandy at this turn of events. "Have you and Connor known each other long?" she asked coolly.

"Not really." Mandy turned to him. "Stan meant well, but if you'd rather go somewhere else, we'll understand."

"I wouldn't think of turning down his generous offer. There aren't many men who would let strangers intrude on a cozy little tête-à-tête. He's a very remarkable man."

Mandy's eyes sparkled angrily, but she matched Connor's smooth tone. "Stan may be lacking in some of the social graces, but he has other things to recommend him." She noted with satisfaction that her barb hit home.

Connor's jaw set grimly, but before he could answer, Stan reappeared. "Great news! A table for four just opened up, and we've got it."

Stan arranged the seating so Connor was on his left and Mandy on his right, which put the two women next to each other.

"This isn't right," Marilee objected. "It's supposed to be boy-girl-boy-girl."

"I know how you gals like to talk." Stan chuckled. "This way you won't have to talk over us."

Mandy knew his real purpose was to pitch a deal to Connor, but there was nothing she could do about it without making a fuss. She clenched her teeth and hoped at least the service was good, so this nightmare would eventually end.

Stan did try to talk business, but Connor cut him off deftly. "Our two lovely guests aren't interested in mergers or takeovers. Mandy doesn't even approve of them." He looked at her across the table. "It was the source of our first disagreement."

"That was just a misunderstanding," she murmured.

"One of many," he remarked dryly.

"How did you two meet?" Stan asked.

"Mandy arranged a business trip for me. She's a travel agent," he explained to Marilee. "We got to be friends through my daughter. There was a mix-up in Tangier about some plane tickets, and Mandy straightened it out."

She couldn't help smiling. "Not exactly. Dee Dee got herself on the plane. I merely persuaded you not to lock her in her room until she was twenty-one."

"I don't know anyone who's ever been to Tangier," Stan commented. "What's it like?" he asked Connor.

"Very romantic. The sky is spangled with stars, and you can swim at midnight," Connor said softly.

Mandy opened her menu. "I think we'd better decide what we're going to order before the waiter gets here."

The conversation became general during dinner, but Connor found opportunities to remind Mandy—in a manner carefully veiled from the other two—of heated moments in their relationship. She either pretended not to remember or reacted indifferently, hoping Connor would be deceived. By the time dessert was served, she had a raging headache.

Connor paid the check over Stan's objections. "It's small thanks for such a delightful evening," Connor said smoothly.

"Then you have to let me buy you and Marilee an after-dinner drink," Stan said.

"No!" Mandy's voice was louder than she'd intended. When everyone but Connor looked at her in surprise, she added, "I mean, I have an early-morning appointment. I have to go home."

Stan tried to change her mind, but, surprisingly, Connor didn't. He'd gotten his revenge, she thought wearily.

As they stood outside the restaurant saying good-night, Connor drew her aside. "Take care of yourself," he said in a low voice.

"I'm fine," she answered curtly. His remorse was a little late.

"You could slow down a little. There's such a thing as having too much fun."

"That's rather amusing, coming from an inveterate playboy."

"I'm concerned about you, Mandy," he answered quietly.

She looked up at him, suspecting some hidden barb. But this was the old Connor, the caring man who'd shown her great tenderness. For one crazy moment, she wanted to put her arms around him and feel his mouth on hers once more, his hard body urgent, the way it used to be.

She managed to control her emotions when Marilee called sharply, "Your car is here, Connor."

His expression changed as he smiled at the redhead. "Be right with you. Goodbye, Mandy. Good seeing you again. Stan, it was an interesting evening."

Mandy didn't sleep all night, and she was violently ill the next morning. After crawling back into bed, she was disgusted with herself. It was ridiculous to let Connor upset her like this. They were bound to meet sooner or later—in fact, it could easily happen again. Was she going to turn into a basket case every time she saw him?

No way! The first time was bound to be the hardest, and he had deliberately tried to provoke her. The next time, she'd be better prepared. Connor was ancient history. She'd gotten her life together and it held limitless possibilities.

Although she covered the shadows under her eyes with makeup that morning, it wasn't enough. Alexandra saw through the thick layer of foundation.

"You look terrible," she exclaimed. "Don't you feel well?"

"I think I ate something that didn't agree with me," Mandy said.

"You went to that new restaurant last night, didn't you? Was the food lousy?"

"No, it was all right." Mandy didn't really remember what she'd eaten. "It was too crowded, though. If you want to try it, I'd wait till the novelty wears off."

When the phone rang, Alexandra said, "That might be the accountant about our taxes. He said he'd call this morning. You'd better listen in, too, so I don't have to repeat everything." She pushed the speaker button without picking up the receiver.

It wasn't the call she expected. "Hi, Alex, it's Dee Dee. Is Mandy around?"

Mandy shook her head and mouthed the words, "Tell her I'm not here."

"Gee, I'm sorry, Dee Dee," Alexandra said. "Mandy's at the bank. Can I take a message?"

"Yeah, tell her to call me. I've left messages on her machine at home, and she never calls me back."

"I've been having the same trouble," Alexandra lied tactfully. "She either needs a new tape or a new machine."

"Well, I wish she'd call me."

"Is anything wrong?"

"No, I just want to tell her about some stuff that happened at school. We used to talk all the time, but I can't get her on the phone anymore and she's always too busy to see me. Do you know if she's mad at me about something?"

"Oh, I'm sure she isn't. We've been awfully busy here at the office."

"Did she and my dad have a fight?" Dee Dee asked abruptly. "Mandy never comes over like she used to, and when I ask Dad about her, he kind of brushes me off. Is that what the trouble is?"

"I don't think there's any problem. Maybe they just decided not to see as much of each other."

"That doesn't mean she has to stop seeing *me*. I thought Mandy and I were friends." Dee Dee's voice was doleful.

Alexandra shot Mandy an indignant look. "I know she's fond of you, honey. Mandy's just been terribly rushed lately, as I told you. I'm sure you'll hear from her soon."

When she got off the phone, Alexandra let Mandy have it. "Aren't you ashamed of yourself? How can you treat the poor kid that way? The least you can do is talk to her."

"You're right." Mandy rested her head on her hand. "I feel terrible about it, but I had to cut all my ties to Connor."

"Isn't that a little drastic? I know the breakup was traumatic for you, but you're over it now. You have everything going for you, a full social life, a successful business. A lot of people envy you."

"If they only knew." Mandy's eyes were bleak. "Why can I convince everybody else that I'm happy, when I can't convince myself?"

"You seemed to have bounced back. I didn't realize," Alexandra said slowly.

"I didn't want you to. I thought I was making progress—until I saw him again." Mandy told Alexandra about her meeting with Connor the night before. "It was absolute torture! Stan latched on to him and wouldn't let go."

"Connor isn't the type who lets people impose on him."

"You've never met Stan! He's like a pit bull when he sets his sights on something. None of the rest of us wanted to have dinner together, but we couldn't do anything about it. It was so embarrassing. Connor kept looking at me as if to say, 'Where did you find this jerk?'"

"There are a lot more frogs than princes out there. You just have to persevere. Dump Stan and move on. Last night was an unfortunate incident, but you'll get over Connor. Just give yourself time. If you run into him again, it will be a lot easier."

Mandy had to believe that. She'd suffered a little set-back, but she would win the war. "I know you're right, but I don't feel up to talking to Dee Dee right now. If she calls again, stall her for a little while."

Mandy's heart almost stopped beating when she heard Connor's voice on her answering machine that evening. He'd only phoned to ask how she was feeling, since she hadn't looked well the night before. He sounded pleasant, nothing more, and he didn't ask her to return his call.

Connor left messages several times in the next couple of weeks, a few short, friendly words. There was nothing in his tone to indicate he felt any deeper emotion.

Even though she'd wanted them to part on friendly terms, she wished now that he'd leave her alone. Hearing his voice—or wondering if she'd hear it, which was almost as bad—kept her off base.

Mandy didn't think things could get any worse, but that was before she discovered the little joke fate had played on her.

In spite of her vow to think positively and believe sin-cerely in a bright future, she continued to sleep badly. And quite often she felt sick when morning came and it was time to face another day.

Mandy was annoyed at herself, thinking it was a sign of weakness. Until another explanation occurred to her. She might very well be pregnant!

A rapid calculation confirmed the fact. She'd missed her last period, but it hadn't seemed significant. Stress could take its toll on the body, and she'd certainly been under enough stress! That didn't explain her other symptoms though. What would she do if she was pregnant? Telling herself not to panic, she grabbed her purse and ran to the drugstore.

A half hour later, Mandy carefully read every word of the instructions on the home pregnancy kit. She reread them again after the result was positive, knowing it was a waste of time. She was going to have Connor's baby.

After the first panic died down, other emotions took its place. She put her hand gently on her still-flat stomach, feeling the ice around her heart start to melt. Part of Connor would always belong to her. Mandy sat on the bed for a long time, making plans. There was so much to do—but first she had to tell Alexandra.

Her friend and partner registered the same shock Mandy had felt when she first found out. Then Alexandra tried to reassure her.

"I'm sure Connor will stand by you. I mean, he'll pay for everything. At least you won't have to worry about money—whether you decide to have the baby or not."

Mandy gave her a surprised look. "I never considered *not* having it."

"Well, I just thought . . . it might be simpler."

"I want this baby desperately. It was conceived out of love, even if Connor's didn't last. That doesn't matter, though. Our child will never feel deprived. I can give it enough love for both of us."

"You'll have plenty of help from your friends," Alexandra assured her. "We'll all be there for you."

This was the hard part. "I know I can count on all of you, but this is something I have to do on my own. I'm going away," Mandy said quietly.

Alexandra stared at her blankly. "What do you mean? Where are you going?"

"Maybe to Washington State or Oregon. I've heard those are good places to bring up a child."

"Are you out of your mind? Why would you want to move away from all your friends? And how about Connor? You're letting him off too easily. This baby is his responsibility, too."

"I don't want our child to be a liability to anyone."

"You're in an emotional state. You're not thinking clearly. Connor is the baby's father. You don't know how he might react when you tell him."

"You mean he might ask me to marry him?"

"It's a possibility," Alexandra said. "You told me yourself that he's an honorable man, and you did have a long relationship."

Both women were so intent that they didn't hear the front door open. Dee Dee could hear their voices coming from behind the frosted-glass partition that divided the office. She was about to call out when she heard something that stopped her.

"Connor might feel an obligation to marry me because I'm pregnant with his child," Mandy was saying. "But I couldn't permit that. It would be torture, knowing he doesn't love me."

"So you're just going to leave your friends and move away?"

"You're all very dear to me, but it's the only way I'll ever get over loving him. Maybe I never will, but at least I have to try," Mandy said bleakly.

Dee Dee didn't wait to hear any more. She closed the door noiselessly and ran to the nearest bus stop.

Alexandra continued her effort to change Mandy's mind. "Moving to another state won't sever your ties to Connor. Don't you think he'll want to visit his child? You'll have to see him occasionally."

"You don't understand. I'm not going to tell him about the baby."

"Now I know you're crazy! What do you plan to do for money? Raising a child is expensive these days, and you won't even be able to work for a time."

"I'll manage. I have some money put aside, and my half of the agency is worth something. I'll sell it or you can buy me out. I don't expect you to come up with a lump sum. Actually, I'd prefer that you pay me monthly. I can live on that when I have to stop working."

"Connor is a wealthy man. Why should you just scrape by?"

"You're talking as if this baby is a burden. It isn't. He or she is a miracle that Connor and I created," Mandy said softly. "I'm happy about it. Be happy with me."

Alexandra's eyes were misty as she put her arms around her friend.

Dee Dee stormed past her father's secretary and into his office, slamming the door behind her.

Connor glanced up and sighed. "What's the crisis of the day? Did the cleaner shrink your favorite sweater?"

"Go ahead, make jokes." She glared at him. "*Your* life hasn't been turned upside down!"

"I presume this is more serious than a sweater. Would you like to calm down and tell me what's bothering you?"

"I just found out about you and Mandy."

Connor's indulgent smile faded. "I know you're fond of her, but our breakup doesn't concern you. You two can still be friends."

"After what you did to her? You're always lecturing me about playing fair and taking responsibility when I goof up. How come you don't have to live by those rules?"

"I like to think I do."

"Then how could you run out on Mandy?"

"That isn't exactly what happened," he said carefully. "Sometimes things just don't work out the way you want them to."

"You still should have stuck by her."

He sighed. "You're too young to understand the complexities of adult relationships."

"I'm old enough to know the stork doesn't bring babies. Even if you don't love Mandy anymore, I should think you'd want to see your own kid."

Connor gave his daughter an incredulous look. "What are you talking about?"

"Mandy's moving out of San Francisco. If she does that, I'll bet we never see her again."

Connor's expression was formidable. "If this is your idea of a joke, you're going to be very sorry, young lady. Where did you get the impression that Mandy is pregnant?"

"I heard her telling Alex. They didn't know I was there. I went to Mandy's office because she didn't ever return my phone calls. She said she had to leave town because it was the only way she'd get over loving you."

"You actually heard her say that? Maybe you misunderstood. Tell me her exact words," he said tensely.

"I just did! That's exactly what she said. Are you gonna let her go away?"

Strong emotions played over Connor's face, the final one exultation. "Stop worrying and leave everything to me. How would you like to be a bridesmaid at your father's wedding? Go home and wait for me, Dee Dee. I'm going to bring Mandy back where she belongs."

Connor broke all records getting to Mandy's office, but she'd gone home for the day. It was one more frustration in a long line of them.

"She hasn't left town yet, has she?" he asked anxiously.

"How did you know...?" Alexandra's voice trailed off.

"I'm just finding out a lot of things I should have known all along. Is it true that Mandy still loves me?"

"Who told you?"

"Never mind. Just tell me if it's true."

Alexandra looked at him gravely. "She's been going through hell without you."

"Strange that we never bumped into each other there." Connor's mouth curved wryly.

"You feel the same way about her?"

"Mandy is the one and only love of my life," he said with deep feeling. "I'm willing to grovel and beg, anything she asks if she'll just take me back."

"I don't think it will come to that." Alexandra smiled. "Just tell her what you told me."

"I intend to. I'm going over there right now."

Alexandra's smile dimmed. "Connor, wait. She couldn't take it if her dreams were shattered again. Maybe there's something I'd better tell you first."

"You don't have to tell me." He grinned. "I was there when it happened."

Mandy was making a list of things to do—shut off the utilities, cancel the newspaper, so many details that had to be taken care of. They couldn't be done immediately, but she might as well plan ahead. It helped take her mind off what a big step she was taking, leaving her hometown and all her friends. Then she thought about the baby and her sadness vanished. Connor's child was worth any sacrifice.

When the doorbell rang, Mandy expected a deliveryman or a door-to-door salesman. She wasn't usually home this early, so it couldn't be anyone she knew. The sight of Connor froze her to the spot.

He stood motionless, too, drinking in every detail of her delicate face. Finally he said, "May I come in?"

She stood aside, not trusting herself to speak. She didn't even think to ask him to sit down. They stood in the middle of the floor, gazing at each other.

After a moment Connor said, "Didn't you think I had a right to know?"

Mandy paled when she realized he had somehow found out about the baby. "I didn't want you to feel responsible," she whispered.

"I'm the child's father, for God's sake! How were you going to raise it alone?"

"I would have managed." They were standing so close that she could feel the warmth from his body. She turned away so her courage wouldn't fail. "I *will* manage."

"The hell you will!" He whirled her around and pulled her into his arms. "You're going to marry me, and we're going to raise this child together."

It was what she'd always dreamed of, but not under these circumstances. She drew back as far as he would permit. "I knew you'd offer to do the right thing. It's the reason I didn't want you to know."

"You think I'm only asking you to marry me because of the baby?"

"Don't bother to spare my feelings. We both know that's the reason. I appreciate the gesture, but it wouldn't work. A loveless marriage must be the saddest thing in the world."

"No, a sadder thing is a misunderstanding between two people who love each other. I don't even know what happened—and I don't want to know. All I care about is having you back." He stroked her cheek, gazing at her in a kind of wonder. "Darling Mandy, love of my life, I'll never let you go again."

She looked up at him uncertainly. "How can I believe you really mean it? You couldn't have cut me out of your life so completely if you really cared."

Connor's face sobered. "I didn't think it mattered to you. When I returned from New York, everything was different. We hadn't been together in almost two weeks, yet you made excuses to avoid seeing me. The bottom dropped out of my world when I came over here and found out why."

"The man you saw was Alexandra's boyfriend. She asked me to go to the ballet with him because she didn't feel well. I tried to explain, but you wouldn't listen."

"I'll admit I was unreasonable that night, but don't you think you share some of the blame? This all started because you were angry at me for not phoning often enough from New York."

Mandy moved out of his arms. "I wasn't getting even."

"What would you call it? You're still miffed because you think I neglected you. It wasn't like that at all. I wanted desperately to talk to you, but not with an audience. Lorna was always there.''

"Don't try to tell me you minded," Mandy said in a small voice. "Dee Dee told me that you and Lorna discussed getting remarried. I don't know why things didn't work out, but I couldn't fight an obsession. She's the only woman you've ever truly loved."

"Is *that* what started all this misery? If you'd only told me! Lorna and I don't love each other—we probably never did. She happened to be between boyfriends, and she remarked that perhaps we should get back together again, since we were both unattached at the moment. It was merely a joke! We both knew it would never happen—and neither of us wanted it to. Dee Dee simply misunderstood.''

Mandy looked at him doubtfully. "She said you told Lorna she hasn't changed in all these years. That means she's the same woman you fell in love with."

"No, darling, I meant she's the same adolescent who refuses to grow up. Her only interests are parties, clothes and new conquests. Her daughter isn't even a priority. I thought our visit might awaken some latent maternal instincts in Lorna, but they just aren't there."

"Was Dee Dee upset that you weren't going to be a family again? I could tell how much she enjoyed being with her mother.''

Connor shrugged. "Dee Dee thinks of her mother as a kind of quirky aunt. She's fond of Lorna, but she knows better than to rely on her for anything."

"That's very sad. You've been wonderfully supportive, but a girl her age needs a mother.''

"You're the one Dee Dee wants. Almost as much as I do." Connor smiled engagingly. "Do you think you can handle two kids and a husband who can't stay away from you?''

Mandy gazed at him with dazzled eyes as she realized that all the things she'd dreamed of had come true. "I'm still trying to get used to the idea that you love me.''

"Will this help?''

He took her in his arms and kissed her with great tenderness. She clung to him, returning his kiss with equal feeling as all the pain and loneliness drained away.

"You'll never know how I missed holding you like this," he said huskily. "I tortured myself by dialing your number just to hear your voice on the answering machine."

"I wish I'd thought of that." She smiled blissfully, twining her arms around his neck.

His hand moved under her sweater to caress her body while he kissed her again, this time with rising passion. Mandy moaned softly with pleasure as his fingers slipped inside her bra to stroke her sensitive nipple.

Connor was slowly gliding her zipper down when the phone rang. "Let it ring," he growled.

Mandy shared his impatience. She had no intention of answering—until they heard Dee Dee's voice.

"I called your office and Alexandra said you'd gone home. This time you *have* to call me back, Mandy. Dad says you two are gonna get married. Is it true?"

Mandy grabbed the phone before Dee Dee could hang up. "Yes, honey, it's true. I hope you're happy about it."

"Are you kidding? I think it's supercool! Dad said I could be a bridesmaid. Is that okay?"

"How would you like to be maid of honor instead?"

"Fantastic! And will you throw the bridal bouquet to me? That ought to shake Dad up."

"Sorry to spoil your fun." Mandy laughed. "It won't be a big, splashy wedding."

"I don't care. I just want to hear all about it. When are you guys coming home?"

"Soon," Mandy promised.

"It was sweet of you to ask Dee Dee to be your maid of honor," Connor said after she hung up. "I know it will mean a lot to her."

"It was the least I could do." She moved back into his arms. "If it weren't for her, we wouldn't be here like this."

His arms tightened. "I can't bear to think of how close I came to losing you. Promise you'll never leave me."

"I couldn't if I wanted to," she said simply. "You were in my thoughts all day, and my dreams at night. I hated to wake up and find you weren't there."

"I'm here now," he murmured, easing her onto the couch.

They moved against each other in remembered ecstasy. Mandy shivered with delight as Connor's erotic caresses made her body pulse with desire.

When he burrowed under her sweater and kissed the slopes of her breasts, she said faintly, "I told Dee Dee we'd be home soon."

"By the time she gets through calling all her friends to tell them the news, we will be." He unclasped her bra and removed it, along with her sweater.

Mandy laughed breathlessly. "Be thankful she practically lives on the phone."

"I have a lot of blessings, but the greatest one is you." Connor framed her face in his palms, gazing at her tenderly.

When his mouth claimed hers, their kiss expressed the love and commitment that would fill the rest of their lives.

* * * * *

COMING NEXT MONTH

FAST CASH 4031 DRAW RULES
NO PURCHASE OR OBLIGATION NECESSARY

Fifty prizes of $50 each will be awarded in random drawings to be conducted no later than 3/28/97 from amongst all eligible responses to this prize offer received as of 2/14/97. To enter, follow directions, affix 1st-class postage and mail OR write Fast Cash 4031 on a 3" x 5" card along with your name and address and mail that card to: Harlequin's Fast Cash 4031 Draw, P.O. Box 1395, Buffalo, NY 14240-1395 OR P.O. Box 618, Fort Erie, Ontario L2A 5X3. (Limit: one entry per outer envelope; all entries must be sent via 1st-class mail.) Limit: one prize per household. Odds of winning are determined by the number of eligible responses received. Offer is open only to residents of the U.S. (except Puerto Rico) and Canada and is void wherever prohibited by law. All applicable laws and regulations apply. Any litigation within the province of Quebec respecting the conduct and awarding of a prize in this sweepstakes maybe submitted to the Régie des alcools, des courses et des jeux. In order for a Canadian resident to win a prize, that person will be required to correctly answer a time-limited arithmetical skill-testing question to be administered by mail. Names of winners available after 4/28/97 by sending a self-addressed, stamped envelope to: Fast Cash 4031 Draw Winners, P.O. Box 4200, Blair, NE 68009-4200.

OFFICIAL RULES
MILLION DOLLAR SWEEPSTAKES
NO PURCHASE NECESSARY TO ENTER

1. To enter, follow the directions published. Method of entry may vary. For eligibility, entries must be received no later than March 31, 1998. No liability is assumed for printing errors, lost, late, non-delivered or misdirected entries.

    To determine winners, the sweepstakes numbers assigned to submitted entries will be compared against a list of randomly pre-selected prize winning numbers. In the event all prizes are not claimed via the return of prize winning numbers, random drawings will be held from among all other entries received to award unclaimed prizes.

2. Prize winners will be determined no later than June 30, 1998. Selection of winning numbers and random drawings are under the supervision of D. L. Blair, Inc., an independent judging organization whose decisions are final. Limit: one prize to a family or organization. No substitution will be made for any prize, except as offered. Taxes and duties on all prizes are the sole responsibility of winners. Winners will be notified by mail. Odds of winning are determined by the number of eligible entries distributed and received.

3. Sweepstakes open to residents of the U.S. (except Puerto Rico), Canada and Europe who are 18 years of age or older, except employees and immediate family members of Torstar Corp., D. L. Blair, Inc., their affiliates, subsidiaries, and all other agencies, entities, and persons connected with the use, marketing or conduct of this sweepstakes. All applicable laws and regulations apply. Sweepstakes offer void wherever prohibited by law. Any litigation within the province of Quebec respecting the conduct and awarding of a prize in this sweepstakes maybe submitted to the Régie des alcools, des courses et des jeux. In order to win a prize, residents of Canada will be required to correctly answer a time-limited arithmetical skill-testing question to be administered by mail.

4. Winners of major prizes (Grand through Fourth) will be obligated to sign and return an Affidavit of Eligibility and Release of Liability within 30 days of notification. In the event of non-compliance within this time period or if a prize is returned as undeliverable, D. L. Blair, Inc. may at its sole discretion award that prize to an alternate winner. By acceptance of their prize, winners consent to use of their names, photographs or other likeness for purposes of advertising, trade and promotion on behalf of Torstar Corp., its affiliates and subsidiaries, without further compensation unless prohibited by law. Torstar Corp. and D. L. Blair, Inc., their affiliates and subsidiaries are not responsible for errors in printing of sweepstakes and prizewinning numbers. In the event a duplication of a prizewinning number occurs, a random drawing will be held from among all entries received with that prizewinning number to award that prize.

SWP-S12ZD1

5. This sweepstakes is presented by Torstar Corp., its subsidiaries and affiliates in conjunction with book, merchandise and/or product offerings. The number of prizes to be awarded and their value are as follows: Grand Prize — $1,000,000 (payable at $33,333.33 a year for 30 years); First Prize — $50,000; Second Prize — $10,000; Third Prize — $5,000; 3 Fourth Prizes — $1,000 each; 10 Fifth Prizes — $250 each; 1,000 Sixth Prizes — $10 each. Values of all prizes are in U.S. currency. Prizes in each level will be presented in different creative executions, including various currencies, vehicles, merchandise and travel. Any presentation of a prize level in a currency other than U.S. currency represents an approximate equivalent to the U.S. currency prize for that level, at that time. Prize winners will have the opportunity of selecting any prize offered for that level; however, the actual non U.S. currency equivalent prize, if offered and selected, shall be awarded at the exchange rate existing at 3:00 P.M. New York time on March 31, 1998. A travel prize option, if offered and selected by winner, must be completed within 12 months of selection and is subject to: traveling companion(s) completing and returning a Release of Liability prior to travel; and hotel and flight accommodations availability. For a current list of all prize options offered within prize levels, send a self-addressed, stamped envelope (WA residents need not affix postage) to: MILLION DOLLAR SWEEPSTAKES Prize Options, P.O. Box 4456, Blair, NE 68009-4456, USA.

6. For a list of prize winners (available after July 31, 1998) send a separate, stamped, self-addressed envelope to: MILLION DOLLAR SWEEPSTAKES Winners, P.O. Box 4459, Blair, NE 68009-4459, USA.

EXTRA BONUS PRIZE DRAWING
NO PURCHASE OR OBLIGATION NECESSARY TO ENTER

7. The Extra Bonus Prize will be awarded in a random drawing to be conducted no later than 5/30/98 from among all entries received. To qualify, entries must be received by 3/31/98 and comply with published directions. Prize ($50,000) is valued in U.S. currency. Prize will be presented in different creative expressions, including various currencies, vehicles, merchandise and travel. Any presentation in a currency other than U.S. currency represents an approximate equivalent to the U.S. currency value at that time. Prize winner will have the opportunity of selecting any prize offered in any presentation of the Extra Bonus Prize Drawing; however, the actual non U.S. currency equivalent prize, if offered and selected by winner, shall be awarded at the exchange rate existing at 3:00 P.M. New York time on March 31, 1998. For a current list of prize options offered, send a self-addressed, stamped envelope (WA residents need not affix postage) to: Extra Bonus Prize Options, P.O. Box 4462, Blair, NE 68009-4462, USA. All eligibility requirements and restrictions of the MILLION DOLLAR SWEEPSTAKES apply. Odds of winning are dependent upon number of eligible entries received. No substitution for prize except as offered. For the name of winner (available after 7/31/98), send a self-addressed, stamped envelope to: Extra Bonus Prize Winner, P.O. Box 4463, Blair, NE 68009-4463, USA.

SWP-S12ZD2